ice contact

Milwaukee Steel Riders

Book One

ellie k. drake

contents

*To all the girls who've been called clingy...don't settle.
Your Hayes is out there waiting for you.*

authors note

Thank you for reading Ice Contact! This is a funny, swoony, and spicy hockey romance. As with any book, you should know what you're getting into. Below are some themes I want to make sure you're aware of.

- explicit language
- multiple open door sex scenes between two consensual partners, for more specifics please visit my website www.elliekdrake.com
- on-page alcohol consumption
- medical emergency including a hospital scene
- gaslighting and degradation in a relationship shown on-page
- emotional scars and healing from past relationships.
- estrangement from family (briefly mentioned)
- mention of being cheated on by former partners, one resulting in a pregnancy

ice contact playlist

So High School - Taylor Swift
Suit and Tie - Justin Timberlake
Sweet As Whole - Sara Barielles
Africa- Toto
Don't Stop Believing - Journey
Passenger Princess - Nessa Barrett
Butterflies - Kasey Musgraves
Here's to Us - Halestorm
Hypotheticals - Lake Street Drive
Talk Dirty to Me - Poison
Legs - ZZ Top
I Wanna Know What Love Is - Foreigner

Listen on Spotify!

1
olivia

"Chest Bush coming in hot," my best friend, and co-worker, Maggie says as she leans across our shared workspace. Gazing across the endless sea of cubicles, I notice our account manager, Bill Stansson, heading this way.

Sighing, I let my head fall back to stare at the ceiling. "Kill me. He *just* sent me an email. I'm sure he's coming by to 'explain it to me' as usual," I say to Maggie. "Why does he have to send it, then come over to tell me about it?" I grumble as I roll my eyes and Bill continues to walk towards us. "We betting coffee tomorrow morning if I'm right?"

"I'll take that bet. Last time he asked if I could show him how to save something as a PDF," Maggie replies with a giant eye roll.

"Olivia," he says, his glasses sliding down the bridge of his wrinkled nose, "did you get my email?"

"I sure did, Bill. Reading it now."

"Great. I wanted to stop by and explain it to you, in case you have any questions." *Of course he does.* I force a stiff smile. "We need to get the final edits for the Bayview Bourbon campaign over to them by EOD," he says. My eyes can't help but stare at the disgusting display of hair pouring out of his polo shirt which always has one too many buttons undone. Bile rises in my throat, and I fight to keep my face neutral enough he doesn't suspect a thing. I barely want to work with this guy, let alone see his curly bush *fully* displayed on a daily basis.

"Yep. I see that information right here in your email, Bill. I'm almost done working on it, and I'll send it over to you in the next hour. You'll have time to review before we need to get it to them," I reply with a passive aggressive tone, hoping he won't pick up on it.

"Great! Glad to have my crack team on it. This is a big account for us, and we need to put our best foot forward," Bill says with a wink as he walks away.

Maggie waits until he's out of sight, and we both roll our eyes with a snort. We have nicknames for almost everyone in the office. It's the only way to keep ourselves sane surrounded by the chaos we deal with on the daily. There's Cowboy, Turkey, Emo Guy, Coffee Breath, Sausage Fingers, and, of course, Chest Bush. We both work for Lakeshore Creative, a small advertising agency in Milwaukee. I am the copywriter, and Maggie is our graphic designer. We instantly clicked the day I started. We have a lot in common, including parents who are not thrilled with our creative career paths. I haven't actually talked to my parents in years because of that and other philosophical differences. It was painful at first, but Maggie volunteered to show me around town and introduce me to some of her friends, helping me find my own sort of family here. I'd just moved to the city, so her kindness was a gesture I wasn't expecting. And now, eight years later, we are still trauma bonding over the ridiculous people we work with.

"I hate being treated like an idiot every time one of these guys talks to me. I know Bill can't read an email to save his life, but I am *quite* capable," I vent. "I'm surprised he even figured out how to send the email in the first place. Earlier this week, he sent one with the entire email in the subject line. Nothing was in the body. It was almost impossible to read, but there's no way in hell I could ask *him* for clarification. He thinks because I haven't been doing advertising for twenty-five years I am a complete moron and he has to mansplain every task to me."

"Ditto, Liv. If Sausage Fingers bitches me out one more time for not checking with her before I add a new client into the account software, I swear I'm going to walk out. I don't understand how some people function acting like they own the entire world and we all have to bow to them. Who made her the Pope?" She groans, digging her fingers into her temples. "I walked by her desk yesterday and, despite my literal hate for her, tried to be the bigger person. I said, 'Hi Angi, how are you?' That bitch looked up at me, rolled her eyes, and went back to work. What the hell did I ever do to her?" Maggie grumbles with a sigh. "At least it's the weekend, so I can drink my sorrows away." She moans, draping herself between our desks and pouting with big puppy dog eyes. "Then, in a few short days, Monday will come again, and we'll be back on this never-ending train ride straight to hell."

I laugh at her and the depressing monotony of our situation.

"You want to come to Walt's for happy hour tonight?" I ask. "Not that you haven't heard me sing before, but there is alcohol and cheese curds available for purchase."

"I wish! I promised my mom I'd go to her cousin's retirement party tonight. I would *much* rather go to Walt's and listen to you belt out some tunes over a drink. But my mom is basically bribing me to attend this party. She said if I go, she'll pay for my flight to our annual Florida trip, and I love you, but I'm guessing you won't be paying me $400 in airline gift cards to come see you perform."

I laugh. "Yeah, if I was making $400 myself I'd gladly help you out. I would go for the free flight, too, if I were you. Besides,

Cayden said he might try and come tonight since it's been raining all day."

"Cayden Banks doing something unselfish? I'll believe that when I see it."

"I know, I know. At least he's making an effort. I'm honestly surprised he hasn't already made plans with his buddies since his softball game got rained out."

"Liv, I *really* hope he shows up for you," Maggie says with a pitying smile. "I would hope your boyfriend would want to spend time supporting your passion when his beer league softball game gets rained out. Then again, I don't even have a boyfriend, so you've got me beat there. Sadly, I'll be at a retirement party with my mom and a bunch of older ladies trying to set me up with their weird grandsons. I certainly hope your night is more exciting than mine."

"Can I get a little more piano in my monitor?" I ask Walt, the owner of Walt's on Water. He flashes me a quick thumbs up, and I hit a few keys on my piano as I test the level. "Thanks Walt. Everyone, give it up for Walt, the best bar owner and sound engineer this side of Lake Michigan!" The crowd hoots and hollers as he shakes his head and rolls his eyes. Walt does not like to be the center of attention, and flips me off every time I give him a shout out.

Walt's on Water is an old-school bar in the Third Ward neighborhood of Milwaukee. As with any bar in the city, the decor is part of what makes it great. Between the dark wood paneling lining the walls, the ancient brown leather bar stools, and the multi-colored Christmas lights providing a soft glow throughout the space, it looks like my grandparent's basement. Some may think it's too kitschy, but it's one of the most popular bars downtown and has been for decades. I personally think it is perfect for a true Milwaukee bar experience. Add in some good music from yours truly, and you've got the makings of a perfect night.

Walt has been gracious enough to let me perform here every Friday for happy hour the last year. It's honestly beneficial to both of us. It's good exposure for my music, and he says my set draws in a good crowd for his happy hour specials.

I'm not sure I believe him. I'm just a local singer-songwriter looking to perform my own music. I'm sure the bar crowd won't be into my moody piano ballads, so I mostly sing cover songs. You've never seen a crowd go wild during happy hour until you bust into an acoustic version of Journey's 'Don't Stop Believing' or Toto's 'Africa'. People can't help but sing along to those songs, they're classics for a reason, but my original songs? I've always longed for an outlet where my music can reach those who truly appreciate the art of songwriting, but it's not Walt's. I weave them into my set list as I can, but no one knows the words. No one knows the melody. No one really pays attention to be honest. A deep ache forms in my creative heart when my songs go unheard. These customers are here to enjoy a drink, and maybe a bite to eat, after a long week of work. Similar to how my life feels most of the time, I'm nothing more than background noise.

The only nights I'm not here are when the Milwaukee Steel Riders are playing. As the NHL team's national anthem singer, and a huge hockey fan, I wouldn't miss those games for the world. Even if I wasn't there for a purpose every game, I'd still be there to cheer on my boys.

Hockey is the *best* sport. I will never comprehend how there are not more hockey fans. It's fast paced, high-energy, and they get to *fight*. And the punishment for fighting? They get to take a break. Sit in a little box all by themselves for a few minutes, grab some water, and chill.

Why can't office jobs be like that? *What if I could punch Coffee Breath from sales?* She always drinks the last of the coffee, then saunters back to her desk without making another pot. What I wouldn't give to throat punch her when she forces me to be un-caffeinated longer than necessary, painfully waiting for the empty pot to fill back up. She makes my blood boil hotter than the drink brewing in the machine. Going by hockey rules, I would smile at her with an evil grin, punch her, then sit in a little penalty box to take a rest while the coffee refilled. Instead, I'd be sent to HR and be packing up my desk before the pot finished. Most days, I slump my shoulders, begrudgingly brew another pot, and sigh…a girl can dream. *And for God's sake, Brenda, just make another damn pot of coffee - it takes two freaking seconds!*

I know hockey players don't see it my way. They are frustrated when they get their little time out, desperate to be back on the ice. But as a fan? I love the fights. I'm not a violent person by any means, with the exception of serial empty coffee pot assholes, but watching hockey players go at it and get roughed up on the ice is one of the best parts of the game. Just the thought of them getting all riled up with their sweaty, ripped muscles under their jerseys gets blood pumping to intimate places in my body.

But today it's a rainy Friday night in early September, and hockey season doesn't start for a few weeks. Even then, there will be pre-season games where one of my fill-in singers will perform the anthem. I won't make my big debut until the home opener when the arena will be packed with anticipations high for a new season.

So, for tonight, I'll play songs for the fifty or so people at Walt's and serve as their soundtrack for the end of the workweek. I'll enjoy performing, soaking in the thrill coming with it, eager to sing with the chill of icy air on my face.

2
hayes

"*Yes*, I made sure to pack enough warm clothes for the Midwest," I say to my mom on the other end of the Face-Time call. "I know I just moved here from Tampa, but you do remember I play ice hockey for a living, right? And that I grew up in Minnesota? Milwaukee is, like, five hours southeast from St. Paul, so *technically* it should be warmer here."

She scoffs, "Yes Hayes, I remember. Who do you think took you to every practice, drove three hours to weekly tournaments, and sat in freezing cold rinks nearly every weekend of my adult life? I'm just saying, you know how it gets up here once winter starts and… oh, for Pete's sake, just let me be a worrying mother for once, okay? If I tell you I'm worried about you being cold, it takes away the need to tell you I'm worried about you getting hurt on the ice. Just let me have my mothering moment."

Laughing, I settle back in my chair, smiling at the woman who has supported me through everything. "Okay, okay, I get it Mom. I will make sure to bundle up once winter hits…in three months."

Even at thirty-one years old, my heart swells knowing she still worries about me on the ice. *Hell, I probably should worry about myself on the ice.* Hockey is a high contact sport, and injuries happen every day. But it's out of my control. I'm a professional athlete; I can't play like I'm scared of getting hurt. I would've never made it to the NHL if that were the case. To be successful, I have to play every game with one-hundred percent focus. There's no room for fear.

I wrap up the call and get ready to head out. After a long day of unpacking at my new place, I take a quick minute to appreciate the amazing view of Lake Michigan from my living room. It's been pouring rain all day, so it's not the most *picturesque* view at the moment. Even still, the sound of the rain beating against my building and the rippling drops cascading on the lake is peaceful. When I visited a few weeks ago to sign the lease there were dozens of sailboats out on the dark blue water. With the cool breeze waltzing in off the lake and the music festival happening down by the shore, I felt like good things were finally ahead for me. It was the perfect mix of everything I love. *They can't call Milwaukee 'the good land' for nothing, right?*

It's my tenth year in the league and I'm just about to start my first season with the Milwaukee Steel Riders. I've been in Tampa for the last few seasons, and Carolina before that. But when my contract was up in Tampa, I jumped at the opportunity to be back in the Midwest to get away from the fucking humidity. Plus, Vladi Volkov is the goalie here. He's one of my best friends and team-mates from college, so I'm pumped to be on the same team with him again. Training camp starts in a few days. Hockey is a long, grueling season and requires the intense amount of hard work and discipline I've maintained for most of my life. From staying in shape in the off season, to sticking to my proper nutrition, consistent strength training, and routine mental health check ins, it's a lot to keep up with.

Tonight though? I just need to relax. I've been cooped up inside all day. I don't even have groceries yet. The internet installer doesn't come until tomorrow, so it's not like I can plop down on the couch to watch TV. Searching on my phone, I find a bar with good reviews just a few blocks from my new place. Glancing out the window, I can't help but grin. The rain has let up, for now, so I throw on a baseball cap and a hoodie, hoping I'm still new enough to the team people won't recognize me yet, and walk to the bar.

This bar is packed tonight, and I grab the only open stool, ordering a Spotted Cow. As I wait for my drink, I respond to a quick text from my agent making sure I got settled in. Tapping out a nameless tune on the bar, my mind is captivated by a sound unlike anything I've ever heard before. This is a noisy bar, but the song cuts through all the commotion. It's one of the most soulful sounds I've ever heard. My eyes, as if controlled by something outside my understanding, land on the stage where a gorgeous woman is sitting behind a piano singing. My mouth goes dry, and the air is sucked from my lungs, like I've just taken a gut punch from an enforcer on the ice. Flowing auburn hair cascades past her shoulders while sun-kissed skin glows under the stage lights; she has stunning crystal blue eyes I can see all the way from here, and I'm desperate to dive into their depths. I don't know what song she's singing, but I know I don't care. She could be singing the names of my teammates, and I wouldn't even notice, the melody she's singing tunneling from my ears straight into my soul.

A tap on my shoulder breaks the trance I'm in, and I turn to see a man with an annoyed look on his face beside me gesturing toward the bartender who's trying to get my attention. The bartender smiles, noticing how distracted I am by tonight's entertainment.

"Want to start a tab or close out?" the bartender asks again.

"Oh, umm…yeah, sure. I'll start a tab," I say handing the bartender my card. "Sorry about that; I spaced out for a second. Got a lot on my mind this evening."

The bartender smiles again. "No problem. Happens more than you think around here."

With a gorgeous girl belting out notes like that up on a small bar stage, I have no doubt.

"You like what you hear up there?" the man beside me asks.

"Yeah, she's really good," I reply, once again entranced by her voice.

"That's my girlfriend, Olivia. She sings here every Friday night. I got her this gig. She's lucky I know the owner," he smugly replies.

She's lucky he knows the owner. What kind of thing is that to say about your girlfriend? I look at him again. Your girlfriend who is *obviously* talented. "You got her this gig? Not her singing skills?"

He shrugs his shoulders, looking at his phone. "I mean she can sing, but talent only gets you so far. You have to know people. And *I* know people." He slides his phone into his pocket. "I'm Banks by the way." He extends his hand and I shake it with a polite nod.

"Hayes," I reply skeptically. I'm normally a 'nice to meet you' type of person, but after what's come out of this guy's mouth, I'm not actually sure it is nice to meet him. *He got her this gig and talent only gets you so far?* I work in professional sports and know a *lot* of cocky people, but this guy…I hide my scoff by clearing my throat. I've known him for less than five minutes, and he takes the gold medal in self-promotion.

"Do you come here every week to hear your girlfriend sing?"

He scoffs. "Hell no. Normally I play softball, but the game was rained out. Damn rain. I'd much rather be playing softball. I'm not into this whole music thing. It's nice she has this to do on Fridays so I can have a night off from her." He groans, rolling his head back to look at the ceiling. "She's so *clingy*. She wants to hang out three or four times a week." He drops his head back, lifting his eyebrows as if I'd understand what he meant. "It's kind of a drag."

Who the hell is this guy? It takes every ounce of my energy to grip the edge of the bar with my hand and not ball it into a fist to punch this guy square in the face. My mother drilled into me that we treat women with respect. *This guy has obviously not met my feisty mother;* Kristine Larson would smack this guy on the side of the head if she could hear the few words he's spoken about his girlfriend.

I take a minute to process everything and decide to prod him a little more about his 'clingy' girlfriend. The one with the killer auburn hair and piercing blue eyes currently singing some sort of siren song and drawing me in.

"Isn't spending time together kind of the point of a relationship?"

He lets out a roaring laugh, clapping me on the shoulder. "Listen man, once you're married to them, you're stuck with them. All day. *Every* day." He leans back in his seat, lifting his fingers half-heartedly at the bartender. "Might as well enjoy my freedom now. You know how these girls are. Always wanting to spend every minute of the day together. I need my time off. Time to hang with the guys. I can't give up all my friends to hang out with my *girl-friend* twice a week…you know what I mean? I'm actually getting ready to pay my tab and head home to play puck with my room-mates after this."

"Puck? As in you play softball *and* hockey?" I ask as I take another sip of my beer, trying to keep my cool realizing he's going to ditch this girl.

He laughs. "No man...we play NHL '94 on an old school Sega Genesis video game console. It's a *classic*, and my buddies and I play it religiously. We made it into a drinking game too, so we load up on beers and play all night long. If you'd like to join us, I can give you the address. If you're into hockey, that is."

Yeah. I'm into hockey. Not fucking 'puck' or whatever the hell he just called it. *Who calls it* puck? This motherfucker apparently. Thanks to my ball cap and nondescript clothes, he is oblivious to who he's talking to. I'm not super famous, especially out of my hockey gear, but most people in the hockey community know who I am and that I just signed for the Riders. Not Banks though. *What kind of a name is Banks anyway?* Too bad we aren't on the ice. I would smash this guy into the boards so fucking hard and take whatever penalty or fine came my way. This guy is, apparently, dating an amazing singer with the voice of an angel and is upset she wants to spend time with him. *Is this guy for fucking real?*

"No, thanks," I reply, "I've had a long day. *Really* great meeting you though, Bart." My voice drips with sarcasm, my frustration and distaste quite clear.

"Oh, it's Banks," he says, his tone filled with irritation.

"Oh gosh, *so sorry* about that. It's so loud in here, I must have misheard."

I didn't mishear shit.

Everyone in the bar is now singing along with the stunning woman on stage, and thanks to jackass over here, I know her name. *Olivia.* It is just as beautiful as she is, and somehow, it's comforting to repeat it in my mind. Her voice fills every inch of the bar, and I realize I know the song she's singing. It's a *Journey* song...*I fucking love Journey.* Goosebumps cover my arms as the entire bar sings along, taking nothing from the beauty of her talent.

She ends the song and the entire bar cheers for her. Well... everyone except for douchebag over here, who is too busy paying his tab to clap for his girlfriend. I haven't even met Olivia yet, and I can tell she deserves better than this asshat trash talking her in a bar to a random stranger.

I would give anything for a chance to show Olivia she's worthy of so much more.

3
olivia

"Gonna take a quick fifteen-minute break, then I'll be back. If you have any requests, write them down and turn them in up here on the stage. I'll get to as many songs as I can!" The crowd claps as I catch my breath after the first set. Needing a refill on my water, I head over to the bar. My boyfriend is surprisingly here and I want to go say a quick hello while I'm on my only break.

The shock of him *actually* showing up tonight sends a jolt of excitement through me as I weave through the crowd, dodging swaying bodies and sloshing beers. Cayden hates this stuff. Actually, he loves the drinking aspect of the bar, but hates the 'me performing music' part. But there he is, at the bar, and my heart skips a beat. *Maybe he cares more than I thought?*

Cayden Banks and I met online a year and a half ago and started dating after quickly connecting through a mutual love of hockey. He's a nice guy, but lately, we haven't been spending as much time together as I'd like. My lips thin, anxiety rushing through me. He has never wanted to spend a lot of time with me, but it's been worse lately. Hopefully after my set is done, we can go back to my place and chill. Watch a movie or something. But as I near the bar, I see he's paying his tab. I freeze, a pit forming in my stomach. He's not one to stop drinking this early in the evening, especially on a Friday, and I still have another forty-five-minute set to play. I blink against the burning in my eyes, already seeing where this is heading.

"Hey, babe," I say, his spine stiffening as I approach. "Thanks for coming tonight. Are you leaving already?" I lean into give him a quick peck on the cheek, my heart squeezing when he doesn't even look over at me.

"The guys want to play puck tonight, so I'm headed out before I have too much to drink. I'd rather get wasted at home; you know that. Besides, the drinks here get more expensive after happy hour ends."

God, he is so cheap. With a last name like Banks, you would think he has lots of money. False. He *never* has money. He has a decent job working in procurement at one of the local community colleges. To be honest, I make more money than he does.

I think he resents me for it.

But it's not like I'm rolling in dough either. I make enough to pay my bills and set aside some money to buy things I want. But Cayden? He is always complaining about how everything we do is so expensive. Unless it has to do with sports or drinking. Anything I suggest we do is an instant no-go.

Once, when we went out for dinner, he ordered an appetizer and a meal for himself. I ordered a salad. He paid. He planned the date, so it seems nice, right? I thought it was. Until we got into the car. He complained about how expensive it was, telling me, "We can't be going out to eat all the time." Apparently, *him* ordering an entree and an appetizer was my fault.

Somehow, everything is my fault.

"I was hoping you'd stay awhile. I'm playing a couple of new songs this next set, and I'd love for you to hear them. And Walt's back is acting up, so he can't help me get all my gear in the car."

He shrugs, pulling his phone out of his pocket. "You've gotten all your equipment packed up here on your own before, why can't you handle it tonight too? It's just part of the job you signed up for. Plus, the guys are going to start playing soon, so I gotta go."

If I had one wish in life, it would be for that damn video game to explode into a million pieces. I know the drill when he plays. He gets wasted. He won't reply to any of my texts or calls, won't check to see that I got home okay, and he'll be so hungover tomorrow, he won't even remember his own name, let alone want to spend time with me. The ache in my chest grows, making it hard to breathe. His unwillingness to help is almost crippling. But, as always, I take a deep breath and smile through my eternal disappointment, my cheeks stiff and my eyes flat.

"Okay. I'll talk to you tomorrow. Be safe and let me know when you get home," I say as he walks away.

"Yeah. Will do. Thanks, babe," he says, typing on his phone as he walks out of bar, the door closing behind him.

"Need a refill on the water, Liv?" Johnny, the bartender asks.

"I may need something stronger than the water tonight, Johnny."

He narrows his eyes, his gazed filled with worry. "I'm not sure it's the drink that needs to change."

I shrug, my smile wobbling. "Yeah, yeah, you say that every week. Just give me my water. And you better have a Strongbow ready for me after I finish this set!" I tease, as he smiles and nods at my traditional post-show drink order. "Don't you worry about me, Johnny. I'm a strong, capable, badass, independent, thirty-one-year-old woman. I'll carry all the super heavy expensive music equipment out to my car. Alone. In the rain. No problem."

"I'd be happy to help you," a deep voice resonates beside me.

4
olivia

There is a guy in a baseball cap sitting at the bar talking to me. Blinking, I suck in a sharp breath. *At least...I think he's talking to me.* I'm watching his lips move, but I can't hear the words. I can't seem to form my own words either. This guy is good looking. As in Zoolander's 'really, really, ridiculously good looking.' And he's staring at me with the sexiest brown eyes I've ever seen. *Okay, Olivia, calm your tits. Stop looking at his eyes and* focus. *He's talking to you. Say something back.*

"What?" is the only word my mouth can form. *Smooth, Liv, real smooth.*

"You mentioned you needed help getting your gear in your car? I can help," he says again with a smile that is both friendly and a little smoldering. I'm not actually sure what smoldering means, but it's in a lot of the romance novels I read. I study him quickly, a small smile breaking through the pain of the night. *His smile is definitely smoldering.* But I cannot let this random guy, with an incredibly chiseled jawline, help me load equipment into my car. Even if he is extremely handsome. *Especially* because he is extremely handsome. After all, I have a boyfriend…who's left me blinking back tears and ditched me to play video games with his friends.

My chest tightens and I swallow the lump in my throat. *Is this how relationships are supposed to be?*

"Oh, right," I reply to Mr. Handsome-Eyes, my smile feeling more forced. "Thank you for the offer, but I don't take random equipment hauling help from strangers."

"That seems like a very specific thing to have a rule about." He smirks, his eyes sparking in the low light.

"Don't you watch Dateline?" He lifts a brow, his lips twitching as he tries to stay serious. "I say yes, and the next thing you know, my family and friends will be talking about how I was the type of person that 'lit up a room,' but I'll be dead at the bottom of the lake." He laughs at my analogy, and my heart flutters at the sound.

"Well, how about we not be strangers?" he teases with a warm smile. "I'm Hayes. And if you don't mind me saying so, you do light up the room."

Heat rushes to my cheeks as he extends his hand, I reach out to meet it for a friendly handshake. "I'm Olivia. Nice to meet you, Hayes."

My pulse races at the roughness of his hands on mine. His grip is firm, yet somehow still gentle. He holds my hand for a few seconds longer than the normal friendly handshake amount of time, and I don't mind one bit, sparks erupting across my body.

"Nice to meet you, Olivia. See, now we aren't strangers. So, like I said, I'd be glad to assist getting your equipment to your car after your set is over."

I look over to Johnny who smiles at me with a wink, as if he's vetted this guy already. Biting my lip, I stare at the water Johnny hands me. *I really could use the help.* Walt is not an option. Johnny can't leave the bar unattended for long. And Cayden ditched me. *Why should I not accept a little help from a willing bar patron?*

I take a sip of my water as I look his way. "I have to go play my next set, but if you're still here when I'm done, we'll get better acquainted so this doesn't turn into a made-for-TV movie."

He looks at me with that damn smile again as he laughs. "I'm not going anywhere."

My face flushes at his words. *Okay, what in the actual fuck is happening?*

"Here's your Strongbow, as requested, Liv. Great job tonight. That new song of yours you sang at the beginning of this last set is catchy! You got talent, girl," Johnny says to me as he hands me my drink. I'm not a huge beer person, but I love a good cider beer, and this one is not overly sweet. It's like a beer with a hint of cider. *Or maybe a cider with a hint of beer?* Regardless, I convinced Walt to keep it on draft, and he was surprised when it became a popular drink here.

"Thanks Johnny. As my bartender, and personal cider dealer, you are required by law to say nice things to me." I wink. "But I appreciate it anyway."

He gives me a snarky look. "You know I do not dole out compliments if I don't mean 'em, Liv." I give him a smile back. He's a sweet older man who knows every person, and their drink, in this bar. He's worked here with Walt since the bar opened and is always great with advice. Unless it's advice you don't want to hear. Even if it's what you *need* to hear.

"He's right, you know," Hayes says. *My new acquaintance is still here. And still talking to me.* A mix of disbelief and warmth floods through me. Cayden never hangs out, never sticks around. This shouldn't feel so surprising, but it does. "You're really talented.

And I *also* don't give out compliments unless I mean them." He raises his glass towards Johnny in agreement.

Why is it suddenly so hot in this bar? Is the air-conditioning out? I haven't even had a sip of my drink yet, so I know it's not that. I'm too young for hot flashes; right? Is this early menopause? If not, this very handsome man just told me I'm talented. *Really* talented. And, earlier, he told me I lit up a room. I glance at him from the corner of my eye. *Did he mean that?* Surely, he's only referring to my singing. Because with those sexy brown eyes, gorgeous smile, and I *think* blond hair peeking out from underneath his hat, this guy is way out of my league. He has to be one of those guys who has a high level of sarcasm. He's just being funny. He's probably like this with his girlfriend all the time. *He has to have a girlfriend.*

"Well, thank you; I appreciate the kind words. I messed up a couple of times. I know I could have done better," I reply as I take a sip of my drink. I've never been sure how to take a compliment. I never know if people mean what they say or if they are just being polite.

"You know, it's okay to accept a compliment without pointing out your mistakes. I was listening quite diligently, and I didn't hear any. Remember, I don't give out praise unless someone is deserving."

I swear I saw him wink as he finished his last statement. And for some reason the word praise makes it seem a bit warmer in here. *What the hell is happening to me?* I'll talk to Walt later about the HVAC needing a tune-up.

"I know, I know. I'm my own worst critic. I'm a bit of a perfectionist, so it's hard to mess up and accept a compliment. Probably why this beer is needed to calm down the adrenaline running through me after I perform," I say as I take a sip, hoping it will steady my nerves and stop my legs from nervously swinging, too short to reach the bar stool's footrest.

Hayes swivels his seat to face me, leaning in and more engaged in our conversation. "It's crazy you get to sing here. Do you ever get nervous performing?"

"I get a little case of the butterflies right before I perform, but I feel like it's such a thrill to sing in front of a crowd. As soon as it's over, I'm exhausted and relieved to be done. But I also can't wait to do it again immediately. When I don't have another gig for a while, I'll just spend my days criticizing my every mistake and working to get better." My cheeks flush as I glance back to the stage. "Sorry, that's probably a weird concept, and *wow*, am I rambling on like a total psycho. I'll leave you to your drink while I go pack up my gear."

He reaches over and places his hand on top of mine, keeping me in my seat. "Do you have to pack right now? Finish your drink, and I'll finish mine, then I'll help you pack up *and* haul your equipment to your car."

My heart pounds in my chest at his touch. *I should say no.* I'll just go pack up my stuff and head home. I open my mouth to tell him no, but, with his sexy eyes staring into mine, the only word I can form is, "Okay."

Hayes flashes his devastatingly handsome smile at my response as his fingers tap along the side of his drink. "How long have you lived in Milwaukee?"

"I've been here about eight years. Moved here from a really small town in Illinois you will never have heard of. Got a job opportunity here and wanted a change of pace from small-town life. Don't get me wrong, growing up where everybody knows everybody is great. But the downside of that, as an adult, is everybody knows everybody." I grimace, feeling the walls close in around me. "They are always all up in your business, telling you what you should be doing, what you shouldn't be doing, and it's... *a lot.* Plus, I'm more of a city girl. There are more things to do here and *way* less corn fields and nosy people. I love the hustle and bustle of the busy city, but also the joy of finding hidden gems where you feel like you're the only person there." I glance around Walt's, feeling at home in the packed bar. "Plus, the weather in the summer is gorgeous. The breeze off the lake…there's nothing like it. It's-" Biting my lip, I feel my cheeks heat as I force myself to take another sip of my drink. *Stop rambling, Olivia. This guy does not care about small towns, wind, or corn fields.*

"How about you, Hayes? How long have you lived here in Milwaukee?"

He looks at his watch, and my heart sinks. He's probably got to go meet his smoking hot girlfriend. Stupid for me to think someone, especially this guy and his smile that won't quit, would actually help me tonight. But he glances up with a shy smile and says, "Exactly twelve hours, thirty-seven minutes, and maybe a few seconds. I just moved to town today."

He's new in town. Interesting. I watch him with a newfound curiosity. There's something fascinating about seeing someone discover this place for the first time.

"What brought you here to the good land of Milwaukee?"

"Same as you," he replies. "I moved here for a job. I also needed a change of pace. Plus, my hometown did not have a lot of opportunities to help haul equipment out of a bar into a non-stranger's car," he says as I laugh. I am a sucker for a good sense of humor, one that gets me to laugh and calm down. I can't help but notice he keeps referring to only himself. Not a *we* to be heard. *That has to be a sign he's single, right?*

I mentally knock my forehead into the wall. *What are you doing Olivia…you are not single.* I need this guy to put some sunglasses on pronto; those brown eyes boring into my soul are not helping me remember I have a boyfriend. One who is currently getting drunk with his roommates who are all too old to be sitting in a living room getting plastered and playing a stupid hockey video game.

"I think you're going to love it here." I smile as I raise my almost empty glass towards him. "Cheers to new beginnings!" I shout with a smile.

He raises his glass to clink mine back. "To not-strangers. I think I'm going to love it here, too."

5
hayes

Olivia is my fucking dream girl. I've always had a thing for redheads, but she's something else entirely. Between her sultry voice, her petite, curvy body that would fit so damn perfectly in my arms, and those beautiful lips. I would give anything to pull her close and kiss her right here and now as I run my fingers through that gorgeous auburn hair.

Fuck. Get it together, Hayes.

You already told her she lights up the room, and now you've volunteered to walk her, and her equipment, to her car. You know for a fact she has a boyfriend. Albeit a really shitty boyfriend. I barely know this girls name, but I know she deserves better than that pathetic excuse for a man. It feels like a punch to the heart whenever I think of her being with him. *What's the male version of homewrecker called?* That's what I would like to do with their relationship. Technically, I don't even know if they live in the same home, but I'd like to be the reason her relationship to that guy fails. *Relationship-wrecker?* I fight to hide the satisfied smirk on my face. That's good. I'll work with my agent on the branding.

On the other hand, I know what it's like to be the other party in a wrecked relationship. My most recent ex, Chelsea, was cheating on me. And the cherry on top was she got pregnant with the other guy's baby. It's the main reason I'm here in Milwaukee. I needed to get away from that life, away from the hurt she caused me. I'm glad it ended before we got engaged. Or married. But the pain from time wasted on someone who wasn't investing back in you hurts like a motherfucker. I suppose every relationship story has two sides, but I really felt like I tried my best. I thought I did right by her. I provided for her even though we weren't legally tied together. I did things I thought were special like sending her gifts or flowers when I was out of town for games. I thought I was a good boyfriend, but it wasn't enough. And that realization has gnawed at me for months. Every moment of silence filled with nagging thoughts of my failures. Even now, as I'm dodging puddles and carrying an enormous speaker, I can't help but think about that toxic situation.

I force myself out of the darkness consuming my mind, gazing instead at a piece of the sun on Earth. Maybe *I* don't want to be the person who wrecks Olivia's current relationship. But the way she smiled at me earlier when I told her she lit up a room tells me she's not getting told that enough. And that doesn't mean I can't hope Banks will wreck their relationship all by himself. My beer sits heavy in my stomach. That actually seems highly plausible if tonight was any indication of their normal interaction.

"How long have you and Banks been together?" I ask as we walk to her car with her equipment. Thankfully the rain let up a bit and is now just a slight mist. *Though…if I learned anything about rain and romance from the movies…*

"Banks?" she replies, her brows dipping together before quickly saying, "Ohhhh, you mean Cayden! Sorry. His name is Cayden Banks, but everyone calls him Banks. Except me and his family. I just always thought Banks was a dumb name, so I never called him that. I don't think some people even realize Banks is not his first name." She rolls her eyes. "We've been together for a year and a half."

Well fuck. That's longer than I was expecting. I hide my disappointment with a nod, thankful that she probably can't see much of my face behind this big ass speaker. That's more in the 'will they/won't they walk down the aisle' territory than the 'we've been together for two months and he sucks ass' territory. But being the gentleman I am, I simply say, "Wow, a year and a half? That's a long time."

I want to tell her every detail about my encounter with him at the bar, but I refrain and relay just enough to let her know I got the gist of his attitude towards her. "He mentioned he got you this gig at Walt's. That's sweet of him. How long have you been playing here?"

She stops, and I walk a few steps past her before I realize what happened. "Wait…you talked to him?"

"Yeah, he was sitting next to me at the bar."

"Oh. Gosh, I guess I didn't notice. But I'm not surprised he told you he got me this gig. *Classic* Cayden." She scoffs, quickly catching up to me. "Walt is neighbors with his parents, and Cayden introduced me to him at a barbecue they were having last summer. Walt mentioned he owned a bar and, somehow, the conversation turned into me stopping by during a happy hour to check it out. He said his usual happy hour singer just moved out of town, and he was looking for a regular replacement. I auditioned, and…well, here we are." A nearly uncontained grin splits her face. *She really loves this place. This job.* "I'm not sure he 'got me this gig,' but he did introduce me to Walt."

The rage brewing in me makes me want to beat this guy within an inch of his life. I officially hate this guy. He's going around telling people he got her this gig when all he did was introduce her to the owner of the bar. My knuckles turn white gripping the sides of the speaker. *I'm going to cut this guy's nuts off if I ever see him again.*

"Well, if you ask me, your talent is what got you this gig. I mean, if you were horrible, would Walt have hired you?" I ask as she opens the trunk of her car.

She looks into my eyes as if she's deep in thought. "Yeah, I guess you're right. I never thought about it that way. He tells everyone he got me this gig, and I guess I just let him. It's one of those 'pick your battle' situations where I give him that win."

But the weight of disappointment I see in her eyes tells me she's not happy he gets to win this battle. And she's right.

"You shouldn't let him win," I say as I help her get the speakers, her keyboard, and other gear into the car. She shuts the trunk, biting her lip and refusing to look at me. "I'm probably over-stepping here…" I pause.

"But…?" Olivia looks back at me, curious to know my thoughts.

"But you should know you're extremely talented. You should be damn proud of that. You can have a God-given talent, and if you don't do anything with it, it just sits there unseen and unrefined. You have to work hard for it. You have to hone your craft to be good. From what I heard tonight, you've done that, Olivia. You're phenomenal. Don't let anyone but you take credit for that."

I don't know how the fuck the universe works, but as I talk to her about talent, I realize my talent and hard work is what got me here to Milwaukee tonight. Every practice. Every game. Every hard hit suddenly has meaning. It's all led me to the back alley behind Walt's on Water, my new favorite bar in the city. Staring at the most gorgeous girl I've ever seen, tears forming in her bright eyes. She jumps, her arms wrapping around me so tightly it feels like she's never going to let me go.

If I'm being honest, I don't want her to.

6
olivia

I'm full-on bear hugging a man I just met in a bar. And, I might add, a very tall, handsome, and muscular man with a killer smile and big, soulful eyes. I don't know what possessed me to wrap my arms around him. Maybe it was the cider beer. Maybe it's the fact my boyfriend ditched me for a stupid video game. Maybe it's because Hayes just said words I've desperately needed to hear for years but never had voiced. Regardless of the reason, I'm holding onto him so tightly I don't want to let go. But a wave of guilt washes over me and I loosen my grip, pulling back from him slightly.

He wraps his warm arms around me and pulls me even tighter into our embrace. One of his hands slowly rubs my back, soothing the pain and loneliness that's been my reality for so long. His other hand gently rests on the back of my head, holding my broken pieces together.

Hayes pulls back and gazes into my eyes with a deep longing, inviting something I feel deep in my soul. His hand cups my cheek as I lean into his touch, my eyes searching his as the sound of rain surrounds us. Hayes slowly leans closer, his lips inches from mine. Heat burns in my core making me have thoughts and desires I should not be having since I have a boyfrie-

"BOOM"

Hayes and I jump back from one another, my cheek cold from losing his heat. I look over to see Johnny walking away from the dumpster. I swear I see the slightest smirk on his face as he quickly looks away and heads back into the bar.

"I should get going," I sheepishly say nervously digging in my purse for my keys. *What the hell am I doing?*

"Olivia, I'm sorry if I overstepped. That's not like me," he says, his face crumpling with remorse.

"You didn't overstep at all. I got caught up in your stellar equipment hauling skills and all your talk about talent," I mumble under my breath. "I'd better get going. It was so nice to meet you, Hayes, and thanks again for helping me with my gear." I open my car door, but I turn back to look at him, my heart not wanting the moment to end, but my head knowing it's the right thing to do. "Seriously, thank you for tonight. Welcome to Milwaukee."

7
hayes

Welcome to Milwaukee indeed. If this is the welcoming committee, I'm going to look for sponsorship deals with the Milwaukee Tourism Board, because *damn*.

But...*fuck*. She has a boyfriend. On the other hand, *she* was the one who put her arms around me and pulled me in close enough I could feel the pounding of her heart. Those soft lips, capable of singing the most beautiful songs, were *so close* to mine. God, I wanted to kiss her. *Fuck her shitty-ass boyfriend.*

And now I'm home in my apartment. Alone. No internet. No TV. Just my imagination. I am definitely not going to lie here in my empty apartment imagining those lips on other places of my body. I shift on my bed, lacing my fingers behind my head. Nope. I'm a respectful gentleman. Staring at the ceiling, I hear the low rumble of the fridge, filling the void Olivia left. My jeans feel tight as I relive the night over and over. I need more alcohol.

And a cold shower.

I strip off my clothes, my phone slipping from my pocket, hitting the floor with a loud thud. Holy shit...I could Google her!

Find her on social media maybe? Snapping my phone off the floor in an instant, I hop back on my bed to do some detective work. *Shit.* We did not exchange last names. *Damnit.* Maybe she's on the bar's social media page? A quick search for Walt's on Water only brings up a few check-ins and one bad review claiming they had the world's worst mozzarella sticks and should be ashamed to serve them in the dairy state, but no actual social media page. *Remind me to stick to the cheese curds.* Turns out Walt's is in the technology dark ages. And no mentions of Olivia. I drop my phone on my stomach.

Fuck.

Maybe I'll go back to the bar tomorrow and see if that bartender, Johnny, will give me the scoop. I think I saw him smiling when he caught us outside. Or maybe it was an evil smile. He does work for Walt, who apparently knows Olivia's boyfriend somehow. Then again, he seemed like he wasn't a fan of Banks. Or Bart. Or whatever the fuck that guy's dumbass name is.

I throw my arm over my eyes, fisting my sheets with my other hand. I can let this go. I'm not here to find a relationship. I just got out of a really shitty one. I'm here to work hard and play hockey, building a new life for myself in a new city. I'm a professional. We hit the ice every day, putting our personal lives aside and focusing on the task at hand. *Speaking of hands…*they were so petite and silky. The thought of what I want her doing with those hands has me hard as a rock.

Fuck cold showers.

Palming my dick, imagining her hands instead of mine, I dream of her soft lips parting to take me in one inch at a time. Wishing her fingers were digging into my ass to pull me further into her mouth. Wanting her to look up at me with those fathomless eyes while she licks and sucks my thickness. I move my hand slowly at first, then faster and faster, longing to have Olivia here, in my bed, lying beside me. On top of me. Beneath me. Every muscle in my body tenses as a warm feeling overtakes my abdomen. Fantasizing about my cum exploding across her tits and her tongue sends me over the edge. Screaming her name, I find my release longing for more of her.

"Fuck. I am totally screwed."

8
olivia

Three Weeks Later

Tonight is the home opener for the Milwaukee Steel Riders. Every game is exciting, but the first *real* game of the season is my favorite. The offseason feels dreadfully long for a fan, making the simple act of being in the arena with fresh ice exhilarating. It's like showing up for the first day of school with your new sneakers and backpack ready for a new start but being nervous to make a good impression. Except this 'class' just happens to be filled with twenty-thousand fans who will rip you to shreds on social media if you don't meet their standards.

No pressure.

Much like the players, I have a whole pre-game routine to help calm my nerves. While I get ready at home, I listen to my hockey playlist and fix my hair and makeup. I drink a cup of tea specifically brewed to prep my vocal cords, then I get dressed, putting on my prized possession, what I like to call my 'work uniform'. I cherish my personalized Riders jersey—the vibrant blend of blue, teal, and white, adorned with the team's striking motorcycle emblem on the front, and the name 'BROOKS' stitched across the back—fills me with pride.

As an added bonus, it really cuts down on the nightmare of deciding what to wear every time I perform for them.

Arriving at MKE Arena, I begin warming up my vocal cords for the national anthem. Cayden has been engrossed in something on his phone since the minute we got here. These last few weeks Cayden has been...off. Every time we talk, his words almost seem rehearsed, nothing like the way we used to talk when we met. My gut has been twisting with unease lately with this sudden change. And that doesn't even account for the fact I almost kissed a random guy in the back alley of a bar. *Now that I think about it like that, it really does sound like an episode of Dateline.*

Of course, I have not mentioned *that* incident to Cayden. He would lose his collective shit. But, sadly, I've only seen him once in the three weeks since my last show at Walt's. He's been distant, and I've been super busy working extra hours on the Bayview Bourbon campaign.

I just can't shake the fact that something seems funny with him. He is constantly on his phone, even more than usual, going to extreme lengths for me not to see his screen, and being more distant and standoffish than usual. I don't have evidence he's cheating on me, but I can't help thinking about that saying, 'where there's smoke there's fire.' *At least he came tonight to support me.* Or, more likely, for the free tickets.

"Hey babe, I'm going to go refill my water and use the restroom. I'll be back in a few." I glance at him, but he doesn't even look up from his phone. Rolling my eyes, I wander off toward the green room.

Pushing open the door with a silent huff, I see they have the usual dinner, snacks, and drinks for the Riders staff. I immediately spot David Green who is in charge of in-game entertainment. He's my 'national anthem boss' so to speak.

"Hey David! Ready for a new season? You didn't find anyone to replace me during preseason, did you?"

"Olivia! Good to see you, too, and no; you have not been replaced by the Singing Granny's Choir," he says, giving me a good laugh and helping calm the pre-game nerves.

"Anything special happening tonight before the anthem? Ceremonial puck drop? Sponsor appreciation?" I ask.

"Nope. Just the usual home opener pre-game introductions. You know the drill; Harley the mascot will skate out throwing t-shirts, they introduce all the coaching, training, and scouting staff, the players, then the starting lineup. Then you're up." He winks, catching me fidgeting with the bottom of my jersey. "I'm heading up to the booth, but I know you'll kill it out there, as usual, and get the crowd pumped up for the new season." He heads out into the hallway, lifting a hand over his shoulder in goodbye. "Make em cry, Liv!"

"You know it!" I yell back. I say a few hellos to some of the Riders staff I've gotten to know over the last few years as I fill up my water bottle and grab a snack, watching the monitor showing the fans in the crowd, Zambonis finishing up on the ice and the pre-game countdown. *Ten minutes till showtime.*

I head back to where I left Cayden. He's talking to some guy in a fancy suit, and I quickly realize it's Zack Reeves. *Oh no…*he's the team captain, one of the Riders best players, but he's recovering from an ACL repair. He's been cleared to practice, so hopefully he'll be back soon. Tonight, he's not playing, so he's walking around before the game in a nicely tailored three-piece suit.

As I near the two of them, Zack hands something to Cayden

and walks off towards the locker room shaking his head with an annoyed look on his face. *Was that a puck? And a marker?*

"Cayden! What were you doing talking to Zack Reeves?" I ask, slightly panicked.

Rule number one of being on staff or singing the anthem or being on the ice crew: No player interaction. If they say hi to you, you can say hello back—they aren't monsters, even if they are intimidating—but otherwise, there is *no* bothering them. They are working and don't need to be hounded for autographs, selfies, or anything else that could distract them. My stomach churns seeing this interaction, unsure about what transpired.

"Yeah. I got him to sign these pucks for me," Cayden replies, a wicked glint in his eyes as he pockets the pucks.

"You did WHAT?" I ask, my voice echoing around us.

"It's no big deal," he scoffs like I'm an idiot for mentioning it. "It's just some pucks."

I snap back. "Cayden, you know I could get *fired* for this right? We are not allowed to bother the players. Especially for autographs before a game. I've told you this!" *What the hell is he thinking?*

"Livy, you are way too uptight about this. It's not a big deal, and no one is going to say anything. Isn't it time for you to go sing now, anyway?"

Rage bubbles to the surface of my skin. This hockey arena is freezing, but right now...

I. Am. Fuming.

As much as I hate to admit it, he's right about one thing. It's seven minutes to pregame, and I have to grab my mic and get my in-ears situated. I *cannot* have this conversation with Cayden right now, who still seems to be engrossed in whatever the hell he's doing on his phone tonight. I have to focus. *Shake it off, Olivia. You can do this.*

Standing in a corner by a trash can just off the ice, I do a final run through of the Star-Spangled Banner. I could certainly find a classier place, but I warmed up here once and now it's part of my routine. I like my pre-game routines; they help settle the last of the butterflies. Even though I'm still fuming mad at Cayden, I have to focus on not screwing up the *one song* I am most known for. At least this song is about war, so I can fuel all my rage into this performance.

The Riders entertainment assistant rolls out a rug onto the ice for me to stand on and motions it's go time. As I walk out to hit my mark, the opposing team hits the ice and whips around the rink doing their pre-game warm up, and my lip curls. We are playing Omaha tonight, and their hideous dark brown uniforms are on full display. They look like giant prunes skating around the ice. *Is it petty to judge them for their uniform color?* Pursing my lips, I hum quietly to keep my voice warm. *Probably.* But vomit brown is just not in my color wheel.

The Milwaukee Steel Riders staff and players are introduced - all except for the starting lineup. The crowd is electric, so excited to see their boys back on the ice. I take in a deep breath and do one last check to make sure my mic is turned on.

The announcer begins the introduction of tonight's starters. "And now, the starting lineup for *YOUR* Milwaukee Steel Riders!!!" he shouts as the crowd cheers. "Starting at Center, from St. Paul, Minnesota, assistant captain, number 22, Hayes LARRRson!" I start to clap awkwardly with the heels of my hands, which is the only way to clap while holding a microphone…*wait a minute. Did he say Hayes?* I swear the announcer just said Hayes. My heart lodges in my throat, my head feeling fuzzy. Like the same name of the guy from the bar? Surely my mind is playing tricks on me, and this is a crazy coincidence. My head whips towards the video board, nearly knocking me off balance on the carpet. Not only is the name Hayes Larson up on the Jumbotron, but so is his picture and those damn gorgeous eyes I can't stop thinking about.

The microphone nearly drops from my grip. My jaw is nearly touching the ice. As I prepare to sing for a sold-out crowd, I stare up at the picture of the handsome man I nearly kissed three weeks ago in a back alley after he told me I lit up a room. Number 22 skates out of the tunnel, speeding across the rink towards me. He stops on the blue line, taking his spot for the anthem, smiling at the roaring crowd. My mouth goes dry, and my pulse races knowing he's standing on the same ice as I am.

Holy. Shit.

9
hayes

Kicking off the season as a Rider is the fresh start I needed. I'm charged up for this new opportunity, eager to leave my past behind. This team has some great talent, and if we can find the right groove, we'll be unstoppable. Being in the prime of my career, I'm excited for what I can bring to this team. Other professions may still see a thirty-year-old as a junior employee, but in hockey - this is it. In another few years, the sports world will be clamoring for me to retire. *But everything in my gut is telling me this is going to be my fucking year.*

I hear the announcer say my name, and I skate my way across the ice. *I'm ready for this.* I stand on the blue line with my stick stretching out to rest on the ice in front of me, taking a moment to soak everything in. The nerves pumping through me as the game is about to start are there, but they are a necessary evil. My anxiety eventually turns into pure adrenaline, and it fuels me while I play. I move my skates back and forth, getting a good feel for the ice, as the other players are announced and skate up in line beside me.

"Please rise and remove your hats for our National Anthem, performed tonight by Olivia Brooks."

Did he just fucking say Olivia? My blood was pumping with anxiety before, now it's full-on racing through my veins like a goddamn cheetah chasing a gazelle. That name and the gorgeous girl it belongs to have been haunting my thoughts for weeks and I cannot, *will not,* get her out of my mind. I don't know how, but that woman is going to be mine.

I gaze up to the top of the arena, then I hear five words I've heard a million times before every game. Sometimes good, and sometimes really, *and I mean really,* bad. Those five words, 'oh say can you see', are always the same. But tonight, those words sound different. They're beautifully sweet, piercing through my ears straight to my heart. Just like that night three weeks ago at the bar. I look down from the flag to the anthem singer.

Holy. Fucking. Shit.

There, on the other side of the ice, is a short girl with cascading red hair wearing a Riders jersey. *My* team's jersey. *My* Olivia. Okay, well, she's not mine…*not yet.* But there she is, standing on a small red carpet, her pipes belting out the most beautiful rendition of the anthem I've ever heard. The girl I've tried, but failed, to get out of my mind for the last three weeks is standing on the same ice I'm going to be playing on. *She's going to watch me play.* What did the announcer say her last name was? *Shit; I wasn't paying attention.* Fuck me man, I can find her now! *How did I not know she sang the anthem here?* As she keeps singing, I am once again mesmerized by this girl. Her voice. Her body. Literally everything about her.

She finally hits the high note, holding it out super long, and the crowd goes crazy as she finishes the song. The guys all tap their sticks on the ice as our way of cheering. My heart skips a beat, and I try to hide the smile creeping onto my face knowing they are all cheering for *my* Olivia. As the song ends, she smiles and waves at the crowd, and I swear, for the briefest second, she looks my way.

Does she know it's me?

My line-mate, defenseman Jordan Boucher, slaps me on the back as I'm still standing on the ice in shock instead of heading to the bench to get ready to play. To, you know, do my *actual* job.

"Hey Larsy, you okay, man?"

"Yep! Just excited for the game. That was…um…just a really good anthem, and being my first game here, I got caught up in the moment," I mumble, avoiding eye contact and adjusting my gloves as we skate back to the bench. I see Vladi cocking his head and glaring at me from his goal. I swear, I can't get anything past that damn goalie - whether it's pucks or me freaking out about a girl from center ice.

"Oh yeah! Our anthem singer is *good*. They call her The Weapon," he replied.

"The Weapon? Why the Weapon? Does she kill people with her voice or something?" *At this point, I wouldn't be surprised if she did.*

He laughs. "No man. I heard she started singing here a couple seasons back, and we won twelve games in a row. So, they called her 'The Secret Weapon,' which eventually shortened to 'The Weapon'. Apparently, she's our good luck charm, especially if we make the playoffs. But hey, let's go man; time to kick some Omaha ass!"

Right. Yes. The hockey game I need to focus on.

How the fuck am I supposed to concentrate knowing the girl who rocked my world with a song and a tight embrace three weeks ago is here in the same arena as me? *You can do this, Hayes. You are a professional.*

A professional who is majorly fucked.

10
olivia

When I sing the national anthem, I am never thinking about the song. My body goes into autopilot, and my muscle memory takes over. Usually, I'm thinking about how my face looks on the Jumbotron or what the rest of my plans are for the evening. *Is my hair okay? Am I smiling? Did I sing the right words? What should I get at the concession stand later?* Then, as I get towards the end of the song, my mind wanders to 'how long should I hold out the word free?' It's different thoughts and little tweaks every game.

But tonight, my thoughts are on none of that. They are focused on the player standing on the ice who held me so tightly three weeks ago, the one I'm desperately trying not to glance at. *Does Hayes know it's me? Was he paying attention?* I thought I would never see this guy again, and now he's here. Literally right in front of me. And, apparently, he's also the new star center for the Milwaukee Steel Riders. I'm tempted to check my watch for my heart rate; I don't think it's ever beaten this fast.

How did I not put two and two together? He almost kissed me for God's sake! I knew we signed a new player during the off season, but I didn't pay much attention. I saw a few news stories come across on my phone, but a lot of players come and go during the offseason. My mind is whirling with confusion, shock, and excitement, all while trying to get through this song. Besides, it's not like he was sitting in his hockey gear at the bar. I think the biggest misconception about hockey players is that they look like pro-wrestlers or football linebackers. They don't. I mean, they are very muscular, but they skate almost five miles during a game. Even tonight, Hayes looks much bigger than he did at the bar, and, obviously, taller on skates. My palm starts to sweat as I grip the microphone imagining how ripped he is underneath all that hockey gear. *Oh my gosh, Olivia! Calm your hormones. You are singing a very patriotic song honoring America; you cannot be thinking about what's under his hockey pads.*

Somehow, I miraculously get through the song like nothing is amiss, turning to walk off the carpet as if this was just another season opener. My pulse races as I catch Hayes looking this way, possibly recognizing me. But I have to get off the ice before the game starts, or I'll have ten players barreling toward me, their sticks clattering and skates cutting the ice, ready to slam me into the boards. My heart races at the thought. There is one player I wouldn't mind slamming me up against a wall. *Okay, Olivia. No more romance novels for you.* I'm switching to non-fiction. Maybe a nice book about Abraham Lincoln, who was apparently one of the more attractive men of his generation, should stop me from lusting after the hot hockey player in front of me. It's not like there are smut books about Abe Lincoln salaciously taking off Mary Todd Lincoln's bonnet. *Is that weirdly hot?* A full body shiver makes me nearly trip as I walk down the carpet. *Nope...nope it is not.* We do not need that book.

As I reach the side of the ice, Cayden is waiting for me. *Shit.* My stomach sinks, embarrassment heating my cheeks. *Cayden.* Kind of forgot about him during the last two minutes of internal drama happening in my head. He's been holding my phone. *Hopefully he thinks my blush is just from the chill of performing on the ice.*

As he hands me my phone, he says, "Sorry; forgot to film you. I got distracted."

Of course he did. Another classic Cayden moment.

But I don't want to argue; not after the euphoria of having sung in front of 20,000 people cheering for me. *One in particular that makes my heart stop.*

I force in a deep breath trying to stay calm in this very public setting.. "No worries. We'll just video the anthem at the next game for my social media."

By the time Cayden and I get to our seats, it's a few minutes into the first period. One of the biggest perks of singing here are the seats ten rows off the ice, just to the right of the opposing teams goal. Neither team has scored yet, but the Steers have a high-sticking penalty, and one of their players heads over to the box, putting the Riders on the advantage. The music director kicks up the power play song, and I raise my arms up and down for the little power play dance they do at the arena.

Cayden yanks my arms out of the air, and snaps, "I told you I hate that dumb power play dance, and my girlfriend is *not* doing the hand motions that go with it."

Tears well up, but I choke them back. "Sorry; I forgot," I mumble, feeling like an idiot. I forgot he hates this dance. I like to cheer on my team, and any way the crowd gets involved is great for ticket sales, team morale, and overall crowd experience. And it's fun! But Cayden thinks it 'makes a mockery of hockey.' *What is so horrible about doing hand motions to a song?* Some days I wish I had the nerve to just say 'fuck it' and do the dance anyway, but I always have this feeling that if I do or say the wrong thing, Cayden's going to leave me. On second thought, would it be such a bad thing? Twisting my fingers in my lap, I focus on relaxing my tense muscles. Maybe I'm just overreacting, *as he oh-so-nicely reminds me every day.* So what if I do overreact? It's not like I'm going to do anything about it. *Am I?* Surely being slightly unhappy is better than being alone.

The fans around me jump to their feet as one of our players flies down the ice towards Omaha's goalie. I stand up to get a better look, peeking around the tall people seated in front of my five-foot nothing frame. It's Hayes Larson. As he races towards me my heart thrums in my ears and my thighs squeeze together. *Why is this getting me so turned on?* Omaha had been in our zone trying for a shorthanded goal, when Hayes snatched the puck, skating full speed towards the Steers goalie. My palms are sweaty and every nerve in my body is on edge as he zooms past me. He dekes once to one side, and the goalie goes for it. I catch myself holding my breath, nearly falling forward as I stretch further on my toes. Hayes dekes again to the other side, shooting the puck right into the net without hesitation.

The horn sounds and the crowd roars. "Milwaukee Steel Riders GOAL! Scored by number twenty-two Hayes Larson."

Milwaukee is up 1-0 over Omaha. I reach over to high-five Cayden, but he's too busy high fiving everyone else near our seats. *Of course.* I watch Hayes get tackled by his new teammates in a group hug, then he leads them in high fiving all the players on the bench. *I bet he would high five me first if he were sitting here.*

As I slump back into my seat, I notice Cayden taking a handful of cash from the guy sitting next to him, then shaking hands.

"Cayden, *what* are you doing?" I say through gritted teeth.

"This guy gave me cash for one of my Reeves pucks! The other ones are listed for sale online. This is gonna bring me in a *nice* profit. All thanks to your little singing thing, Livy," he says as he pats me on top of the head.

I grip the seam on the side of my jeans with white knuckles and take a deep calming breath. "I have asked you *repeatedly* to please stop calling me Livy. And you're selling the pucks? Jeezus! What the hell are you thinking?"

"Chill, babe! It's fine. People sell pucks all the time."

Leaning back in my seat, I cross my arms and stare into the rafters of the arena. *I can't freaking deal with this shit right now.*

The horn sounds as the first period ends, and the players head back to the locker room. The arena hums with fans heading to the concourse for snacks or a bathroom break. But my eyes are fixed on number twenty-two, and I manage the slightest smile at the way he skates off the ice with confidence after scoring his first goal of the season. *What I wouldn't give to have him sitting here next to me right now.*

My phone buzzes, pulling me out of my wishful thinking. I have a text from David.

> DAVID
>
> Hey Olivia, can you meet me down in the green room after the game?

That's weird. I usually don't see David after I sing, but maybe he wants to do something different with the anthem at the next game? *Oh God does he know Hayes and I know each other? About the pucks?* My worries turn into instant diarrhea stomach as my shaking fingers type back to let him know I'll meet him there. *Shit.*

"Hey, I have to go meet with David after the third period," I shout to Cayden, trying to be heard over the break antics on the ice.

"Seriously? So, we have to stay late after the game? Why can't he talk to you now? You know I like to leave early to get a jump on traffic," he grumbles with irritation. I try to contain my eyeroll and annoyance, knowing this is not going to end well.

"Because he's *working* through the entire game Cayden. He directs the entire in-game show, including everything happening during the intermission. He's the one in charge here, so I need to go. It won't take long, then we can head back to my place and relax," I say, hopeful some alone time will help smooth over the pain and frustration of the night.

"Yeah, *about* that," he mutters, shifting awkwardly in his seat to face me. His eyes dart around before he finally settles on me. "I'm just gonna drop you off. The guys are hanging out tonight, and I don't want to be too late."

"Sure, Cayden," I say, my sigh dripping with sarcasm, "Noooo problem. I'm sure you'll have a great time with your *friends*" *While your girlfriend sits at home. Alone…*again.

"You're the best, Livy. I'm gonna go get another beer before the second period starts," he throws over his shoulder as he slaps me on the back, like I'm one of the guys, making me spill a little of my drink.

As he walks away, tears well in my eyes again. I don't know how we got here. I guess it doesn't matter. *I will not cry alone in my seat.* I chug the rest of my beer as a fiery rage ignites in my belly. I'm nothing more than background noise in my own boyfriend's life, and I'm not sure how much longer I can take it.

11
hayes

"Great game, boys! You were buzzin' tonight!" our coach, Gordon Calhoun, whoops as he comes into the locker room after the game. We beat Omaha 3-1, and I had a fucking hot stick tonight. "Game puck tonight is going to the guy with two goals and an assist, already making his mark on this team. This one's for you, Larsy!" All the guys cheer in deep voices, my nickname echoing around the locker room, and those around me pat me on the back, huge ass smiles on their faces. Being the new guy on the team, it's a big deal to get this game puck.

Jordan Boucher stops by to congratulate me. "Way to fucking start the season, Larsy! We're all going for drinks after the game; you wanna join?"

Bougie is a rookie this season, already earning his nickname from his obsession with designer everything. We all have to wear suits to the games, but he takes it to the next level wearing every designer label he can. He has Gucci belts for fucks sakes. I like nice clothes, but I'm not about to shell out fucking five-hundred dollars for a belt.

"Thanks man, but I'll pass tonight. Hit me up next time though," I reply.

He pouts, sticking out his lower lip like he's not an adult playing a professional sport. "Come on, Larsy; don't be a pussy! Have a few drinks, unwind, maybe meet a few puck bunnies…" he says in a sing-song voice.

I let out a laugh, my stomach clenching at the idea of chasing anyone but Olivia. *"No thanks.* I've had my fill of puck bunnies, Bougie. Now I'm an old man who just wants to go home and chill."

"Okay *Grandpa,*" he says walking away with a fake limp using his stick like a cane. "Be a fucking Wheel Watcher and go home. Just know that while you're trying to buy an 'o' to solve the puzzle, I'll be balls deep in a sexy woman giving her the best 'o' of her life."

I roll my eyes and shake my head. *Oh, to be twenty-one again.* So full of yourself without a care in the world.

"Ignore him," Vladi says, coming up beside me. "Fucking rookies." I snort, remembering what I was like freshly drafted to the ice. "That one especially. He's cocky as shit, and it doesn't help he's a trust fund baby and doesn't need a dime of his salary. If he doesn't do his job and keep the puck away from my goal, he's getting a fucking beating."

"Always so kindhearted, aren't you, Vladi?" I say with a wink.

"Just call it like I see it," he says in a monotonous tone, his voice having the slightest hint of a Russian accent.

"You going out with them?"

"Fuck no; I'm going home too. My old ass is tired," he yells over his shoulder, walking towards the showers.

Stripping down and heading towards the promise of relief for my sore muscles, I finally have a moment to think back to seeing Olivia tonight. She's our *fucking anthem singer,* which means I finally found my dream girl. The way my heart and my dick, got an instant hard-on when I heard that voice and saw her across the ice made it hard to breathe. Then, I saw that bitch-ass boyfriend of hers off the ice, on his damn phone the entire time she was singing. My mood sours, my face falling flat as my jaw ticks. I channel all my rage into soaping up and rinsing off, my fingers leaving marks against my skin with how much I fucking hate that guy. If I start thinking about the girl I've been obsessed with for weeks while I'm showering, it's going to be evident *real fast* I'm not replaying my goals from tonight's game. The *only* goal I'm interested in is finding Olivia and making her mine.

Bitch-ass boyfriend be damned.

I finally dress back into my suit and head down the long hallway leading to the underground players' parking area. Walking past the staff green room, I hear someone crying as they try to talk. *I wonder what that's about.* As I walk past the door, I can't help but take a quick peek inside.

And there, sitting in a chair crying, is Olivia.

My chest tightens as I try to reign in my protective instincts that are screaming at me to run to her. Then I hear her douchebag boyfriend say, "Stop crying. Will you just stop crying, please!?"

I swear to all the hockey Gods listening, I'm going to punch this cocksucker in the face. *Fucker deserves it.* Everyone knows the cardinal rule when a girl is crying is you never say, 'stop crying.' I continue walking past the door to the green room but stop to listen, leaning against the wall next to the door. I know I shouldn't be eavesdropping, but I need to know why Olivia is crying. I need to know if she's okay.

"How could you do this to me, Cayden?"

I stand up from the wall and move a little closer to the door. *Should I do something?*

"What's the big deal anyway? It's not like you get paid to sing here or anything."

Olivia scoffs. "What's the big deal?!" she mutters as I hear her fighting back tears with a tightness in her throat, "The big deal is you got me *fired* by bringing pucks with you to get autographed when you *know* that's against the rules. My boss found out about it. He actually showed me a screenshot of the pucks posted for sale online, and now I'm done. No more games. No more singing for the Riders. I love this team and the staff here; it's an amazing opportunity to get my name out there, and you blacklisted me from the entire organization. That's what the big deal is!"

Holy shit why does her standing up to him get me a little turned on.

"It's not like your music career is going anywhere anyway," Cayden whines.

"Oh, hell no," I whisper to myself. All of my restraint flies out of the window. I can't stand here for another second and act like I'm not hearing this asshole talk to her like this. I ball my hands up into fists, my knuckles going white as my hands shake, trying to contain my rage as I storm into the room looking only at Olivia. "Are you okay?"

She looks at me with those same longing eyes from a few weeks ago, stunned, but doesn't reply. Eyes that are now bloodshot and glistening with tears. My chest aches seeing her broken heart so exposed.

"Oh, wow! Hayes Larson!" I hear douche canoe say from across the room.

I don't give him the courtesy of looking his way; I only focus on Olivia as I softly ask again, "Olivia, are you okay?"

"Yeah, I'm okay," she mumbles, but the tense and overwhelming sadness in her eyes tell me she's anything but okay.

As if ignoring this fuckwad wasn't a hint enough, he is, somehow, still talking. "Hey man, you had a great game tonight. Two goals! Wait a minute..." He gasps, and I see him covering his mouth out of the corner of my eye. "That was you! Sitting next to me at Walt's a few weeks ago. I didn't recognize you with the hat on! Dude, no fucking way I shared a drink with Larsy! Could you sign my jersey?"

Slowly and methodically, my hands still squeezed into tight fists, I turn to face him, hoping he can see the rage filled daggers I am shooting his way. As I try and compose a response to his auto-graph request, Olivia speaks instead, surging from her seat with newfound confidence and rage.

"Seriously, Cayden?! You *just* got me fired for asking Zack Reeves to sign pucks for you, and now you're asking Hayes Larson to sign your *jersey*?!"

"Yeah, you got fired, so it's not against the rules anymore, right?" Cayden barks. I crack my neck from side to side trying to keep my cool, but also preparing myself to knock this motherfucker out.

"This is another *perfect* example of Cayden Banks only caring about himself," Olivia snaps, trying desperately not to cry. The asshole just gapes like a fish, his mouth opening and closing without saying anything. "Why can't you ever just want me?" she whispers, tears streaming down her face.

"Livy, I didn't want to do this here, especially not in front of Hayes Larson, but we need to breakup," Cayden snarks, pulling his phone out and swiping through it for a moment.

Olivia stops crying, silence blanketing all of us, and says, "What? You're breaking up with *me*? After you just got me fired? Wow, as always, this is *amazing* timing on your part."

"Yeah, I've been meaning to tell you, but I just got distracted. I think it's for the best, given how upset you are," Cayden says, smirking at something on his phone. "Also, do you think you could take an Uber home since we're not together? You know I'm hanging out with the guys tonight. Larsy, you're welcome to join us. We're going to the casino to have some drinks and gamble."

Olivia collapses back into her seat, a blank look on her face as tears continue to cascade down her cheeks. *Is this fucking guy for real?* What is the actual penalty for murder, because I am about to destroy this idiot. I grab a fist full of his shirt, yanking him towards me, my six-foot height towering over his short frame.

"Get the fuck out of *my* arena before I call security. You are not credentialed to be down here, and if you *ever* speak to Olivia that way again, or call me Larsy, it will be the last thing you ever say," I hiss through gritted teeth.

"Okay, okay. Geez man. You're awfully sensitive for being the new guy on the team." His eyes bounce back and forth between mine, seeing the absolute certainty I could end him without giving a flying fuck. "Fine! I'll leave, but seriously, let me know if you ever want to hang out man!" Cayden says as he pulls his shirt from my grip and trips out of the room, his nose once again glued to his phone.

Olivia stares down at the floor, seemingly embarrassed and trying to choke back more sobs. I grab a chair, spinning it to face her, my palms itching to hold hers. She is somehow still the most stunning woman I've ever seen, even with puffy eyes and smeared makeup. Olivia, *my Olivia,* is hurting, and it's killing me to see her suffer.

"Hi; I'm Hayes Larson." I reach my hand out to shake hers. "My new job in town is being a center for the Milwaukee Steel Riders. I'm sorry I didn't mention that the other night. And *you* are welcome to call me Larsy anytime you like. That name is only for people I respect, and no offense, but I don't respect that guy."

She smiles and gives a half laugh as she shakes my hand. "Hi Hayes. I'm Olivia Brooks, and one of my many singing gigs is…*was* being the anthem singer for the Milwaukee Steel Riders. I'm sorry I didn't bring that up after you almost stranger-danger kidnapped me in a back alley, then I almost kissed you and fled the scene mortified before I knew you were a big deal hockey player."

"I did *not* almost kidnap you. We established we were non-strangers after exchanging names," I playfully respond, my heart racing looking down at her lips at the mention of the almost kiss we shared.

"I guess you're right," she smiles, but only for a second, and I can see the gravity of her reality setting in.

"Can I ask what happened tonight? You got fired?"

Olivia takes in a deep breath, then slowly lets it out, her body collapsing on itself, before she begins to tell me what is going on. "When you sing for a team, you're not allowed to hang out with, or bother, the players. *Especially* not for autographs. If they say hi, you can say hi back, but we are not allowed to go up to them and ask for stuff. And I get it; you guys are working. If every person who worked here asked you for an autograph, it would take all three periods for you to sign their stuff. And, apparently one of the ice crew on another team got knocked up by one of their married players. It was a huge scandal, and she accused him of pressuring her. So, as you can imagine, they are super strict about it now, which makes sense."

This girl is just so damn sweet. And practical. And probably a little bit of a rule follower too. But after we almost kissed the other night, I smirk, far too curious to see if she likes to break some rules once and awhile too. *Fuck...focus, Hayes.*

"Apparently, Cayden saw Zack Reeves in the back of the arena before I went out to sing. I had no idea he brought pucks with him, or that he asked Zack to sign them. I was refilling my water before the anthem when it all happened. I barely saw Zack hand him the pucks and walk away as I got back. I wasn't even there, but he posted the freaking pucks for sale online, and someone sent it to David. He asked me to come down here after the game and told me I couldn't sing for the Riders anymore. He said he was really sorry, but he can't make any exceptions. I don't know what I'm going to do," she says as the tears well in her eyes again.

"Is there anything I can do to help? Do you want me to go talk to David? I don't know him well, since I'm so new, but I'm sure he'd listen to me. This was obviously not your fault."

"Oh my gosh, no! You do not need to do that. It'll probably make things worse. I should just go home and contemplate what to do with my life." She pulls out her phone, her hands shaking as she unlocks the screen. "And now I have to get an Uber home…so that's fun," she says as she slumps forward looking away from me embarrassed as if she's about to cry again.

"I can give you a ride home. My car is in the players' lot, and I don't mind at all. I won't even charge you surge pricing." Olivia looks at me for a minute, stunned, before her face morphs and she starts to laugh.

Then she punches me in the arm.

"Hey!" I gingerly rub my shoulder, a smirk lifting my lips. "I don't have my pads on anymore! That's the arm of tonight's first star of the game; you better be careful," I say playfully.

"Oh no," she pouts, fluttering her lashes as she cocks her head to the side. "Is the big, bad hockey player sensitive? Hope you don't hurt your arm opening the car door for me."

I didn't know anything could top her smile, but the smirk and sassy attitude she's giving me goes straight to my heart…and my dick. *I'm going to have* so *much fun with this girl.*

"So, can I drive you home then?" I ask, my voice a little shaky hoping she won't say no. *I do not want to chance her getting away from me ever again.* "I'd love to make sure you get back okay after every-thing that happened."

"Are you sure? I don't want to hold you up any longer." She bites her lip, and I need to remind my libido she's not mine *yet*, my cock eager to put her mouth to use. "You've already stuck around to make sure I was okay after this mess. You are probably tired after the game and need to rest, and I can just get a -"

"Olivia", I stop her mid-sentence. "It would be my pleasure."

12
olivia

I am *terrified* to walk by a mirror right now. I probably look like a dying clown. I'm on the verge of a crying headache, my eyes are swollen, and the chaos spinning in my head from the last ten minutes is overwhelming. But Hayes Larson is walking *me* through the players' parking lot. He puts his hand on the small of my back, guiding me toward his car. My skin ignites from his touch, and the ache in my heart quickly morphs into gratefulness toward the man driving me home. On a normal night, I would never be allowed to talk to a player, let alone get a ride home from one. But…I *technically* don't work for the Riders anymore, so I guess there is one bright spot in the evening.

I jump at the honk of a vehicle passing by us. *God, I'm on edge right now.* Coming to a stop next to us, the window rolls down.

"You still headed home, Larsy?" Vladi says with a smirk and one eyebrow raised at Hayes.

"Yes Vladi, just giving Olivia a ride home first. Olivia, this is my best friend, and nosy bastard, Vladi."

"Pleasure to officially meet you, Olivia. Don't let Larsy use that hockey player charm on you."

Oh my God. My eyes widen in shock and embarrassment. Is Vladimir Volkov, aka *The Wolf,* hinting at the tension between Hayes and I? The air leaps from my lungs at the thought of Larsy using his charm, or honestly any part of his body, on me.

I finally compose myself enough to respond. "Nice to meet you too Vladimir."

"You are The Weapon. You have my respect. You may call me Vladi."

Well, I was The Weapon. Still…it's nice of him to say. I give him a soft smile at the kind words, nodding at his request.

"Okay Vladi," Hayes says trying to shoo him off. "Thanks for stopping to say goodbye. See you at the airport in the morning,"

"Yes, Larsy. I'll save you a seat on the plane. *Right* next to me. I cannot wait to catch up," Vladi says with a wink as he drives off. Hayes looks up to the top of the parking garage and shakes his head, and I can't help but let out a little giggle.

Arriving at his parking spot, Hayes opens the door for me. The smell of crisp leather and Hayes' cologne engulfs me as I slide into the passenger seat. *This is a nice, black SUV.* I'm not a car expert, nor do I have any interest in cars, but I think this might be a Mercedes. Clasping my hands in my lap, too scared to touch anything, I watch Hayes jog to the driver's side. I basically know two things about cars - what color it is and how much gas is in the tank. And yes, I'm one of those 'driving on fumes' gals, knowing exactly how far I can drive after the gas light comes on. I'm going to guess Hayes is one of those guys that never lets his car get below half a tank.

"No equipment to haul tonight?" Hayes jokes after we're both settled.

"Nope! Luckily, MKE Arena has its own built-in sound system.

Otherwise, you'd be up in the rafters on a catwalk unhooking my speakers to pack in the car," I say as he laughs.

"Well, equipment or not, I am more than happy to drive you home. But, I do need to ask you something," he says with a serious, deep voice that makes my heart skip a beat.

Oh my gosh. Is he going to ask for some big favor for this? Is this going to turn into an episode of Dateline? Do I look so hideous from crying he's changed his mind about the ride home? Flinching, I look in the rearview mirror to make sure I don't look like an actual monster. Then I look at him stunned, not knowing what to say.

"I need to know your address," he says, a ridiculous smile stretching across his face.

I awkwardly laugh with a relieved smile. "Yes, you do. I can put it into your GPS."

He hands me his phone, starts the car, and nods toward some of his teammates as we drive by. "Go for it. You should add your number in there too."

"Why would you need my number, Hayes?"

"In case of emergencies," he says, completely serious as we pull out of the parking garage.

I glare at him. "Emergencies? What kind of emergency would you need my number for?"

"First of all, I don't know many people in town, and I may need someone to help me haul my gear to my car," he says with a smile. "Or someone may try to kidnap me and hold me for ransom. You can never be too careful with stranger danger in this town." He glances at me out of the corner of his eyes. "Or some asshole could call me Larsy and ask me to autograph their jersey, and I accidentally punch them in the face, ending up in jail and in need of someone to bail me out." He looks at me a little sheepishly, clearing his voice to get rid of the growl he fell into. "Too soon?"

I stare at him for a minute…then burst out laughing, my eyes watering as I struggle to catch my breath.

"No. Not too soon at all. I would *definitely* provide bail money for that," I giggle. "You should *for sure* have my number for that reason alone. I don't want you sitting in a cell overnight thinking of which guy will make the best prison boyfriend." He laughs from deep in his belly, warming mine as I hand him his phone back with my address in his phone GPS and my number in his contacts. I bite my lip trying to hide the excitement of him having my number.

"So, you sing *and* you're funny?" he says, glancing at his screen and lane changing for our exit.

"Yeah, I guess. Thanks for laughing at my jokes."

"You're funny, Olivia. I thought you were funny a few weeks ago at Walt's too."

"Cayden never laughed when I said something funny, but then he always tried to steal my jokes and use them as his own. But, with jokes, it's all about timing and delivery, and he just didn't have the delivery, so no one ever laughed. But he still took the credit for it. I'm sorry, I should stop. I don't want to talk about Cayden all night; he's wasted enough of my time."

"Me neither," Hayes replies with a gentleness in his voice I didn't expect.

The miles seem to pass by in a flash, Hayes' music playing quietly in the background. 80s rock is a genre I wouldn't expect he'd enjoy, but now that I know him a little more, it's the perfect fit.

"I know there was a lot going on tonight, so I haven't gotten a chance yet to tell you how awesome your anthem was. I've have heard a lot in my career, from middle school bands that make your ears bleed, to electric guitars that don't make sense, to famous popstars merely doing it for the exposure, but yours tonight was the most beautiful version I've ever heard."

Heat floods my cheeks, and it feels unbearably hot in this car.

"You think so?" I whisper, twining my fingers together in my lap. "I was a little distracted when I saw you skate out on the ice, if I'm being honest, and all the puzzle pieces started clicking into place that you were the same Hayes from Walt's. So, I wasn't sure if it was one of my best performances."

"Olivia," he says in a deep, serious tone, turning his head long enough to make me lift mine and stare back. "Do you remember me saying I don't give out compliments I don't mean? Please believe me when I say you are amazing."

Where did this guy come from? Cayden never once told me my singing was beautiful. *He never actually told me I was beautiful either.* It was always 'you look nice' or 'I like that outfit.' And now, here I am, getting a ride from a pro hockey player who thinks my singing is beautiful.

"Plus, that anthem literally gave me chills. It got me and the whole team pumped up for the game. You're definitely the reason why we won," he says with a smile, taking a quick glance at me.

"Oh, stop it; that's not true," I scoff, trying to give him another smack on the arm. But as I do, he takes his hand off the steering wheel and grabs mine before I can playfully punch him. And then he just…holds my hand. I swallow hard as heat creeps into my cheeks. I try and hide my smile, but it's no use. He rubs his thumb along my knuckles and gently sets our clasped hands on my thigh as he continues to drive towards my place.

Then I realize two things at once:

Cayden broke up with me. He is no longer my boyfriend, and I'm single for the first time in eighteen months.

Hayes Larson is holding my hand. On. My. Thigh. And he's not letting go.

13
hayes

Olivia's hand is silky smooth and absolutely tiny in my massive hockey mitts, her fingers fitting in mine like a missing puzzle piece. I'm not exactly sure what all went down with her and Douche-A-Roni before I showed up, but I want to show her there are other options out there besides dickwads and assholes. And with the help of my fantastic athletic reflexes and peripheral vision, I grab her hand before she hit me in the arm again. I'm getting major brat vibes from my little siren, and I am fucking here for it. Now I'm driving with her perfect hand in mine, and the best part is - she's not pulling away.

"FUCK!" I yell as some dumbass in the right lane does an illegal turn across my lane, making us almost t-bone his truck. I drop Olivia's hand, my reactive hockey instincts kicking in, and I swerve to miss running head on into the back side of this guy's souped-up pickup truck. I lay on the horn, letting this idiot know he almost caused a major accident, and pull off to the side of the road, trying to calm myself down and get my bearings straight.

"Fuck! What the hell was that guy thinking? Shit, Olivia, are you okay?" I turn towards Olivia, my heart breaking as I see her white knuckle gripping the side of the door, her face pale as her breaths come in sharp pants. "I'm so sorry for that. I can't believe that guy whipped around out of the blue like that."

She takes a deep breath, slowly prying her fingers off the door. "Yeah, I'm fine. Just startled. Thank God we didn't hit that guy. The last thing you need is to get in a car accident with the season just starting."

"You don't need to get into an accident either. A broken arm seems like it would be extremely unhelpful for playing piano. Then I would have to play for you, and no one wants to hear that." I see a smile as I look over to make sure she's safe, settling the pounding panic in my own heart. "You sure you're okay?" I ask her one more time, cautiously reaching over to place a hand on her shoulder.

"Yes. I promise. Just shaken up," she says, placing her hand on top of mine. "But thanks; I'm okay. God, it's been quite the night. I don't know how things could get any worse. I'm really sorry."

"What in the world do you have to be sorry for?" I ask, worry and confusion thrumming through me.

"If you wouldn't have been driving me home, or if I hadn't been joking around and trying to smack your arm, you could have seen the guy sooner," she says, hanging her head down and biting her lip.

"Olivia. Look at me," I say as I grip her chin, tilting her face towards mine. "This was *not* your fault. You didn't distract me. Nothing could've prevented this besides that fucking idiot knowing where he was going. I could have just as easily gotten in a close call on the way back to my apartment," I reassure her as I move my thumb from her jaw line to brush the bottom of her lip. "This is not your fault, okay?"

"Okay." She looks at me with a half-smile, almost like she

doesn't believe me. *I swear I will find a way to undo these bruised pieces of her confidence.*

"Okay then. You're good. I'm good." I search her eyes, desperate to see her relax and believe me. She doesn't. Not fully. "The only guy at fault is that asshole in the other car. God, my heart is still racing."

My heart is racing from the adrenaline of almost getting in an accident, but it's also racing from the touch of the gorgeous passenger in my car with beautiful, soft lips I've been dreaming of kissing for the past three weeks. She leans into my palm more, closing her eyes for a moment and taking a deep breath. I can see the tension start to bleed from her, and my muscles relax a little more, my eyes locked on her delicate mouth. I sigh, breathing her in. She's had a rough night, and she just ended things with a giant douche, so, for now, I'll give her some space. *I can behave if I need to.*

"Let's get you home."

She smiles as I reluctantly pull away and hit my blinker to merge back onto the road. My hands are cold and empty without her touch, only the soft sound of the ballad on the radio heavy between us. I can sense her stress and heartbreak, and *fuck* I just want to hold her and not let go until I know she's okay. If only I knew what she's thinking in that gorgeous head of hers. *Is she truly upset about her breakup?* I grip the steering wheel tight, still shaky, and frustrated I'm not a mind reader.

"Hayes?" she asks, breaking the silence between us. "I actually haven't had a chance to tell you something yet either." My heart rockets in my chest, my eyes almost incapable of staying on the road, too anxious to see what she's going to say. "You were *fantastic* on the ice tonight. Two goals and an assist at your first Riders home opener? That's unheard of. You played a phenomenal game tonight. That fast break you got at the end of the first, when you deked and faked the goalie out to score the first goal, was unreal!"

I can't help the dumb-ass grin on my face as she compliments my game. Olivia was watching me play. *And it sounds like she was actually paying attention.* I risk studying her in the low light of the car, completely enraptured by the siren sitting next to me. *Did she just use actual hockey terms?* I never thought the word 'deke' would do it for me, but suddenly my dick is awfully tight in my pants, and I subtly shift to give myself some relief. Most girls just say things like 'when you hit the puck with your stick, that was awesome.' This girl knows what a deke is.

Could this girl possibly get any hotter?

"Thanks; I actually felt really good tonight. It's nice to be in a new city with a solid start to the season. I'm starting to gel with my teammates, finding my place on the first line. I think I'm going to be happy here in Milwaukee."

"Well, if you ask me, Milwaukee is lucky to have you here, Larsy," she says with a wink.

"You think so?"

"I know so."

"You can drop me off here. That's my place on the right," Olivia says as she points to the building my GPS has taken us to. It's a cute older house that looks like it's been recently redone. *From what I can tell in the dark anyway. I'm not sure exactly what part of town this is, but it looks reasonably safe.*

Fuck. I have no game plan here. It's not a date by any means, she literally just ended a relationship less than an hour ago, but why does this feel like a first date? *What do I do? Do I try and kiss her? Do I ask to see her again?*

I put the car in park, feeling like it's a step in the right direction. "Can I walk you to your door?" I ask, my heart pounding in my chest like I'm back in middle school asking a girl to slow dance.

"Oh gosh, you really don't have to do that. I appreciate the ride, and I don't want to take up anymore more of your night," she says, her cheeks flaming in the dark.

I'm noticing every time I offer to help, she makes it seem like she's inconveniencing me. *Man, that fuckwad really did a number on her.*

"Olivia, remember how I told you I don't give out compliments unless I mean them? I also don't offer anything up that I don't want to do. I would like to walk you to your door, if that's okay with you." She looks stunned at my words, but I can sense her trying her best to hide a smile. *That mix of emotions on her face makes the list of things I want to do with this girl grow by the minute. Not to mention my fucking dick matching my thoughts.*

"Okay."

"Okay." I jump out of my car and race to meet her on the passenger side to open the door, fighting a smile the whole time.

Calm the fuck down, Hayes.

"This is a cool place," I say as we walk toward her house. "How long have you been here?"

"Almost a year. I used to have a small one-bedroom apartment, but my lease was ending, and it was time for a change. My landlord rents out this place, too, so it was an easy transition. This is two bedrooms, just a few blocks from the lake, and I wanted a little more space. Originally, I was going to move here with the 'person that shall not be named' but he wasn't sure if he wanted to live so far away from his friends," she says, rolling her eyes. "I was devastated when he wouldn't commit to this place because the rent was a little high for me by myself, but I asked my landlord if he could lower it, just a bit, for me. I don't know if he took pity on me or what, but he said I'd been a great tenant, and he would drop the rent so I could afford it. And I'm so glad he did - I *love* this house. Plus, I have the extra bedroom set up like a little music studio, so I can practice and work on my songwriting."

The way she talks about this hidden gem of a place is adorable. I want to ask to see the inside, but I also don't want to be too forward. But oh, how I want to comfort her in *so* many ways. This being a gentleman thing is a bunch of horseshit. *God, why can't I be more like Bougie and just go for it? Okay…no. Too far, Hayes. Too far.*

"It must be nice to be able to practice at home. Sadly, an ice rink in my second bedroom would be a little impractical," I say as she laughs beside me, walking the steps up to her place. Out of the corner of my eye, I notice a porch swing, and I gesture to it. "Want to sit and talk for a little longer before I officially drop you off at your door?"

14
olivia

Hayes is beside me, my pulse racing as our thighs touch on this *very small* porch swing. He's still in his suit from the game. It's royal blue and nicely tailored, and he's paired it with a crisp white dress shirt and a navy tie. He's also wearing some surprisingly trendy black dress shoes with no socks. Most men's dress shoe selection is lackluster, but Hayes' shoes are sharp. I don't know why the dress shoes with no socks and a suit does it for me, but oh…it *does* it for me. I'd be lying if I said I haven't thought about Hayes these past few weeks. I've woken up several times, my heart pounding against my sweat-slicked skin after having feverish dreams about what might have happened if we hadn't been interrupted that night at Walt's. The emotional roller coaster of the past few weeks has been crippling, a constant tightness in my chest draining me of all energy. The weight of suspecting my boyfriend was hiding something, the guilt of dreaming about another man, and the deep ache of wondering if the relationship needed to end, all while fearing the uncertainty and loneliness that might follow, has been overwhelming. But right now, I just feel…safe.

"What made you get into hockey?"

He shrugs as he pushes his feet on the ground to rock the porch swing back and forth. "I went to a friend's birthday party when I was really young. Five or six, maybe? It was an ice skating party, and I remember being super excited about getting cake. I have a bad sweet tooth."

"Fun fact - I happen to be an *excellent* baker. You like peach pie? That's my specialty."

"I *love* peach pie. Any pie actually. Especially when it's warm with a nice scoop of good quality vanilla ice cream. Not the cheap generic ice cream. It has to be one of the good brands where you can see the little flecks of vanilla bean in it. That's my dream cheat day. How fast can you whip that up? Like ten minutes or so?"

I laugh at his intimate description of the good vanilla ice cream and his dessert request. "Sadly, it takes a couple of hours, but I'll make you a deal. If I buy some peaches, and you can help me peel them and cut them up, I'll make a peach pie for you."

"Deal. I'm a horrible cook, but I can totally peel your peach."

I sit up straight at the thought of him peeling anything off of me. "Actually, wait right here," I say as I head in the house. I come back out with a plate of caramel brownies I baked yesterday. "It's not peach pie, but I made these, and they are sweet."

Hayes' eyes grew wide. "Oh. My. God. Seriously? These look dangerous. I'd better sample them to make sure," he says, taking a brownie and inhaling it in almost one bite.

"Hory shiiii. Eese are 'elisious," he tries speaking with a mouth full of brownie crumbs spraying across the porch. He swallows, his fingers dancing over the plate as he fights with himself over eating another. "These are definitely dangerous," he snatches another one off the plate, "but I cannot stop eating these."

I smile, pride filling my chest at his compliments, knowing he means every word. I take the final brownie for myself, setting the plate on the wicker table beside me. "Glad you like them. Now that we've gotten your sweet tooth settled, finish your story about the skating birthday party. I want to hear how you fell in love with hockey."

"Oh, right! So, when we got to the party, I got my rental skates on and went out on the ice. I stumbled for a few minutes, but I caught on and got the hang of it quickly. The only way my mom got me off of the ice was by reminding me about the cake," he continues, and I chuckle at his serious love of sweets. "After the party, I asked my mom if I could take skating lessons or something, and she found an intro to hockey program. Thankfully, it's a big sport in Minnesota because they don't have these programs in every part of the country. I was just one of those kids who had a natural knack for it. And now, here I am, an opening night MVP for the Riders. Overnight success," he says as we both laugh.

God, I am a sucker for a guy with a great sense of humor. Add together a nicely tailored suit, trendy dress shoes with no socks, a sweet tooth, and a sense of humor, and I'm lost. This has been a rough night, but it's surprisingly trending upward.

"Yeah, I'm sure the league had you in their draft at age seven, right? No hard work after the pee-wee leagues at all," I taunt, my voice thick with sarcasm.

"Yep, no hard work at all. It's a miracle," he replies, raising his hands in the air like he's at church. "Seriously though, it's like I said the other night at the bar. You can have God-given talent, but it's up to you what you do with it. I worked hard, *really* hard, and ended up at the top of my game at the right time. I was drafted right out of high school, went to college for development, and then finally got the call up to the big show."

"So, all that talk about talent and hard work the other night wasn't just about me. You've done the same thing?"

He smiles and nods, his leg resting fully against mine.

"I can only imagine the amount of hard work required to be a professional athlete. I do a thirty-minute workout on my spin bike and want to die. I can't imagine skating up and down the ice as fast as you do. I would pass out after one trip across the rink."

Hayes' laughter fills the air, gently shaking the swing beneath us. "It's a lot of hard work, that's for sure, but I love it. I love the game. I love the look of the ice right after it's been resurfaced by the Zamboni. I love the camaraderie with my teammates. It's indescribable, just a great game. But *you* seem to know a bit about hockey yourself. Did I catch you using the term deke earlier? How do you know so much?"

My cheeks flush, my eyes staring out at the quiet street. "Only from the Mighty Ducks movies. Gordon Bombay and his famous triple-deke," I say as he laughs. "I mean, it's only *the* greatest movie of the 90s. I always imagined I'd be Julie 'the Cat' Gaffney. Except, I'm a horrible skater. I look like a baby giraffe learning to walk. So, my hockey dreams, along with my dream of being an astronaut when I realized I wasn't great at science, quickly vanished. If I wasn't on a little rug when I sang, I'd probably fall flat on my face."

He laughs, his joy contagious as a smile spreads across my face. "Well, maybe I can help you with the skating since I have a *little* experience with that. Or, at least, help you learn to walk on the ice and not fall."

"I may take you up on that," I say with a nervous smile. "But, seriously, I probably do know more than the average person when it comes to hockey. When I was younger, my dad used to take me to games at the local college. He knew the coach, and that's where I fell in love with the game. And, as a teenager, there was a cute goalie I wanted to see."

Hayes raises an eyebrow, a smug look morphing his face. "Oh, do tell me about this cute goalie. Have you always had a thing for hockey players?"

"I don't have a *thing* for hockey players," I grumble, crossing my arms over my chest and bumping his arm in the process.

Well, maybe I have a small, teeny-tiny thing for one *hockey player.*

He waits, lifting his brows in mock intrigue and interest, leaning in closer than I expected. *I can smell his shampoo and see how the ends of his hair curl as they're drying.* I sigh, rubbing my hands along my legs as I suck in a fortifying breath.

"I was fifteen, and it was a cute college guy. I honestly only saw his picture in the program since he was wearing a goalie mask during the game, so I can only assume he was cute in real life. But lil' ol' fifteen-year-old Olivia didn't care." I lapse into a comfortable silence, the memories of that game skating through my mind. "The game was fun. I loved the violence and the fights; they were exhilarating. It's probably my favorite sport."

"Probably? It is *going* to be your favorite sport now. Don't make me put you in the penalty box for liking a sport more than hockey," Hayes replies playful, nudging me with his elbow and adding a little gruffness to his voice.

"Oh, I didn't realize there was a penalty for such a thing. I *really* enjoy college basketball. March Madness can get pret-ty crazy, especially when my bracket is winning at the office. But..." I cheekily tap a finger against my chin, pretending to be deep in thought, "which sport do I like better? They both have a lot of action. Basketball has more scoring, but the hockey scoring is way more intense, *and* I get to see grown men brawl." I peek at Hayes out of the corner of my eye, his gaze locked on my lips. "How. To. Choose?"

"Olivia," he says in a much more serious tone. "Let me walk you to your door."

"Oh. O-okay," I say, shocked and a little nervous. My eyes widen and my stomach churns as I stand and move towards the door. *Did I say something wrong? I hope he knew I was just joking.*

Biting my lip, I fight the growing panic in my chest. *Oh God, now you've done it, Olivia; you've pissed him off.* "I'm sorry. I was just joking; I didn't mean to -"

Hayes places his hands on my face and presses his lips to mine. My heart races as his kiss calms all of my worry. My body struggles to stay standing as I melt into his touch. If I'm being honest, I've been dreaming about this for weeks. I wrap my arms around him as I open my lips to deepen the kiss, his tongue stroking mine. *Damn*…his tongue is powerful. I'm not sure if this is a muscle needed for hockey, but he's got skills. He's kissing me as if I'm the last person on the earth, and he's been starved of human contact for *years*. He tips my head back to press against me fully, and I let out a small moan, craving the feel of his muscles against the curves of my body.

Dear God, how does this man do these things to me?

As he pulls away, he takes a step back. "I hope that made your favorite sport decision a little easier," he says with a smirk while I wipe the drool from my face, a little stunned and in disbelief.

"Jury's still out."

He laughs a deep belly laugh and smiles back at me, his eyes practically sparkling. "Olivia, thank you for the pleasure of driving you home tonight and allowing me to walk you to your door."

"No, Hayes, seriously, thank *you*. After everything that happened today, this was exactly what I needed."

"And what is it that you needed?"

I think for a second, a small smile twisting my face. "Perspective."

15
hayes

I should win a fucking award for the amount of willpower I just used not asking Olivia to invite me inside. *Or inside her for that matter.* I have no clue how I left her with just a kiss on the porch. As I drive home from her place, part of me, a better-than-average-sized part of me begging for attention, thinks I am a giant dumbass. I tuck my cock into the waistband of my slacks, knowing she needs time to process things. I don't want to be a random hookup after she had a crazy breakup with her boyfriend less than an hour ago. I want her future. I want her smiles, her joy, her *everything*. I flex my fingers against my steering wheel, my body begging me to turn around and give her the care and attention she deserves. I know I can't, but I couldn't leave without a kiss. She is too special. Too perfect. Too beautiful. *I want a lot more than kisses with Olivia Brooks.* I've never been one to believe in love at first sight, but this girl, this siren, has burrowed deep within me and might make me a changed man.

As I practically stumble into my apartment and climb into bed, I take a quick peek at my phone to see if she did, in fact, add in her number. That sweet little brat put herself in my phone as "Olivia Brooks - ICE" and listed the company name as "Emergency Contact". My cock twitches, begging for my siren to come and play. Sexy with a snarky attitude is *exactly* my type. *Olivia has* no *idea what she's in for when number twenty-two skates down the ice looking to score in the five-hole.*

"Time to text my emergency contact."

HAYES

Hi, is this my emergency contact, Olivia Brooks?

I have an emergency I'd like to report

OLIVIA

Yes, you've reached Olivia Brooks. What's your emergency?

HAYES

I just realized I haven't been to any fun places here in Milwaukee, and I've lived here for nearly a month. I need a chaperone, someone who knows the city well, and I was wondering if you had time to show me around next weekend?

OLIVIA

That's an emergency?

I can picture her delicate brow raised in a severe arch, her lips twitching as she tries, and fails, to hide the smile desperate to peek through.

HAYES

Yes. If I don't see some of this beautiful city, I'll die.

OLIVIA

LOL. What happens when you have a real emergency? What if you're dying and bleeding on the side of the road, and I think you're crying wolf?

HAYES

I'm willing to risk it.

OLIVIA

I'll have to check my schedule.

HAYES

Got a lot going on next week?

We leave midmorning tomorrow for a hellish travel schedule of nearly back-to-back games. It's a fucking brutal way to start the season, but with one win under our belts already, the momentum is in our favor. *Too bad we can't take our secret weapon with us.*

OLIVIA

There's a Dateline marathon on. 24-hours of people who lit up a room then were brutally murdered.

HAYES

That's a very morbid thing to watch for 24-hours.

OLIVIA

True. I guess I could take a break and interact with the real world.

My heart races in my chest, my body feeling warm as adrenaline rushes through me. *Who needs pre-workout when all I need is a shot of Olivia Brooks?*

HAYES

Perfect. The real world will be happy to have someone who lights up a room. Pick you up Saturday around noon?

OLIVIA

Works for me. Any requests where you'd
like to go?

HAYES

Nope. I'm completely at your mercy.

OLIVIA

Oh really????

HAYES

Really.

My body begs to feel her skin along mine, my free hand fisting my cock and relieving some of the pressure and desire of a woman I'm sure I'll never get out of my system. I watch the dancing dots appear and disappear again and again, my breath catching in my throat as I wait for her response. When it never comes, I suck on my teeth, realizing I may have pushed too hard, too fast. *Stupid, Hayes; she* just *broke up with the wet bag of a douche nozzle. Time to pump the breaks.* My body flushes at the shock I can hear in her response. *For now.*

HAYES

In regard to where we go.

OLIVIA

LOL. Even with your limitations, I have a
few ideas.

HAYES

Sweet.

OLIVIA

🙂

HAYES

Goodnight Olivia

Ellie K. Drake

OLIVIA

Goodnight Hayes

78

16
olivia

ayes. Larson. Kissed. Me. *Me.* It's late but I am *wide awake*, wired as if I just downed six espresso shots. I dance ridiculously around my house in my pajamas, brush my teeth, turn off lights, and double-check the locks on the doors. *How in the world am I going to sleep tonight?* He wants me to show him around town! *I have to fill Maggie in on all this.* I pick up my phone to text her, but another one comes in.

HAYES

Hello? Emergency contact? I need your help.

Oh my God. We *just* said goodnight and he's texting me again. I can't help the giant smile on my face, *especially* after that kiss my lips are still tingling from.

OLIVIA

It's getting a little late for that, don't you think?

HAYES

As part of my emergency contact duties,
you'll need to be available 24/7.

OLIVIA

That's a steep expectation. How do you
know I'm up for that task?

What's wrong now? Did your nightlight burn
out again?

Can't sleep without your security blanket
you've had since you were a baby?

HAYES

Dammit! No one was supposed to find out
about Mr. Blanket! What do I need to do to
swear you to secrecy??

OLIVIA

LMAO. Okay, okay…what is your
emergency now?

HAYES

See? I knew you'd come around to being
stuck with me 24/7.

I just wanted to tell you I'm excited to see
the city with you.

OLIVIA

Really?

My breath catches in my throat, warmth spreading across my cheeks. It's been less than an hour, and I'm already giddy at the thought of seeing him again. *This is going to be a long week.*

HAYES

Really

And I really enjoyed our kiss earlier. Will that
be a part of the tour?

Oh. My. God. Does that mean he wants to kiss me again? My thighs squeeze together, wetness pooling between my legs at the thought of kissing those sexy lips once more and his muscular arms wrapping around me. Finally lying down in bed, I glance over at my nightstand. *I may have to open that drawer to help myself fall asleep tonight.*

OLIVIA

I'll have to see if I can fit that into our agenda, but I make no promises.

Get some rest, Hayes. I'm planning an entire afternoon of fun where you'll need a week's worth of sleep to prepare.

HAYES

Well, damn…now I really won't be able to sleep LOL.

OLIVIA

Snuggle up with Mr. Blanket and go try for me :) Goodnight Hayes

HAYES

Goodnight Olivia

17
olivia

"Okay, *wait*; let's go over it one more time," Maggie says with a mix of shock and excitement as we sit at Walt's for emergency drinks after last night's flurry of events. "That fucking prick Cayden got you fired from the anthem gig, dumped you *at the game*, and then Hayes, like...*the* Hayes you almost kissed...is a Rider? *And* he drove you home, then you *did* kiss? Holy tits, Liv! This is...I don't even know what this is, but I'm so excited!" She whips around, her eyes sparking with mischief and squeezing my fingers as if what she's going to say next is the most important thing in the world. "Is Hayes a good kisser? Was there tongue? Did he press up against you so you felt his hardness like they do in romance books? *Please* tell me that happened!"

"Oh my God, Maggie, *reign it in*," I say through gritted teeth, glancing around the bar as my cheeks heat. "We're in a public place. I *sing* here. But...yes..." I look down at my shoes, hardly believing I'm saying this out loud at Walt's. "There was tongue."

"I fucking *knew* it! Oh my God, this is the most fantastic thing since pumpkin spice lattes came back."

"What's all the fuss about, you two troublemakers?" Johnny teases, stepping toward us with an arched brow and wiping down the bar with a towel.

"Cayden dumped Liv at the Riders game last night!"

"No shit?" Johnny says with a wrinkled brow. "You okay, Liv?"

I know he's never been a fan of Cayden, but the way this sweet old man looks out for me gives me the warm fuzzies. "Yeah, Johnny, I'm good."

"She's *good* because she made out with the new Riders player afterward."

"MAGGIE!" I smack her arm, mortified she announced that.

"What? Johnny should know all the facts," she says, giving him a wink as she chugs the rest of her drink.

I take a sip of my own drink, trying to hide the pleased smile on my face. *These two are going to be the death of me.* I give up trying to mask my joy. *At least my death will be a fun one.*

"I do enjoy it when you *spill the tea,* as you kids call it these days," Johnny says as he reaches under the bar and pulls out a small bottle of champagne, practically slamming it down in front of me.

"Johnny…what is this?" I ask, extremely confused.

"I've been saving this for the day you finally got that no-good fool out of your life. Sorry it ended the way it did, sweetheart, but you'll be better for it in the end."

"Alright, what's all the commotion about?" Walt says, approaching Johnny and cuddling up next to him. "Does that bottle mean what I think it does?" He glances between the champagne, Johnny, and my shocked face, a dazzling smile overtaking his. "You and Cayden finally over, Liv?"

I sigh, leaning my elbows on the bar and dropping my face in my hands in sheer embarrassment. "Yes," I groan, "We're done."

"Well, hot damn! This calls for a celebration." He knocks his knuckles on the bar, playfully nudging Johnny. "Round of drinks on the house, folks!" Walt calls out as the bar patrons cheer, none of them having any clue why they're getting a free drink.

"Hell yeah, Walt!" Maggie says raising her glass and tipping it towards him.

"Jeezus, was *everyone* waiting for this to happen?" I gape, my eyes skating between my friends. "Why did no one say anything to me?"

Walt puts his arm around Johnny's shoulder and gives me a sweet, sorrowful look. "You can't see it from the inside, honey. We were just hoping, one day, you'd realize you were worth a hell of a lot more. We want you to be happy, and we could tell you weren't."

My heart melts, their kindness and understanding more than I could ever ask for. These two are so sweet. Everyone knows they've been together forever, but for some reason, they don't make a big deal about it. Yet, I see their love for each other in the most mundane actions. The way they smile at each other from across the bar. The way Johnny always has a shot of whisky ready for Walt before they close every night, or Walt restocking low bottles before Johnny even realizes. The fact that they want me to have the same kind of love they share makes my heart swell. They created this safe space for me and everyone else in this town, and that's why this bar is such a treasure.

There's no other place like Walt's.

"Well, I appreciate all of your kindness. I don't know what I'd do without you and this place," I say as Walt reaches his hand across the bar to give mine a little squeeze.

Johnny leans over, making a show of looking around the bar before talking to me in a quiet voice. "Now…tell me about this hockey player you were *smooching* with. I assume it was the one here at my bar a few weeks ago?"

My eyes widen as he winks, and I give him an evil look for him keeping this information from me. "What the heck, Johnny? You *knew* who he was?"

"Listen, missy, I've been a hockey fan since before you were born, and I watch the sports channels religiously when I'm not here. Trust me to know when a Rider sits at my bar. I knew that was Hayes Larson the minute he walked in."

"Why didn't you say anything?" I ask, half not wanting to know the answer.

"Sweetheart, sometimes it's better to figure things out on your own. Plus, I wasn't about to out the newest athlete in town to a bunch of drunk fools."

Maggie slams her hand down on the bar, pulling Johnny's attention to her. "Well, if another hot-as-fuck hockey player comes in here, Johnny, would you please point them out? I could use the help," she says with an overly dramatic sigh, draping her body across the entire bar. "I can only be so patient." She keeps her face squished against the wood, her words mumbled as she looks to me. "Back to you and your love life, Liv."

"In case you forgot, I currently don't have a love life." *Or do I?*

"Oh yes. You. Do. *You're* showing the new player for the Riders around town next weekend, *and* you two have already played tonsil hockey. This has *major* potential, girlfriend, and I'm going to live vicariously through you until I find my own super rich hockey player." Maggie looks at her phone as a text comes through, jolting up in her seat. "Shit, I gotta go. Sunday dinner at my parents' house tonight where their lawyer asses will passively-aggressively lecture me about my poor career choices. Jesus, take the wheel."

I laugh as we hug goodbye, feeling the best I have in a long time. "Thanks for meeting me for a drink this afternoon, Mags. You're the best. See you at work tomorrow!"

"Love you too, Liv! You know I'm never one to turn down drinks and gossip," she says, making her way toward the bar door.

"Oh…Emo Guy said he's bringing in bagels tomorrow…save me a blueberry one!"

As a musician, the one good thing about a breakup is the songwriting material. Finally having some time to sit down at my piano, I pick out a bass line my grandpa and I used to play together as a duet. It's a boogie-woogie tune, which seems odd given the complex emotions I'm feeling. Sadness. Confusion. Loneliness. Heartache. It all seems to lead toward a moody ballad, but I'm drawn to a fast-paced rhythm, the chaos leading my fingers across the keys.

As my heart pounds through this simple bassline, I start to realize what a complete tool Cayden is. Last night I cried. But today? Today I'm filled with rage.

How did I navigate a gauntlet of unhappiness and let him *be the one to break up with me?*

Memories creep up of all the terrible things he used to say to me - things I had long forgotten about - flooding my mind and fueling my anger. I remember *everything*. Every time he ditched me to hang out with his friends. Every time he made me feel bad for wanting to spend time with him. Every time he said something I wanted to do was too expensive, but anything he wanted was a can't miss opportunity no matter the cost. I pound the keys harder and harder, playing through the outrage coursing through my veins, feeling myself healing with every note shattering the stillness of the room.

All this time I thought I was an inconvenience to him. I always seemed to be in the way of whatever he wanted to do. But in reality, *he* was the one standing in *my* way. Being with him caused me to place limitations on myself. I was never enough. I couldn't compete with anything in his life. I wasn't worth the time, energy, or effort. *I was a girlfriend in name only; a convenient excuse if he needed one.* The lyrics begin pouring out of me, and I hit record on my phone, capturing anything I might miss. After a few hours, and some tweaking, a new song is written. One I'm happy to have purged from my soul.

Not every song happens this fast. Sometimes I work on something for weeks, or even months, before it's where I want it. But with all the pent-up sadness and frustration from everything Cayden put me through, this song poured out of me like a waterfall - crashing down on the remnants of our shitty relationship and wiping it from existence.

Last night with Hayes gave me a fresh perspective of what a good relationship could be like. *Oh my God, Olivia, it was* one *kiss; you are not in a relationship.* Biting my lip, I upload the recording to the cloud, making sure my new song is saved in a safe place. *Maybe I am clingy.*

No, no, no. New mantra. *I am* not *clingy. Cayden just wasn't enough for me. He wasn't worthy of me. He was nothing more than a lesson of what I truly deserve from a partner.*

My stomach growls, and I realize I've been writing all afternoon since I got home from Walt's. I order takeout from my favorite sushi place, and once it arrives, I plop down on the couch to eat and find something to watch on TV. A few minutes later, I hear a knock on the door. Glancing at the bag, my brow furrows. *Did the delivery guy forget to give me part of my order?* Peeking through the blinds, I see a different delivery man holding a package. I open the door.

"Olivia Brooks?" he asks, looking down at the package.

"Yeah that's me, but I wasn't expecting anything. You sure you have the right address?"

"Says your name right here on my packing slip. Just need your autograph here please," he says, holding out his electronic pad for me to sign.

Scribbling quickly, I grab the package and head back inside. *Did I drunk order something online?* I open the box and inside is a card, along with fabric I recognize immediately, my breath catching in my throat. *A Milwaukee Steel Riders home jersey.* Quickly taking it out of the box, I flip it over and, sure enough, across the back in big letters is "LARSON" with the number 22 beneath it.

Holy shit. I hug the jersey to my chest, unable to help but take a quick sniff. A smile stretches my cheeks. It's not like I don't have a ton of Riders gear due to my singing gig. Well…former singing gig. I groan, dropping my head back and staring at the ceiling. *Already forgot about that.* But I've never worn anything other than my own jersey. I gently set it down and rip open the card as fast as I can.

Olivia,
I know you already have a jersey, but I thought you might like this one too. There's no other siren I'd rather see wearing my number.
Hayes

My heart leaps out of my chest as I stare wide-eyed between the note and the gift it was attached to. *He wants me to wear his number.* I feel like I'm back in high school. Except I was not popular enough for any guy at my school to want me to wear his jersey. I remember always longing to be asked but always knowing I wasn't cool enough, skinny enough, or pretty enough. I look back on that version of myself and wish I could tell her to hang in there. To tell her that one day, a sexy man with blond hair, brown eyes, and a smile that makes you weak in the knees will give you a jersey with his name on it.

I put the soft fabric over my head and walk across the creaky hardwood floors to my full-length mirror. The warmth of it soothes my bruised heart. It's huge on my tiny frame, the sleeves hanging down past my short little alligator arms. It's much larger on me than the custom-tailored one I sing in. This is more like the size an actual player would wear.

I love it so much.

As I'm admiring my reflection, my phone buzzes with an incoming call, and I can't help but smile when I see who it is.

"Well, if it isn't Hayes Larson calling his emergency contact. To what do I owe this pleasure? I do hope everything is alright."

"Hello, Olivia Brooks. I was just calling to see if you got a little gift delivered to you today." He laughs, the sound making me press my legs together. "Actually, I know you got it because I just got a notification."

"Oh my gosh, Hayes. *Thank you*. This is too much and too sweet, and I…I absolutely love it. I'm actually wearing it right now."

"For real?" he asks excitedly. "Can you show me?"

Oh my God, he wants to FaceTime? Shit. Do I look okay? I reluctantly hit the video button to switch the call and walk back over by my full-length mirror.

"Oh my God, Olivia. That jersey has never looked better on anyone. Not even me. Turn around; let me see the back," he says as I turn around, trying to figure out how to get the camera to face the right way so he can see his name splayed across my shoulders.

"My little siren, you look beautiful wearing my number, and I'm pissed I'm a thousand miles away so I can't enjoy it in person," he groans, and I nervously laugh. I bite my lip as I look away from his gaze in the little window on my phone.

Did he just say I looked beautiful?

"Seriously, Hayes, this is incredible. I'm going to wear it when I watch the game tomorrow night."

"Please take a selfie of that," he says with a deep voice. *Oh my God,* the gruff tone of his voice makes my entire body shiver, and I hope he can't tell how strong of an effect he has on me. "It's a game-worn jersey from pre-season. I wanted you to have one."

"So, you sweated in this? Gross," I joke, trying to play off the fact that this conversation has me extremely turned on. Thankfully he laughs, doing nothing to help my ever-growing arousal. "I'm just teasing; I freaking love it. How's Denver?"

"Much better now that I'm talking to you," he says. "It's been a long day between travel, practice logistics, and dinner. Glad to finally be at the hotel to get some rest. How was your day?"

"Good! Went to Walt's this afternoon for a drink with my best friend Maggie, then I came home and worked on some music for the rest of the day. Got a new song knocked out I'm excited about," I gush, recapping my day.

"You wrote a song? Today? An entire song?" he says, seemingly in shock.

I laugh, touched that he seems as excited as I am. "Yep, a whole song."

"What's it about?"

Shit. Do I tell him it's about Cayden being a dipshit? Will he be mad? Will it upset him that I wrote a song about my ex? I really need the number to Taylor Swift's songwriting hotline so I can ask her these kinds of questions.

"Well...it's kind of about my recent past relationship with a giant douche. I literally refer to him as a douche in the song," I nervously tell him. "Is that weird?"

Hayes sits for a minute, a myriad of expressions flashing across his face. "It's not weird at all; I love that you call him a douche in your song. Can I hear it?"

Oh. Double shit. I don't play my songs for people one-on-one. It's awkward. I can sing in front of 50,000 people, no problem, but singing in front of a small group, or even just one person, makes me unbelievably nervous…like, puking nervous.

"You want to hear it? Like, hear me play it for you? Now? Over the phone? Just you and me?" I ramble.

"Olivia, I love hearing you sing. You could sing the words to the Declaration of Independence, and I would probably be a sobbing mess," he says, making me laugh.

I love the way he makes me laugh.

"Funnily enough, this song starts with 'four score and seven years ago.'" He laughs again, and if I keep smiling like this, my cheeks are going to ache.

"That's the Gettysburg Address."

Damn…he's right. "Potayto, potahto," I grumble as Hayes lets out another laugh, his video shaking as he looks at me expectantly.

"*Okay*, I'll play it for you. Just know singing for only one person makes me super nervous, and I might vomit," I relay, my voice shaky.

"Why does it make you nervous?" His brows come together, an adorable tilt softening his face. "I would take you to a skating rink and show you how I shoot a puck into the goal. What's the difference?"

"When I sing for a small crowd, everyone is staring at me, and they are, like…*right there.* They don't stop staring. The *entire* time. Then I finish the song, and they are *still* staring at me, and no one knows what to say or do. It's *so awkward* to pour your emotions out in an intimate setting. There's a lot less emotion involved with shooting a puck."

"I beg to differ. I'll show you how emotional it is to hold my stick and shoot a puck sometime." *Did he just say hold his stick? Jeezus, get your mind out of the gutter.* "But seriously, Olivia, there's no need to be embarrassed or nervous around me. I'm literally you're biggest fan."

Why does this man make me feel safe being vulnerable with him? "Well, when you put it like that, I can't disappoint my fans. Hold on," I say, walking into the music room and setting my phone at an angle so he can see me sitting at the piano. *God am I really doing this?* I swallow the giant nervous lump in my throat and begin to caress the keys.

(View the lyrics to Olivia's song at the end of the book)

"Well…what do you think?" I ask, a sick feeling in my stomach and more nervous than I've ever been in my life. "I know it needs some work, and I could maybe tweak some of the lyrics, and …" I groan, covering my face with my hands. "I shouldn't have played it for you."

He takes a minute and looks at me over the phone with fierce sincerity. "I have a few thoughts," he says tentatively. "First, you are so fucking talented. The fact you wrote that song in a day, start to finish, is incredible. It's going to be stuck in my head our entire trip. Second, it makes me want to go to that douche-nozzle's house and beat the ever-loving shit out of him for *ever* making you feel like that. And third, my dick is so hard right now. Watching you sing while wearing my name across your back unlocked a fantasy I never knew I had."

Oh. My. Lanta.

I was *not* expecting that. Any of that. My eyes are about to pop out of my head, and I have no idea how to respond, but his words go straight to my core, igniting a heat low in my stomach and making me shift on my piano bench.

"Really?" I sheepishly reply.

"What did I tell you about compliments, Olivia?"

"That you don't give them unless you mean them."

"Exactly. And I meant *every* word of what I said."

I blink, my heart pounding against my chest. *Like when he said his dick was hard? I mean…I'm not mad, but…what the* hell *is happening?*

I swallow back the lump in my throat, trying to recover from all the dick thoughts bombarding my mind. "Thank you. It means a lot. And so does this jersey."

"I'm glad you like it. Would you do me a favor, Olivia?" His deep, gruff voice has goosebumps prickling across my skin. "Will you sleep in my jersey tonight?"

Oh my fucking God. My core clenches around nothing, desperate for this man halfway across the country. I've only met him twice, but the way he talks to me makes me think he could ask me to rob a bank and I would do it without a second thought. *Also, I could use the money.* Still in a state of shock, I nod my head slowly.

"I may never take it off."

18
hayes

We beat Denver 2-1 in OT tonight. I'm exhausted from the game, but I head down to the weight room to get a few reps in to force out the lactic acid while my muscles are warmed up. Otherwise, I'll be sore and stiff as fuck in the morning. *Well... not that I'm* not *stiff every morning thinking about what my sweet little siren's lips will feel like on my dick.*

Walking into the visitor's gym, I feel the base thumping in my chest as Russian metal music blares through the speakers. *Fuck.* I've been avoiding Vladi's meddling self all damn day. I spin on my heel, beelining back to the cardio area, when I'm yanked back by my shirt.

"Well, well, look who it is. You're just in time to spot me," he says, dragging me over to the squat rack, my eyes nearly popping out of my head from the force.

Could I get away from him? Yes. But I don't need an angry Russian chasing me through the underground tunnels of the arena.

"Why are you avoiding me, Hayes Larson?"

Double fuck. He didn't use Larsy, which means he's pissed. Full name means he's inching toward blowing up entirely. *Mother-fucker…someone send help.*

"Vladi," I awkwardly laugh, gently yanking myself from his grip, "I am not avoiding you."

"The fuck you're not! I saved a seat for you on the plane yester-day, but somehow *Bougie* sat next to me and talked my fucking ear off about his millions of social media followers. Do you *know* how much vodka you owe me to make up for that little seat switch?"

I can't help the evil smile spreading across my face. *The plan fucking worked,* and *it didn't totally fuck us for the game today.* I planted Bougie for him yesterday, knowing it was risking a full Vladi melt-down that would bleed into the game. "Alright! Alright," I hold my hands up, trying to smother my smile, "I owe you vodka."

"A *lot.* And top shelf. None of that shitty American crap. Moth-erland vodka; the water you idiots drink tastes like piss," he grum-bles, sliding more plates onto the bar. "Now, tell me about you and The Weapon?"

"I just gave her a ride home. That's it. What's it to you?"

"She looked upset. And you just got out of that shit-show of a relationship with C-3PO, so I wanted to make sur-"

Holding my hand up, confused as fuck, I halt him mid-sentence. "Wait, wait, wait…C-3PO?"

"Cheating Cunt Chelsea, Pregnant and Obnoxious." He blinks at me, settling under the bar and setting his feet. "You know this nickname, yes? We used to just call her C3, but then…well…you know."

The dead-serious look on his face, paired with his wide-eyed disbelief that I didn't know how my friends referred to my ex, makes me burst into laughter. "I didn't," I say, still chuckling, "But it's fucking brilliant."

He nods, stone faced as he drops into a series of punishing reps. "As I was saying, I wanted to make sure you were thinking with your brain, not your lonely cock. Also, I'm your fucking best friend, which means I get to know what the fuck is going on in your life. Lie to me again, asshole, and I'll throw you through a goddamn wall."

Damn. He's right.

"Remember me telling you about the girl I met the first night I was in town?"

He grunts, dropping into a deep squat with controlled precision. "Yes. You haven't stopped droning on. You talked my goddamn ear off the entire first day of training camp. I'm tempted to start wearing earplugs around you, brother. What ever happened with that situat-" Vladi stands up fully from his squat, standing strong under the bar flexing under his warmup weight as his eyes widen with realization. "Oh, *fuck*. You said she was a singer. It's her, isn't it?"

"Yep." I lean my head back against the rack, not bothering to fight the goofy ass grin stretching my cheeks.

"You said she was your dream girl, but she was dating some other guy. You said you weren't going to get in the way. What happened to him?"

"Cocksucker dumped her after the home opener. And got her fired from the anthem job. That's why she was crying."

"He got her *fired*? What the fuck? She can't be fired. She's part of the Riders."

"I know. I asked if I could talk to someone about it, but she said no. I wanted to respect her wishes. And you know…I'm kind of the new guy."

"Right. Nothing to do with your panty-dropping good looks swooping in to be her hero?"

"There was no panty-dropping involved." *Not yet anyway.* I sigh, standing up from the squat rack as my heart races just thinking about being Olivia's harbor from the toxic shit she was evicted from. *Little victories, even if it comes from a painful place.* "This girl is *different.* There's something about the way she crinkles her nose when she laughs, the way her eyes light up when she talks about hockey, the way the entire room stops to listen when she sings. She's funny, smart, and wicked talented. Even in the short amount of time I've spent with her, I feel like she's my equal instead of someone trying to be with me because of my job. I don't want anything to jeopardize this. I don't want to be her rebound or a random hookup. She deserves so much more than that. I just want to be…I don't know…"

Vladi's eyes meet mine in the mirror, understanding and concern coloring their depths. "You want to be hers."

"Yeah." My heart pounds in my chest as I swipe a shaky hand down my face. "Permanently. I'm playing for keeps this time."

The clang of metal plates pings through the room as Vladi adds more weights, his breathing steady as he waits for me to go on.

"Shit, Vladi; I'm fucking losing my mind over this girl! I can't think of anything but making her mine. Giving her everything that asshat never did. Never could." I collapse against the bench, staring at the ground between my feet. "How am I falling for a girl I barely know?"

"You know, Larsy, there's a saying in Russian. *Yesli lyubov' ne bezumna, to eto ne Lyubov.* When love is not madness, it is not love."

"Fuck, man, that's deep." And surprisingly fitting for my situation. *How does he always know?* It's madness that her smile, her voice, and her scent consume my every thought. The emptiness I felt after our embrace at Walt's vanished with one touch of her luscious fucking lips on mine. And now I am a madman willing to do anything to make her mine. Even that first day of training camp, when I was rambling to Vladi, I was already a goner.

Wait…*son of a bitch.* I jump up from the bench, adrenaline pumping, and block Vladi from moving out of the squat rack.

"Mother*fucker*…I told you about a redheaded singer named Olivia, and you didn't *think* to mention our anthem singer matched that description to a fucking T?!"

Vladi stares back at me with the same evil grin I gave him earlier. "Larsy, I am in my own world during pre-game. It's just me, my net, and the fresh ice. I know they call her 'The Weapon,' but I never paid attention to her name. Brother, I tuned you out when you were rambling on and on and *on* about this *dream girl* of yours. So, I may have missed some details. I blame the vodka."

"Buy your own vodka, motherfucker. And I'm going to figure out how to get her back singing for us, so pay attention to the damn anthem next time."

"I will now that I know you're trying to get into her five hole," Vladi says with a wink.

"I need to get my reps in too, Vladi, finish your damn squats."

19
olivia

"Are you sure this looks okay?" I ask Maggie, turning side to side in my full-length mirror to show her outfit number seven I've tried on. *What does one wear to casually show a super handsome, fabulous kisser, pro-hockey player around the city?*

I have on a pair of black leggings, a black and white v-neck t-shirt, a navy bomber jacket, and white tennis shoes with a leopard print logo on them.

"I'm acting like this is a date. Is it a date? Do you have to use the word date for it to be a date?" My breath catches in my chest, the edges of my vision going fuzzy as I continue to spiral.

"Olivia. Girl, *breathe.* You worry too much. You look fabulous. Smoking hot, if I do say so myself. It's just the right amount of sexy, sporty, and chic. I would think a certain pro athlete would go crazy over an outfit like this. As long as *you* are comfortable in your outfit, that's what matters," she reassures me, some of the fear and tension leeching from my body. "Whether you call it a date or not, this guy went out of his way not only to ask you to show him around the city, but to give you a jersey *he* wore in a game. If you ask me…he's got it bad for you." She scoffs, pretending to pout as she eyes me up and down. "You and your damn red hair. Why can't I have red hair?"

"Mags, your chocolate brown hair is to die for, and you know it. You can't go anywhere without turning heads, but if you want red hair, they have this new thing called hair dye; have you heard of it? You think my hair is actually *this* color red?" I joke, my lips twitching as I try to hide my smile.

"Whatever. You know I tried red and it wasn't a good color for my skin tone. You and your forever tanned skin with fucking gorgeous red hair is impossible to compete with as a single girl living on the streets looking for a man," she replies as I laugh once again.

"Mags…it's a spray tan. My pale skin is my least favorite feature, and I feel more confident in myself with a little glow. I know there is a great guy out there for you. We'll keep looking." Maggie smiles, some of the life and confidence bleeding back into her.

"I expect to hear about every second of your day date at brunch tomorrow! Mimosas are on me, so I can get you nice and relaxed and you won't even bat an eye at giving me all the sordid details."

"Maggie, we are going to *lunch*, then I'm showing him a few places around the city. How sordid could that get?"

"There are a *lot* of sordid things you can do in broad daylight, Liv."

I roll my eyes, "He's going to be here soon, and I need to finish getting ready *without* thinking about starring in my own romance novel. I'll see you tomorrow." The thought of doing *anything* with Hayes from one of my books sends my stomach into a whirl of nervous excitement.

"Bye Olivia! Don't do anything I wouldn't do!" she teases as I end the call and roll my eyes with a smile.

Will we be doing sordid things? This is just a friendly tour of the city. It's going to be fine. Tame. *Right?* Simply riding around in a car with an unbelievably handsome man who I'm a little desperate to kiss again.

What sordid things could possibly happen in the middle of the day?

Hayes pulls up to my house a few minutes early. *Damn, I like a punctual man.* I grab my bag and head out the door. He is, of course, outside and opening the car door for me. It's not that a girl can't open her own car door, but it's a nice gesture. *He Who Must Not Be Named would* never *open a car door for me. Or any door, for that matter.* And dammit, I could use some nice gestures. My pulse races through my body at his touch on the small of my back as he guides me into the car. *Why is the small of my back suddenly the most eroge-nous part of my body?* He's wearing black, slim-fit joggers and a cream-colored, long-sleeved hooded shirt that is casual but looks expensive. *His shirt costs more than my entire outfit.* Probably more than my rent. Sliding into my seat, I can't help but swoon as his cologne hovers around me. He is just as sexy now as he was in his tailored suit.

"Sorry to hear about the loss last night. I would have been there, but since I wasn't singing the anthem, I picked up the happy hour gig at Walt's."

He shrugs, and he drums his fingers along the steering wheel. "It is what it is. Losing comes with the territory, and we worked out the kinks at practice this morning. All I can do is shake it off and focus on the next game."

I twist my fingers in my lap. *Should I have brought that up before our date?*

Taking a deep breath, he asks, "Alright, tour guide, where to first?"

"Are you hungry?" I buckle my seat belt, needing to do something to help settle my nerves.

"I'm always starving after practice, but I do need to eat healthy-ish since I'm in season, if that's okay," he says a little sheepishly.

"I mean, you do have to keep up your girlish figure," I say with more sass than needed, and he laughs. "I figured you'd need something better than a corner hotdog, though those are amazing here, so I made us a reservation at The Harbor. It's a seafood place right on the water downtown with lots of grilled fish and vegetables. It's good food and amazing views, so I figured it would be a perfect place for lunch."

"I love it already," he says as he puts the restaurant address into his phone.

We enjoy a lovely lunch at the restaurant, seated at a window table with a stunning view of the lake, the northern Milwaukee skyline, and the art museum. Hayes and I both ordered the salmon special, and it was to die for, both of us groaning at the first bite.

We talk about everything and nothing, topics normally brought up on a first date. I'm still unsure if this *is* a date. I am *technically* available right now, so I'm definitely not opposed to calling it that. *But...is it too soon?* We sip on our drinks and talk about our favorite movies, books, and TV shows. He laughs that Muppets Take Manhattan is in my top ten movie list but agrees Elf is a classic regardless of it being a Christmas movie. We also agree to disagree that Die Hard is a Christmas film. I'll forgive him, just this once, for being wrong. Hayes and I discovered that we are both avid readers; I like romance and he likes American history. I proceeded to call him a nerd for reading a book about Hamilton before the musical came out *and* the fact that he still hasn't seen the musical. *We're going to have to remedy that.*

Time flies by as the server stops at our table to ask how we enjoyed our meal and sets the check down between us. Hayes reaches over to pick it up, and I instinctively say, "No, let me get it."

Hayes raises his eyebrow. "Seriously? There's no way we are leaving this restaurant with you spending a dime of your own money."

"But this place is *expensive.* I would never bring you somewhere like this and expect you to pay." I reach for the bill, but Hayes stops me in my tracks and puts his hand on mine over the little black leather restaurant bill thingy. Goosebumps crawl across my skin at his touch as his intense gaze locks on mine.

"Let me ask you a question, Olivia. Have you ever Googled me?"

Oh God. My eyes widen with panic as my brain scrambles for an answer to his question.

"Have I googled you? Um…*maybe*? Just a little bit, not a deep dive or anything," I stammer, knowing I totally googled him. Who *wouldn't* google the professional hockey player who gave them a ride home and kissed them on their front porch?

He laughs, his body relaxed despite my confession, and says, "It's okay; it's not a test. Did you happen to see the latest contract I signed with Milwaukee?"

"No." My brows draw together as I bite my lip. I actually, for real, did not see that. I was looking for any skeletons in his closet, but I was not going to admit that. I didn't find much anyway, except a few pictures of an ex-girlfriend named Chelsea.

"I just signed a three-year, nine-million-dollar contract."

Holy shit-balls. My mouth drops open, the reality of how different the two of us are truly setting in. Damn, I did not know that.

He continues, glancing down at our hands, "I don't say that to brag about being able to cover our lunch, but to let you know that when you are with me, you are not paying for anything." The way this man makes my body quiver with his words is making my nether regions wetter than the lake outside the window.

He takes the black bill envelope and opens it. "This check is for $180." His eyes meet mine. "Do you think that will even make a dent in my bank account? I want to pay for this meal. And anything else we do today. And anything we do next time. Can we just make that a rule for whenever we hang out? Don't even offer to pay. I've got you taken care of," he says with a soft smile. "Okay?"

"Okay. I'm sorry, I –" Hayes interrupts me mid-sentence, holding up a finger between us.

"Another rule," he says gruffly, but with a tinge of worry. "No more saying you're sorry. Last week, you apologized for things that were not your fault. Not in any way remotely close to being your fault. Stop apologizing for everything. Live your life without fear."

What the hell alternate universe have I walked in to? Is this guy imaginary? Is he a serial killer? If there was a polar opposite to my douchebag ex-boyfriend, Hayes would be it. He reads me like a book, and he's already gotten to the chapter about my self-deprecating tendencies.

And he's still choosing to read.

"I'm sorr-" I stop mid-word, catching myself using the s-word. "It's a bad habit. I will let you pay for things, and I will try my best to stop apologizing," I say politely.

"Good," he says as he sets his card in the bill - *does this thing have a name?* and hands it to our server walking by. "Now that we have that settled, what if we make things a little more interesting? Let's make a bet."

"A bet? A bet on what?"

He continues, his smile positively sinful, "If you can go the rest of the day without saying the s-word, I will give you a prize."

"A prize? Are we at a 5th grade carnival? Are you going to win a little plastic spider ring to put on my finger?" I say flashing a feisty grin.

"I mean, if that's what you'd like your prize to be, I can arrange that," he says with a smile. But this time, there's a hint of deviousness in his eyes as well. Something I thought only existed in my books. "But...I have some other things in mind."

Well, now I'm intrigued. I cock my head to the side with my eyes narrowed in on his. "And if I fail, then what?"

"Well, as most bets go, you'll have to endure some sort of punishment," he says.

Oh. My. God.

Heat flushes my face at the thought of winning anything from this man. Even a punishment. *Why is it so hot in here? Does every establishment in Milwaukee County need their air-conditioning tuned up?*

"Do I get to know what the prize or the punishment is?"

He settles back in his chair, crossing his arms over his chest with a smug smirk. "Nope. It's a blind bet. Take it or leave it."

"And what about you, Hayes? What's your prize going to be?"

He looks at me with his smoldering brown eyes, making me press my thighs together as my breath catches. *I think I'm starting to understand this smoldering word a little better now.*

"I've already gotten my prize," he says with a wink as the

server walks back to the table with his card. "So, my little siren, are you in or out?"

With slickness between my legs and desire thrumming through my veins, I don't hesitate. I look him straight in the eyes, matching his smirk with one of my own.

"I'm in."

20
hayes

The next destination Olivia has me put into my GPS is a bar she tells me is in the Brady Street neighborhood. I have no clue what to expect, but she says it'll be fun. Fuck, the way this girl makes my heart race makes it hard to keep my dick in my pants in public; she's already got me wrapped around her damn finger. To be honest, we could go to a garbage dump right now if she wanted, and I would thank her for the adventure.

I would go anywhere with her.

We pull up in front of a grey brick building with a giant neon sign that says 'Button Bashers.' Walking through the giant glass doors, my eyes widen as I do a double take. In front of me is a bar fully stocked with a nice collection of liquor and quite a few brews on draft, but that's not what stops me in my tracks. Beyond the bar, lining the walls is nearly every arcade game known to man. My fucking heart skips a beat at the symphony of electronic sounds pouring from the consoles bringing me back to my childhood. Except instead of being with my buddies, I'm standing beside this amazing woman who brought me to a fucking arcade bar. I feel like a cartoon character with little hearts in my eyes as I look back and forth between her and the video games with a giant dumbass grin on my face.

This is definitely better than a garbage dump.

"I hope you like arcade games," she says, beaming and waiting to see how I react. "I swear they have every game ever made here. They also have skeeball, that dance game I'm horrible at, basketball, and, of course, all kinds of pinball machines."

"Oh. My. God. Olivia, this is *amazing*!" I bounce in place like a kid in a candy store with a hundred-dollar bill. "What should we play first? Can we win prizes? Let's go get some tokens!"

"Okay, don't be mad, and I promise this isn't me trying to pay for things," she says timidly, "but I have some leftover tokens from the last time I was here for a friend's thirtieth birthday. It's not me paying! It's us being fiscally responsible with tokens I previously acquired."

I pause for a moment; then a roaring laugh pours out of me. "Olivia, you are adorable," I say with a smile as I put my arm around her shoulders. *God, she fits so fucking perfectly in my arms. I need to wake up like this.* "We can use your tokens until we run out. And we *will* run out, then I'll buy us more." I glance around the bar, stuck in place with what might be the best choice known to man. "Should we hit the pinball machines first? Or would you like me to beat you at skeeball as a starter?"

Olivia laughs; the tinkling sound makes my cock twitch. "Your competitiveness is already coming out there, Larsy. You seriously think *you* can beat *me* at skeeball? You're on, sir," Olivia replies with a feisty smile as she grabs my hand and drags me over to the game. *Did she just call me sir? Fuck, this woman is my every dream come true.*

Olivia proceeds to beat me at skeeball three times in a row, and I have discovered she is not a gracious winner. Her calling me competitive was the pot calling the kettle black. She's ruthless as hell, jumping up and down as she celebrates and rubbing in her wins by getting all up in my face and asking me what it feels like to be a loser. I'm loving every single minute of it. Watching her be so joyful after being devastated last week makes my heart soar. If I have any say in it, she will never experience that kind of agony again.

But after three losing rounds of skeeball, I'm ready to find a game I can beat her at. Scoping out the games around us, I pull her in close, trapping her in my arms. "Yeah, yeah, yeah. You win. How are you so good at skeeball anyway?"

"What can I say? I guess I'm just good at handling balls."

My eyes pop fully open and my pants feel tight as fuck at her words. *Did my sweet siren just make joke about handling balls? God, I cannot wait to get this girl in bed.* I try to compose myself, try to keep from losing control at the thought of what she could do to my balls, but her eyes spark as she lays the challenge down at my feet with a simple lift of her brow. *Fuck. Focus, Hayes.*

"Enjoy it now, Miss Skeeball, because when we hit the dance game *you're horrible at,* you're going to regret this little gloating session," I say as I watch the blood drain out of her face at the mention of DDR, grabbing her hand and dragging her across the bar.

As we step up to the platform, I put the tokens in and gesture for her to play. "Ladies first."

She hesitantly steps onto the game, looking back at me with fear in her eyes. "There's room for two players up here, you know."

"*Oh* no. I'm watching every single minute of this performance. We'll see who has the higher score at the end."

With that, she faces the game and hits start. She looks so timid up there; I almost feel bad for her. *Almost.* Until the music begins, and I realize I've been played. *Again.*

Olivia is stomping so fast on those light-up squares on the game platform that she seems to be floating above them. I shake my head with a smirk. She is the most adorable, flirty little brat up there dancing on that machine. And now, she is in so much trouble.

She hits the final pose, not even breathing hard. "Your turn, Hayes," she says with a mischievous smirk on her face. "You think you can top that?"

I flash her my best cartoon villain smile. "No." Glancing around once more, I quickly grab her hand and walk her toward the dark hallway leading to the restrooms. I spin around as I press her up against the wall. "You think you can get away with playing me like that, Olivia? That was some long con you pulled back there."

"What can I say? I have mad skills," she says like the brat I have been longing for my entire life. She's trying to get a rise out of me. *And oh, is she getting* exactly *what she asked for.*

I press my body closer, crowding her against the wall and placing one of my legs between hers as I lean in to kiss those supple lips. This isn't like the playful goodnight kiss on her porch. This a fierce claiming. *Olivia is mine, and it's damn time she learned.* She presses back against me, grinding against my leg as she lets out another one of those goddamn moans I've been playing on repeat for a week. I pull back from her lips and kiss her neck as she quietly moans again. I press her harder into the wall, desperate to get a little relief of my own. *So much for calming down…*fuck, *this girl does something to me, I swear.*

"Fuck, Olivia, that moan of yours is going to unravel me. And," I say between playful kisses along her pulse point, "if I didn't know better, it seems like you're *wanting* a punishment from this bet we made."

She gasps as she struggles to find her words. "I didn't say…I'm not...," she gasps with a shaky, yet excited voice. I interrupt her words again, unable to resist, pressing my lips against hers. She wraps her hands around the back of my head, pulling me deeper as her nails give me shivers.

A forced cough disrupts our moment. "Excuse me," an unfamiliar voice says. Olivia and I quickly pull apart, and there's a gentleman standing in the hallway trying to get past us to use the restroom.

Embarrassed, we move to opposite sides of the hall to let the man pass, and Olivia says, "Sorry about that," as he enters the men's room. She slowly turns back to look at me, sheer mortification at being caught swirling in her eyes, but I'm not focused on that.

I'm focused on the one little word that just slipped out of her gorgeous mouth.

I step toward her, a feral grin on my face. "What did you say, Olivia?"

She immediately puts her hand over her mouth, and I hear a muffled 'oh shit' behind her fingers.

"Oh, you're going to get it now," I taunt as I start to tickle her and she squeals. I laugh at her antics, but don't know what possessed me to tickle her...I think I simply had a hunch she might be ticklish.

I was right. Wonder what else I'm right about.

"But we really *were* in his way," she whines as she playfully squirms to get away. "We *should* apologize for something like that, *right*?!"

I hum, my hands stilling around her waist. "Good point. Your penalty challenge is under review. I'll let you know the results later today," I say to her with a sneaky grin. "Now, let's get out of here before that guy leaves the bathroom and catches us again. I'll go grab some more tokens and find a game I can actually beat you at."

She smiles at me and laughs, bringing a smile to my own lips. *I love her laugh.* I love *making* her laugh. I love the way she makes me laugh too. I'm beginning to think I love a lot more about this redhead than I should in such a short amount of time. She may be teetering on the edge of the penalty box right now, but I am the one who is in big trouble.

21
olivia

"Are you up for a bit of a drive?" I ask as I put the last of our destinations into Hayes' GPS. "It's about thirty minutes, but I promise it'll be worth it."

"Well, if you *promise* it will be worth it, I suppose I can't pass this up. Let's do it."

I should be a tangled mess of emotions right now based on what's happened in the last few weeks. But hanging out with Hayes and getting to know other pieces of this sweet, sexy man, has been the best treatment for my not-so-broken heart. This is honestly better than sitting on the couch eating ice cream straight out of the container with Maggie while binge-watching some sappy show and ugly crying.

Sitting beside him now, Hayes' hand on my thigh loosens the tension in my body, and his calmness wraps around me like my favorite blanket. I can see why he's been named an assistant captain his first year here. Being a good leader requires a certain amount of composure when facing something as unpredictable as a storm. He doesn't seem like the type to get rattled easily. *Except when you hustle him into thinking you're horrible at a dance game and show him up in spectacular style.* I may not be a good skater; honestly, I'm not even a good dancer, but I'm excellent at lighting up those little squares as they pop up. And that rattled his cage. *Mission accomplished.* He practically dragged me into the hallway to devour me with the most passionate of our two kisses to date.

Am I counting kisses? *Perhaps.*

Am I dreaming? *Dreaming would be an understatement.*

Am I wishing he would kiss me right now? *More than anything in the world.*

Arriving at our final destination, we drive down the long hill towards Grant Park Beach. *This place is breathtaking.* It has a gorgeous view of the crisp, blue water of Lake Michigan, white, rocky sand lined with tiki torches, a pier to walk out and see the water up close, and a cute little hamburger stand to grab a snack.

I look over at Hayes, whose eyes are wide and full of awe. My heart swells, and I can't stop the smile spreading across my cheeks at watching him instantly fall in love with this place like I did.

"Wow. You weren't kidding when you said the drive would be worth it."

"Do you remember when I told you I love finding hidden gem spots in the city? This is the best one in Milwaukee." I beam as he parks, and we hop out to see this gorgeous beach in person.

"Olivia," he breathes, unable to tear his eyes away, "This place is unreal. It's…it's beautiful. It's like I'm on vacation."

"Right?! That's how I felt the first time I came here too. It's my favorite place to sit and listen to the water."

We step out of the car and walk towards the beach as I continue to ramble about all the reasons I love this place. "The water is too cold to swim in most of the time, but the breeze drifting off the lake is cooling even on the hottest days. There's nothing better in the middle of the summer. The locals don't like tourists to know about this place because it's so peaceful and doesn't get overly crowded."

Hayes takes out his phone to snap some photos of the picturesque beach. "Thank you for trusting me with the secret location of this hidden beach. It's amazing. Let me just post this on social media quickly to let all my two hundred thousand followers know I'm here," he says with a wink.

I prepare to give him one of my famous punches, but his quick reflexes grab my hand before it reaches him, quickly pulling me towards him in an embrace I was not expecting but maybe hoping for.

"You've already gotten in trouble once today, sweet girl. Are you going for a record?" he murmurs with a raised eyebrow.

"Maybe I am," I respond with a shaky breath. He stares at me with heat burning straight into me as thousands of butterflies float around my stomach. A current of sexual tension pulses between us, my body anxious to pick up where we left off in the hallway. I break the heady silence surrounding us. "Let's go for a walk."

We walk along the shoreline, his rough hand holding mine, before finding a picnic table somewhat secluded from the others enjoying the lake. We sit side by side on the bench facing the water, leaning our backs against the table and watching the waves crash on the shoreline.

"Can I ask you something?" Hayes asks, my body tensing at his words. "You don't have to answer if you don't want to."

Calm your tits, Olivia…Hayes is different. He's not an asshat more interested in video games and getting drunk with his friends than spending time with his girlfriend.

"Sure. Ask me whatever you want."

"Why were you and Cayden together for so long?"

That's…not what I was expecting.

Taking in a deep breath, I calm myself knowing Hayes is just curious why we were together. *So am I.* "Honestly…that's a great question." I sigh, not feeling brave enough to face Hayes as I respond. "I haven't had any serious boyfriends until Cayden. I would meet guys, and we'd go out on a few dates, but things would fizzle out, and we'd move on. It was fun, but it didn't feel right. When I met Cayden, he was nice for a while. He got along well with my friends. But, looking back, there are a lot of red flags I should have seen sooner." I grumble as I stare into the vastness of the water, embarrassed admitting all this, not only to Hayes but also to myself. "He was constantly talking about his friends and how he could never miss an event they had, or he'd be banished from their group. Who lives their life like that? And what kind of friends banish you if you miss a 4th of July cookout?

"The last few months things got worse. I caught him lying a couple of times. Several weeks ago, he was supposed to be at work, but he called in sick. The whole day he was texting me like he was super busy, but I found out from his roommate's girlfriend he was home all day playing video games with his roommates. He just… didn't want to see me. I'd been trying to figure out how to ask him about it, but we barely saw each other for a few weeks, so it never came up." I pause, nervously rubbing my hands up and down my thighs, realizing this is way too much information for me to be sharing with someone I barely know. *Even if it feels like I've known Hayes for longer than a month.* "I could go on all day about this," I peek out of the corner of my eye, "you don't need to listen to me ramble on about my horrible past relationship all night."

"Olivia, it's not too much. I happen to be a good listener. You said his name was Brayden, right?" he says as I smile and nudge him with my shoulder as a gentle thanks for the comic relief.

"Yes, *Brayden.* I think because it was my first long-term relationship, I didn't know what to expect. I got into a headspace where I thought…maybe, this is as good as it gets." My fingers tangle together in my lap, my knuckles white as I twist them together. "I wondered if this is simply what every relationship is like. I know my romance books and movies are just entertainment and nowhere close to real life, but I figured at least the person I was with would *want* to spend time together. Then I went down this whole rabbit trail of *what's wrong with me* knowing someone who's choosing to be with me doesn't want to see me."

Hayes reaches over and grabs my hands, giving them a gentle squeeze. His warmth fills me with a sweet comfort, and I let out a deep exhale at his soothing gesture, finally feeling like I can breathe again, purging all these emotions to someone who actually cares.

Hayes turns toward me, compassion flowing from his warm hands into mine. "You should never have to feel that way Olivia. And, believe it or not, I can relate."

I blink, surprised someone like Hayes would ever have experienced someone like Cayden. "You can?"

He nods, his features softening as a somber expression crosses his face. "One of the reasons I was excited to sign with the Riders was to get away from my ex-girlfriend and the life we had in Tampa. I feel a lot of the same things. My ex, Chelsea, cheated on me. I knew something was up, but I chose to ignore the voice in my head warning me something was wrong.

"Being in the league, I obviously travel a lot. It's part of the job that can be tough on the people you care about. You have to miss birthdays, anniversaries, and special events that are important to them. It sucks. It's the most difficult part of the job. I always tried to find ways to arrange for special things when I'd be gone and to be together as much as possible when I was home." His hand shakes against mine, and I interlace our fingers, reminding him I'm also here to listen.

"I thought things between Chelsea and I were good. Until I got home from practice one day and picked up her MacBook to start planning a surprise party for her birthday. There, on her screen, was a string of text messages from a contact saved as 'Spam Risk.' The messages were racy, but the icing on the cake was her trying to figure out how to tell me she was pregnant with *his* baby. My heart sunk straight to the pit of my stomach, and all I could think is *well, cat's out of the bag now, Chels*."

My heart drops at the pain Hayes must be going through. I want to take this grief from him, but the only thing I can think to do is grasp his hand tighter and I rub my thumb across his knuckles.

"After I confronted her about it, she blamed me for being away so much. She said she was lonely. Then she had the *nerve* to ask me for money to help her with the security deposit on a new place because baby daddy *Brian* was between jobs.

"As much as it hurt, and God, did it hurt, looking back it was for the best. She was living off my salary and trying to be an influencer. I'm not even sure if she cared about me or just thought I would be her sugar daddy and get her more social media followers." He sighs, his head dropping back as he closes his eyes. "The timing of me signing with the Riders was a good excuse to get out of town and away from that train wreck. Get a fresh start."

"Oh my God, Hayes, that's awful! I can't imagine what that must have felt like. That's way worse than Cayden treating me like shit."

He lets out a small chuckle. "It's not a contest, Olivia. It sucked, that's for sure, but like I said, I can relate. From what it sounds like, we've both had some shitty relationships, and it's probably a good thing they are over," he says, looking out toward the water again, a small smile on his face. "Had things not ended with her, I might never have moved to Milwaukee. I might never have ended up at some bar, hearing a gorgeous voice coming from the most beautiful woman I've ever seen, and I wouldn't be sitting here with her at this very moment."

The rapid fluttering in my heart floats deep into my core at his words, my breath catching in my chest.

I can hardly find the breath to speak, staring at the ebb and flow of the water, willing my lungs to find some air. "You…you think I'm beautiful?"

He drops my hand, gripping my chin and tilting it towards him. "How many times do I need to tell you I don't hand out compliments unless I mean them? Not only are you beautiful, you are *the* most beautiful girl I have ever laid eyes on. As if I needed another reason to want to kiss you every time I see you; you are smart, funny, and insanely talented. You deserve to be with someone who appreciates that and wants to spend time with you."

My heart soars at his words, excitement building in my chest. "You want to kiss me again?"

"Out of that entire speech, *that's* what you picked up on?" he says, laughing.

I bite my lip, trapped in Hayes' orbit. His pull. His everything. "I only asked because…I'd like for you to kiss me again."

I have no idea where this boldness is coming from, but it's pouring out of me like a dam that's suddenly broken wide open.

And there is no holding back this water.

Hayes leans toward me and places his other hand on my cheek, gently dragging his thumb across my lower lip as I shudder at his touch.

"Olivia, I could kiss these lips all day and never come up for air." My heart races as he leans in, pressing his lips to mine. He's gentle, delicate - cradling me as if I'm the most precious thing he's ever held. Calming every fear, every worry, every bit of self-doubt constantly plaguing my mind. He's kissing me with a quiet passion in my favorite spot in the city. It feels like it's just the two of us on earth. Everything else fades away as I run my hand through his tousled hair, exploring his mouth with my tongue.

But it's not enough.

My emotions and hormones are raging like wildfire. *I need more.* More of Hayes. More of this. More of everything. I pull back from the kiss, not giving myself time to second guess as I straddle him on the picnic bench. I drop my forehead against his, instantly enveloped by his woodsy spice smell. *God, I could drown in this man's scent.* I lean in to kiss him as he wraps his arms around my back, pulling me tight against him.

Oh my God. I can *feel* his excitement pressing against me. I wiggle, just a little, to let him know, and now *he's* the one moaning. Knowing I am turning him on is getting me even more worked up. I can't stop my hips from grinding against him again, teasing both of us.

God, he feels so good pressed against me like this.

"Olivia…" He moans my name, interrupting the kiss. "I do not want to stop what we are doing for *any* reason. But…we are in public. And seeing as there are people on the beach, it might be a crime for me to walk back to my car with what's happening in my pants right now."

I giggle, letting my head fall to his shoulder. "Good point. I guess I got a little carried away there." I bite my lower lip in attempt to hide the embarrassed grin on my face. I have zero regrets about what happened, ignoring the voice in my head, sounding a lot like Cayden, telling me I'm *too much.*

He leans in to give me a kiss on the cheek. "Alright, let's get out of here. But could you walk in front of me? Kind of like a shield in case anyone sees us."

I laugh hysterically, crawling off his lap and offering him a hand. "I'm happy to serve as your boner shield anytime."

22

hayes

A s we walk back to the car, two things are on my mind. First, the girl holding my hand, who is the best part of Milwaukee, is shielding me from a world of embarrassment. Second, a long list of things I'd like her to do with what she's shielding.

But it dawns on me that I fly out in the morning for a road trip for the rest of the week. *Fuck.* I don't want to come across as being too forward, she's got a lot going on emotionally, and I want to give her space, but I also don't want to drop her off at her house. I don't want this night to end before I'm gone for five days. I slow my steps as we near the car, an idea popping into my head. Hopping into the driver's seat, I wonder...would she go for it? Only one way to find out.

"I have another question for you, and again, you can say no if you aren't comfortable." I glance at Olivia as we drive out of the park, my dick twitching at the thought of what I'm about to ask. "How would you feel about coming over to my place and staying the night? I know that probably sounds presumptuous, and I promise we don't have to do anything other than hang out and talk until we fall asleep, but I leave in the morning for a road trip. I'll be gone most of the week, and I...I don't want to miss another moment with you."

Olivia is quiet for a moment, her fingernails nervously tapping out a rhythm on the door handle, my palms fucking sweating while gripping the steering wheel as I wait for the gears in her mind to stop turning.

"Can we do more than talk?"

"We can do anything you want. Just so you know, I'm trying to calm down what's going on below my waist right now, and comments like that are not helping," I groan, glancing over to her as she fights back a grin.

"Sorry, I didn't mean to cause any more tension in those pants."

I tilt my head, glancing at her from the corner of my eye with a raised eyebrow, a smirk twisting my lips. "What did you say, Olivia?"

"Damn...I said it again, didn't I?"

"Yes, you did. And unlike the earlier incident, which I'm still taking under advisement, you should *never* have to apologize for getting me turned on." I adjust my length, unashamed, as she nods in agreement trying to hide a smile. *I hope she is beginning to see there is no need to walk on eggshells around me.*

"Sooo..." she hesitates before she speaks, nervously rubbing her thighs. "I can't believe I'm about to tell you this. But...since we've shared a lot of relationship scars today, what's one more?" She takes a deep breath. "Cayden always complained I had too high of a sex drive. He was always too tired to keep up with me, so I constantly felt like I was bothering him by making suggestive comments."

"I'm sorry...*what*? He actually said that to you? A *human man* told you your sex drive is too high?" I scoff as I white knuckle the steering wheel to avoid driving straight to this guy's house and punching him square in the dick he clearly doesn't know how to use.

"Yep. He said my sex drive was ramping up in my thirties, which was unusual, and his was winding down, which was to be expected. It was just one more way I was too clingy for him," she replies with a hint of regret. "The kicker is, the last time I was at his place, he opened his laptop and there were all these porn sites pulled up, which he quickly closed. But I still saw them. While I have no problem with porn, I mean we're all human, the pain of him being too tired to be with me, but not tired enough to jerk off to those videos, made me feel even worse about myself."

"Are you sure he was attracted to women?" I ask as she lets out a boisterous laugh. "I have never heard of a man saying his girl-friend wanted to have too much sex."

"Apparently it was too much for him, and he couldn't keep up. You know, the one night a week we'd even see each other," she grumbles with annoyance.

"Well," I growl flashing a devilish grin. "there's something you should know about me, Olivia."

"And what's that?"

"I *love* a challenge."

We stop by Olivia's place for her to run in and grab a few things, along with her car so she can drive home in the morning, then she follows me back to my place in the Third Ward. The elevator ride from the basement parking garage to my 5th floor apartment seems to take an hour, the two of us standing in heavy silence. I look over, finding those longing eyes gazing back at me.

DING.

The sound of the elevator arriving breaks our gaze, and I place my hand on the small of her back, leading her toward my apartment. The lock sounds impossibly loud in the quiet hallway, and inside I drop my gear bag in the entryway as we both slip off our shoes. Olivia sets down her bag and jacket there as well. *She fits so well in my space.*

"Would you like a tour of the apartm-"

My words are interrupted by Olivia slamming her lips into mine. She runs her fingers through my hair as she moans into our kiss, her body flush against mine. *That moan is going to be the death of me.* As our tongues collide, I pick her up and she immediately wraps her legs around my back. *My God, this woman is fucking perfect in my arms.* I carefully carry her toward my bedroom. The passion building between us this week – fuck, since we met - has all been leading to this moment. This glorious, torturous, sexual tension *finally* has an outlet. We enter the bedroom, and I gently set her on the bed, standing between her legs.

"Olivia. I want this. I want you. But I want to be sure this isn't too fast for you. I know you've got a lot going on. Shit, we both do." My hands fist at my sides as I fight against the need to touch her. "I don't want to push you into anything you don't want."

She pauses for a moment, her eyes darting around the room as if she's looking for answers. *For the love of all things hockey, let her answer be wanting me inside her.*

"Hayes," her eyes lock onto mine, "I *really* appreciate the respect and space you're trying to give me. I mean…maybe this *is* too fast. We've both just ended some emotionally complicated relationships," she says, and my heart sinks. But if she wants to slow things down, I'm not going to fuck this up. *She deserves* everything.

"Honestly, I don't know what's come over me, but ever since you sat down at Walt's during my gig, I've felt a different kind of confidence building inside me. I feel like I can finally be myself." I step closer, our legs pressed against each other. "Somehow, you've made me realize I'm tired of living for what other people want. I want to start living for what *I* want. What I need. What makes me happy." I kneel on the bed, towering over her as my body burns. "And right now, what I want…is you."

23
olivia

Hayes presses his rough lips into mine as he gently leans me down on his bed. I shiver as he leans over me, shuddering at the heat of his body. He moves his lips to my neck, lightly sucking on my pulse point and drawing out a moan from deep within my chest.

"Your neck is sensitive, isn't it?" Hayes asks in a soft voice

"*Very*. How did you figure that out so fast?"

"Every time I kiss your neck, you let out that sexy moan, and I almost come in my fucking pants."

Wetness rapidly builds between my legs knowing that any part of me, or what I'm doing, is turning him on, and I can't help but let out another moan knowing what it does to him. *He's already figuring out the most sensitive parts of my body faster than anyone I've ever been with.* He runs his wandering hands up and down my arms, barely touching me. Goosebumps erupt across my skin, Hayes' rough fingers slowly running down the deep v of my shirt. My body shivers, wanting him to touch every part of me, as his hands reach my heaving chest.

I've never been touched like this, such a tender worshiping of my body nearly brings tears to my eyes. He's teasing every inch of me with just a whisper of his fingers. Finally, he reaches the hem of my shirt and pulls it up as far as he can before helping me sit up to peel the barrier up over my head.

I move my own hands to the hem of his shirt and do the same. *I need to see this man shirtless.* It's only fair.

Oh. My. God. This man is mus-cu-lar. His pecs are toned and defined, the flat planes begging for my lips to touch. His fucking washboard abs, and the v-cut trail carving a path below his waistband have me moaning once again. Hayes takes good care of his body, and it fucking *shows.* I run my hands across his chest, needing to feel his muscles ripple as he leans over me. *I am starving for this man.*

He reaches over and slides his fingers between my shoulder and the strap of my bra. "This needs to come off," he says in a deep, gruff voice.

"Luckily for you, this one clasps in the front," I tease as I unclasp the clip, remove it from my arms, and lay bare chested before him. I see a sparkle in his eyes as he gazes at what's displayed before him, the man is almost salivating as he leans down to touch me.

"You are so fucking beautiful," he whispers as he kisses me, grazing his hand over my neck and exposed chest. He squeezes my breast as he licks my nipple, forcing a whimper from my throat.

"Holy shit. Hayes, that feels incredible."

He lifts his head, his eyes locking with mine. "You are what's incredible, Olivia."

My hips lift up as if they have a mind of their own, reacting to his every word and anticipating the feeling of grinding against him. *This man is going to be my undoing.*

As he moves to tease my other nipple, I run my hands through his messy hair, pulling him deeper into my chest. My hips grind against him, and I gasp at how worked up he's getting me, even though he's barely touched me.

"I think these need to come off next," he growls, his fingers dipping beneath the waistband of my leggings. I push my hips up to help him slide them off, realizing too late Hayes is a sneaky bastard. He not only pulls off my leggings, but the black underwear I had on as well. He gazes at me with a feral look in his eyes, taking in my fully naked body. Surprisingly, I notice his attention linger on my legs, fingers twitching as they reach out, then pull back, hovering in the air with hesitation. *Damn, is Hayes a leg man or am I imagining things?*

"Every time I think you couldn't possibly be any more gorgeous, you prove me wrong. Your body is…" his eyes trace over every inch of me, leaving fire sparking across my flesh, "exquisite."

This man clearly wants *me*…and I am here for every moment of it.

I haven't felt wanted in a long time.

"I need these to come off too," I say, tugging at the waistband of his joggers. "Fair is fair." He flashes me a devilish grin as he stands, sliding his pants and boxer briefs down, letting them pool on the floor.

Holy soda-can Batman. My jaw is on the floor. I've been imagining his naked body for weeks, even more after feeling him pressed against me, but this…this is more than I was expecting. I've seen my share of dicks, and his is *the sexiest* I've ever seen. More than anything, his girth is…wow. Guys get so caught up on length, but for me, girth is the difference maker. *Who cares about inches?* My vagina is only so long. And, as if this man's girth isn't enough, he also has the biggest set of balls I've ever seen in my life, and I am *here* for it. The thought of those slapping against me as he takes me from behind sends me almost over the edge, my body arching off the bed, craving his touch.

"Olivia, my eyes are up here," Hayes growls, and I realize I'm still staring at his manhood. "You like what you see?"

My tongue wets my lips, my eyes glancing between his face and his cock. "Yeah." I gulp. "I...um....how do you walk with that?" I ask, and he laughs, moving back on the bed and laying on his side next to me.

"It's one of my many talents," he says.

"Oh, yeah?" I reply, "What other *talents* do you have?"

Hayes slowly slides his hand from my knee to my thigh. "You're about to find out," he says as he ever so lightly places his hand at the apex of my legs, his eyes rolling to the back of his head as he grunts. "Olivia, you are fucking dripping for me."

I melt at the way he says my name, touching me in the most intimate of places as if I'm to be treasured, admired, *enjoyed*.

"Hayes. *Shit*. You make me feel...amazing."

"My new mission is to make you feel this good all the time."

"I am fully onboard with that," I say through panted breaths, reaching down and gripping his rock-hard cock, ready to hold on for dear life. "I want to do the same for you."

24
hayes

I don't know what in my life I've done to end up here, but thank fuck I did. I'm in bed with the woman of my dreams, her moans echoing around my bedroom as she grips my dick like it's the last one on earth and she doesn't ever want to let go. Her tiny hand around my thickness is unbelievable. The way she stared between my legs when I dropped my pants, that look of shock, longing, and *desire*, tells me she likes it as well.

How could that fucking douchebag ex of hers not worship the very ground she walks on? I'm not even sure how I'm going to be able to leave this room - to leave for days without her touch, her smile, her laugh, and now her fucking pussy. I want to spend every minute showing this woman she deserves to be pleasured, to be fulfilled, reminding her that she is worth more than that asshole, or anyone else, refused to see in her. *She deserves to be treated like a queen, and I intend to do just that.*

"Olivia, you *know* what a bad sweet tooth I have. Do you taste as sweet as I think you do?"

She gasps, squeezing my cock still in her hand. I lean down

between her sexy-as-fuck legs, peppering them with kisses working my way higher toward her gorgeous pussy. Olivia is writhing and squirming as I tease her. *She* is loving *this.* "I *need* something sweet, and *you* are the perfect dessert." I part her lips with my fingers, finally tasting her sweetness. *Goddamn...I could survive off of nothing but this woman.* I slowly run my tongue up her cunt, still taunting her until I finally swipe along her sensitive, swollen clit. I'm paying attention to every one of her moans, her twitches, her gasps, taking a mental note of what makes her tick, noticing each time she writhes into me with her hips. I find one spot that really makes her squirm. I dart my gaze up to watch her expression as she groans and squeezes one of her tits. *Holy fucking shit. Why is that so damn hot?* I slowly slide a finger inside her. *Fuck.* I can feel her pussy squeezing me. I've got to calm myself down or I'm going to explode before I get inside her. *Focus, Hayes; eyes on the prize.*

"Oh, my feisty siren," I come up for air from the ocean I could easily drown in, "You are the sweetest thing I've ever tasted," I confess, rubbing my fingers over her clit, kissing my way up her body until I reach that sensitive spot on her neck.

"That feels...oh *shit,* just like that. I'm so close."

I lean in close to her ear and whisper, "Are you going to come for me like a good girl?" Olivia's moan echoes around us as she finally goes over the edge. She grabs my balls and squeezes while she rides out her release; my pulse races as I try to make sense of what's happening.

Holy fuck.

Watching her shatter as she's holding my balls is one of the hottest things I've ever experienced. Her entire body quivers, the vibrations pouring into me through our connection.

"Hayes," she pants, trying to catch her breath, her face flushed and her lips trembling as she tries to recover from her climax.

I smile at her with pride and a sense of accomplishment, admiring the afterglow on her face.

"That was incredible. Phenomenal. You were *not* wrong about having many talents. Is there anything you don't do well?"

"Skeeball," I reply, and we both laugh. I lean over and kiss her before reaching for a condom in my nightstand. She is wet and so ready for me that I'm about to come undone at the thought of her fluttering around my cock.

"Olivia, you are so fucking beautiful," I say, gazing into her eyes as I slowly press myself up against her entrance.

"Hayes, I want this. I *want* it hard. I want it fast. I need you inside me, all of you, *now*. So please …fuck me," she says with desperation.

The fucking dirty mouth on this sweet girl. I am not one to argue with a woman pleading for me, so I slowly press just a little of myself into her. She is fucking wet. *Dripping.* She gasps, arching her back as I slide in a little farther.

"Please, Hayes; *please.*"

Fuck. It takes every ounce of my restraint not to slam into her.

"Olivia, I'm *not* going to rush this. I know my good girl can take this cock, but I'm savoring every moment of feeling your warm pussy for the first time." Her back bows off the bed as I move another inch.

"Shit. Hayes, you are fucking huge," she says, her hands gripping the sheets pressing against me more. "You are going to rip me apart. I want to be ripped apart."

"You and that mouth of yours are going to be the death of me," I growl as I let go of my restraint and slide fully inside her.

She lets out a sound somewhere between a moan and a scream, and I still for a moment, letting her adjust. With every fiber of my being, I know this act of connection between us is going to change everything. *This girl is fucking perfection. And she is fucking* mine.

She is *so* tight. My hips snap against hers, my body stringing tighter and tighter as we come together again and again. "I'm not sure how long I'm going to last, and I want to make you come again. I *need* you to come on my cock. Are you going to come for me again like a good girl?"

"Yes," she cries out, her voice shaking. "Your cock feels good, so *fucking* good, inside me. Like it was made to fill my cunt. I'm so fucking close. Just, *please,* fuck me hard and fast."

I thrust in and out of her, reveling in how tight she feels around me. *Nothing has ever felt this good.* Pounding into her with a quicker, rougher rhythm, desperate to take her with me, I finally explode with a roar threatening to shake the windows. My sexy siren finds her gorgeous release seconds later, the feel of her squeezing around my dick has me seeing fucking stars. This has been every dream I've had the last few weeks, and it's finally come true. Except it's better than my dreams. She's right here. Laying here - me still inside her. Right here.

Maybe I am still dreaming.

"Olivia, you are incredible. Beyond incredible actually. I don't know what the word for that is, but that's what you are." I collapse beside her, leaning over to pull her close and kiss her as she somehow looks even more sexy than before - and well taken care of. "I'll be right back," I say with another kiss as I walk into the bathroom to clean myself up.

When I return, my little siren's snuggled under the covers, her breaths even as I lean against the door frame and admire the view. *I just fucked her into oblivion. Maybe Vladi was right about the panty dropping.* I climb in to join her and spoon her from behind, placing gentle kisses on her neck.

"Hayes," she mumbles, shifting deeper into my arms, "*you* are incredible. No one has ever gotten me off like that before. In fact, … you are the *only* one who has ever gotten me off before."

"What?" I jolt up in bed, leaning over to see her face. "Olivia, are you serious? No one? Ever?"

"Dead serious. I usually fake it because no one seems to know what they are doing and it gets boring," she says as she lets out a sexy, devious laugh.

"Well, having firsthand knowledge of your acting skills, I have no doubt you can fake it with the best of them, but please don't ever feel pressured to pretend with me. I only want to make you feel good, and if something doesn't, you let me know. Promise?"

"I promise," she rolls over to face me, a playful grin on her face. "Besides, if you keep doing what you did tonight, *twice*, I won't need to fake anything."

I stroke the back of my hand along her flushed cheeks. "Oh, my sweet, sweet Olivia, I haven't even gotten started with my bag of tricks yet."

25
hayes

I'm dead. I'm done for. I officially have died and gone to Olivia Brooks heaven. My siren is here, in my bed, and a missing puzzle piece has finally snapped into place. Someone is going to have to pry me off her because she's become a life force I can't live without. I want to sink into her every night and wake up to her every morning. I want her in my jersey, in the stands, at every game I play. I want *her*. Except my fucking idiot stomach is growling, begging me for actual food. *Although, I'm not complaining about having dessert before dinner.*

"Join me in the kitchen for a little after-sex snack?"

"After sex-snacks? You might actually be the whole package," she says.

"Drink it in, siren. Drink. It. In."

Getting out of bed, we throw some clothes on and head to the kitchen. She looks adorable in nothing but my Riders t-shirt as she pads barefoot across the hardwood floor, completely at ease in my space. She snoops around my home, peaking in boxes I've yet to unpack as I grab some carrots, hummus, and pita chips, swiping a few bottled waters as well.

For someone who is only five-feet tall, she has legs that go for days. I am a leg man, and Olivia's legs…dear *God,* they are sexy-as-fuck. Tits are a wonderful, fantastic part of the female anatomy, ones I immensely enjoy. But a woman with killer legs is my weakness. Knowing they lead straight to the promised land makes my dick swell faster than my slapshot. Seeing Olivia prance around my apartment already has me standing at half-mast.

"Do you workout a lot?" I ask, unashamedly staring at the lower half of her frame.

"Not religiously," she says, crunching on a carrot. "And nothing compared to how much you workout. I like to lift weights, sometimes, and I have a spin bike at home. But, honestly, it's hit or miss. Totally depends on my mood and how absorbed I am in my music. I should be more diligent about it. Working out always makes me feel good, but it's getting motivated to do it that is tough."

"No judgement here. I get paid to workout, so that's my motivation," I say, getting a laugh from her. "I was mainly asking because your calves are amazing. Do you do some special calf workout? As someone who's in the gym every day, I must say, I'm fascinated by your leg muscles. Honestly, I need your routine. Some of the guys on the team *desperately* need your secret."

Olivia lets out a roaring laugh. It's always sudden like a firecracker. Her eyes crinkle in the corners, and her head falls back to look at the ceiling as if she's sharing an inside joke with someone above. I could listen to that laugh all day long.

"You know, it's funny, people comment on my calves all the time, but I've never specifically trained them. *Ever.*" She scoffs, her brow lifting high in amusement. "Don't think I didn't catch you staring. Want to know my secret?"

Guess the jig is up. I smile deviously at her. "I'm a sucker for a nice pair of legs Olivia, and yours are…they are….” I swallow hard unable to form words. “Okay, just tell me already.”

“It’s stilettos. I wear heels to work every day. Swear to God, that’s how I have calves of steel. You’d be surprised at how many comments I get. It’s only weird when it’s creepy old dudes, but they usually leave me alone if I just smile and walk away.”

Fire burns inside my chest at the thought of anyone but me catching even a glance of those perfect legs. I set my water down on the counter and take a possessive step toward her. “I don’t want *anyone* looking anywhere near your legs,” I say a little sterner than I mean to.

She hums, sucking her teeth with a smirk. “You jealous Hayesy-poo? Think some creepy old dude is gonna come sweep me off my feet while you’re out of town this week?” she teases, playfully poking me in the chest with her finger. She leans in close, teasing me with a look of pure need and desire, before pulling away with a loud crunch of her carrot. Her bratty tone gets under my skin, my dick twitching to show her how she’s driving me crazy.

And she knows it.

I groan, glancing around for something to throw over her legs. “Can you just wear pants this week while I’m away? Maybe turtle-necks too…none of those v-neck shirts like you wore today. I will not be held responsible for my actions if someone sneaks a peek down your cleavage.”

“Oh? And were *you* peeking down my shirt today?”

“Nope! Not me. I would never do that.” I trace an X over my chest before holding my hands up and taking a small step back. “I was a complete gentleman. Even when you were jumping up and down and basically shoving your tits in my face after you destroyed me in skeeball, I kept my eyes toward the sky.” She laughs again. “However, I *am* concerned about the ‘creepy old dudes’ you mentioned trying to sneak a peek.”

"How about I rent a nun costume for the week?"

"You would do that for me? I mean, we could call around and see if there's one available." I smirk, seeing her playful punch start to head my way. *I'm onto her little trick now.* I easily grab her hand pulling her into me. "My, my, Olivia. Always so violent. I may need to tie you down to protect myself."

"I'm violent?" She scoffs, her eyebrows raised. "You play one of the most *violent* sports in the history of sports."

"Well...true," I laugh, backing her against the counter.

"How do you always know when I'm about to punch your arm?"

"Olivia, my *literal* job is learning to anticipate other people's movements."

"Well, shit...I need to come up with some new moves. I bet I can think of something you won't see coming."

I flash her a devilish grin. "Speaking of bets, Olivia, we still haven't discussed your punishment yet," I tease, and the desire in her eyes tells me all I need to know.

I think Olivia might enjoy a little punishment.

Good, little siren, me too.

26
olivia

"I was *kind of* hoping you would forget about that," I say with a nervous laugh, looking away from his gaze. Truth is, I was hoping he hadn't. My heart is beating so fast there are spots coloring my vision. *Punishing me?* I've never done anything like this before. And I don't even know what *this* is yet! I bite my lip, trapped between Hayes and the counter. But from the vibes he's been giving off, I didn't want to give him *that* much encouragement all at once or this man may go full-on fifty shades.

"Oh siren, I did *not* forget. You know what I think?" Hayes says, slowly running his fingers down my cheek, his rough thumb tracing across my lips, releasing my flesh from my teeth. "I think you *want* to be punished," he says, his voice down a full octave. I can barely breathe, my wide eyes staring into his. *He's not wrong, but…how does he know?* "Do you trust me, Olivia?"

"Yes," I say with a shaky breath. My thighs squeeze together as heat intensifies between them. He's barely touched me and I'm already starting to come unglued.

A girl could get used to this.

"If I ever do anything you don't like, or you don't want, you tell me. In fact, why don't you pick a safe word so you don't feel self-conscious about letting me know."

I swear to God this man can read my mind. He's right; I'll absolutely feel awkward speaking up. The curiosity I have about what we would even *need* a safe word for has me intrigued. My breath catches in my throat and my nipples harden imagining what he has in mind.

"Okay," I whisper, thinking for a moment. "How about... Zamboni."

He lets out a belly laugh, his body vibrating against mine. The sound melts my heart just a little bit more.

"Alright. Zamboni it is," he says as he calms, his eyes still sparking with laughter.

"Is that going to make you have a zam-boner, Hayes?"

He lets out a more villainous laugh, my breath catching in my chest. "You just keep pushing the envelope, don't you sweet girl? You know what happens to sirens when they keep acting up like this?" he says, all lightness suddenly gone from his voice as he leans into me and whispers, "They get spanked."

I gasp, heat building in my core. My body stiffens as I stand like a deer in headlights unable to remove myself from his gaze. I've never done this before. I've never done *anything* like this before. But, for some crazy reason, I trust Hayes. I know his intentions are more for my pleasure than his. *Though I can't imagine he's not finding some pleasure in this as well.*

Flashing me a devilish smile, he sheds me of his t-shirt and I stand naked before him. We stand-off against one another, his eyes darkening as they take in every inch of my flesh before he turns me, my hips digging into the island.

"Close your eyes, and keep them closed. No peeking. Do you understand?"

My legs wobble at his stern rumble. *My God, his serious voice is sexy as hell.* I take in a shaky breath and reply, "Yes".

Standing behind me, his fingers skim up my spine, goosebumps pebbling my flesh as he places his hand between my shoulder blades and gently bends me over the countertop. He takes his time, delicately rubbing his hands down my back, following the trail of his fingertips with gentle kisses along my spine. Every inch of my skin he crosses ignites a fire. A shiver runs through my body as my nipples press against the cold granite. My core is annoyingly empty as his calloused touch teases dangerously close to my ass.

"Olivia, have you ever been spanked?"

Holy fucking shit; this is happening. I breath out a quiet, "No," as I whimper at the thought of what is about to happen.

Hayes palms my right cheek, his heat comforting until he pulls away, quickly smacking my ass, my body jolting against the granite. The slight sting hits me, but the impact goes straight to my clit. He gently rubs my cheek to soothe the sting, and I writhe at his touch.

More. I gasp, surprised. *I want more.*

Is there pain? Yes. But it's like biting into an apple; your gums ache, but somehow it hurts and feels good at the same time. *My God, do I want to take another bite of this apple.*

"You like that?" Hayes asks, his voice nothing more than a growl.

"Yes," I breathe, barely able to speak.

Hayes lets out a guttural sound from deep in his throat. "I *knew* you'd enjoy this." His hand caresses me once more. "You are such a rule follower, aren't you?"

"Yes."

"You don't like to be in trouble, right?"

"Yes."

"Yet, you've been misbehaving all day today, my sweet siren.

Tricking me. Taunting me. Saying you're sorry for things you shouldn't." He groans, his heat washing over me as he kisses my neck between his words. "You need a few more spankings to truly learn your lesson."

"Yes. I've behaved badly today."

SMACK!

He spanks me again right as I finish that sentence. God, the way he brings forward pain then lovingly rubs over my ass has my soul melting and my cunt dripping.

Hayes moves his hand down to the wetness between my legs, my body opening for him. Desperate for him. Desperate for release.

"*Siren,* look how wet you are. Is this turning you on? Do you want more, Olivia?"

"Yes," I say, my eyes rolling back into my head. "God, yes, Hayes."

Why is *this turning me on so much?* His fingers tease, dancing around where I truly want him before lifting away. Maybe it's the idea of letting go. I whimper, seeking his touch. Maybe it's because it feels fucking amazing. Maybe I love the thought of Hayes being in control. My body stills, anticipation hanging heavy in the air. Maybe it's just this sexy-as-fuck man and the dirty things I would let him do to me.

SMACK!

Hayes rubs his hard cock up and down my slit as my legs shake. Pushing my ass back toward him, I moan, "Hayes, I need you inside me."

He leans down, whispering into my ear, "Such a greedy girl, aren't you? You want this dick? You're going to have to beg me for it." He slaps my ass once more, the timber of his voice echoing around us.

My cunt is aching for his cock once more, and I am barely

holding on. "Please, Hayes, please fuck me. I need to feel your cock inside me again. Please!"

His hardness presses up against me, letting me know just how turned on he is. He's turned on by *me. Is this really happening?* My pulse quickens at the thought as his woodsy sent surrounds me. "That's my good girl. I'm gonna fuck you from behind, while I spank this gorgeous ass of yours."

I moan as he starts to push inside me, but he stops and sighs, my entire body going rigid at the sound.

Oh shit. Did I do something wrong? I've never done this before...did I say something wrong? I force myself to relax, my body tense against the frigid counter. *This is a horrible time to mentally spiral.*

I clear my throat, Zamboni sitting on the tip of my tongue. "Everything okay?" I nervously ask.

"Yeah. Just...*fuck.* The condoms are in the bedroom. Hold on," he says in a frustrated breath, hesitating before pulling away.

I breathe a sigh of relief, reminding myself, once again, Hayes is not going to make me feel embarrassed. He's not going to make me feel judged or less than. *He isn't* him.

"Hayes," I turn my head back to face him and grasp his wrist, "I'm on the pill. I just got tested a few days ago at my doctor appointment, and I'm all good. And I haven't been with ...you know...in well over a month. *Months* actually. Not trying to pressure you at all, but just so you know...I'm fine with it if you are."

"I just got tested for everything as well before the season started, so I'm all good here too." Unsure silence blankets the two of us, my heart racing as I wait. "Olivia, are you sure? I don't want to make you feel pressured either."

"Hayes, I'm sure. I...I just don't want you to leave me right now."

I can't see him from this angle, but I can sense the sweet grin on his face. And he doesn't hesitate a moment longer, pressing inside me with a gentle snap of his hips.

"Oh, dear God in heaven, Olivia you feel even better like this. You are so fucking tight on my bare cock," he says as he pumps in and out of me. And, oh my fucking God, he's feels *much bigger* inside me from this angle. He smacks my ass again as he picks up his pace and I arch my back, feeling his balls slapping near my clit, nearly sending me into orbit.

"Holy shit. Hayes, that feels incredible…" I say with a whimper, my body shaking with pleasure.

Hayes lets out his own loud, growling moan as he pounds into me. Harder. Faster. Deeper. *My God, this man has skills.*

"Olivia, you're fucking killing me with that dirty mouth of yours. You are my perfect little siren," he says almost breathless. I arch against him, my fingers curling around the edge of the counter as my eyes roll into the back of my head. Digging his fingers into my hips, he holds me steady, finding his release as he explodes inside me.

Still inside me, he places soft kisses along my shoulders. The pleasure and safety I feel with this man have my heart beating like it's found a new rhythm it can't live without. And feeling him come inside me, no barriers between us, my pulse slows and my body relaxes against the counter as my mind settles. I have never felt more complete in my entire life.

27
hayes

"What time do you have to leave in the morning? And when are you back in town?" she asks, the two of us laying in bed. She's nestled in the crook of my arm, her body pressed tight against me as her fingers idly trace shapes on my chest.

"I head out around seven, so not *too* crazy early. The nice thing about the team plane is we go through TSA screenings before we get on the bus, so we get dropped off right on the tarmac to board.

"Tomorrow is our travel day, then Monday we have our game in Dallas. After that, we fly to Columbus. Tuesday we'll practice in Ohio, then have the evening off since the game is Wednesday. Then we fly back after the game, so I'll get home super late Wednesday night. Actually, it will probably be Thursday morning."

"Wow, that's a long trip."

"It is. Definitely the biggest downside of the sport. But I've been doing this for a while, so I'm used to it. Also, the insane amount of money they pay us makes it hard to complain," I say, both of us laughing. Inside, I wince remembering road trips when I was with

Chelsea, especially when I started to suspect something was up. The tension of wanting to trust her, but knowing maybe I shouldn't was stressful. As much as I try to not let things like that affect my game, I will admit the last season in Tampa wasn't my best. I quickly shake away those cobwebs in my brain, knowing that the most perfect woman is cuddled in next to me. She looks up with a smile, her eyes holding a serious gaze as they meet mine.

"You also love it," she says, tapping her hand over my heart.

I smile back at her, knowing that she is different than any other woman I've been with. "Yeah, I do. It's all I've ever wanted to do with my life." The words, 'until I met you' daring to spill out of my mouth. *Play it cool Hayes.*

"I don't blame you one bit. You're incredibly talented. You should enjoy this as long as you can."

My sweet siren gets it. I lean down to kiss her forehead, the comfort of having her in my arms fills me with certainty that she'll stand by me, no matter what.

"I appreciate that. Most players only play at the top of their game for a few years. I've really hit a groove the last few games. It's great to be back on a team with Vladi and getting to know the other guys on the team. Even the rookies...shit even Bougie and his pompous ass has a lot of talent. We're finally starting to gel as a team. I have a hunch it's going to get even better here in Milwaukee."

"As I've said before," she replies, "Milwaukee is lucky to have you."

"Just Milwaukee, huh? No one else is lucky I'm here?" I jab, lightly squeezing her arm.

"I mean, maybe a few interested parties might be glad to have you here in town. The team owner. The GM. The coach. The fans. You know...interested parties," she says with a wink, a devilish smirk lifting her lips.

"You wouldn't happen to be one of those 'interested parties,' would you?"

"Jury's still out," she teases.

"Olivia Brooks, you are such a lying little brat," I say, leaning in to kiss her passionately once more. *I can't help it; the air is better when it's surrounding Olivia Brooks.*

"I think the jury might be leaning toward a yes on that one," she says breaking the kiss. "But they need more evidence before they officially decide."

"Good," I say, capturing her lips once more. "Because, as of this moment, you're *mine*."

I flinch at my alarm going off. I try to silence it before Olivia wakes up, but I see her stirring. "Hey, sweet girl. I'm not leaving yet, just going to shower and pack. Stay here in bed; I'll wake you up when I'm heading out."

"Mmmffkay," she mumbles as she snuggles in closer to me. *God, I do not want to leave.* She is so beautiful all curled up in my arms. Her red hair is adorably tangled, and her long eyelashes flutter as she struggles to try and open them this early on a Sunday morning.

But sadly, I have to get up. I sweep a stray piece of her hair off her face, leaving a kiss behind in its place, then torturously drag myself away from the siren lying in my bed.

When I'm dressed and ready to go, I check on Olivia still passed out in bed. I hop in bed sitting beside her gently stroking her back.

"Hi," she says as she groans with a sweet morning smile, her eyes barely cracked open, "You can leave the money on the nightstand, big boy. I'll call when I need you again."

I can't contain my laughter, the sound filling the room and lightening the weight on my chest. "You are such a little brat," I say, reaching down to run my fingers over that ticklish place that makes her squeal.

"Hayes, stop it!" she begs, giggling as she tries, but fails, to wiggle free from my torment. "I can't defend myself before coffee!"

"Good thing there's coffee brewed in the kitchen; help yourself. How do you take your coffee, by the way?"

"Black. My favorite is an Americano." She groans, her eyes going out of focus. "I just want pure unadulterated coffee," she says. "How about you?"

I raise my eyebrows with the discovery of another similarity we share. "Same, actually. I was going to apologize for not having creamer, but seems I'm in good company," I say as I give her a quick kiss. "Seriously though, help yourself to some coffee after I head out. Go back and sleep some more first."

She starts to scramble out of bed, "Oh! I can go now if you're leaving…" I place my hand on her arm to stop my spiraling little siren. My face falls, my heart crushed at how broken she is. It's going to take some time to heal the scars of her past relationship. I'm going to show her everything she's deserved for so long.

"Please, Olivia, stay. I left a spare key on the counter, next to the coffee pot. Sleep in and head out whenever you like."

"You're leaving me a key?" she says looking up at me with her eyes almost as wide as the lake outside. "You trust me to just stay here without you?"

"Were you planning to rob me?"

"I mean, you do have some nice stuff," she says, making a show of glancing over my shoulder, "But I was a little busy last night, so I haven't had time to fully case the joint."

Why does this woman make me laugh more than anything else?

"I trust you, Olivia. Plus, you know what will happen if you misbehave."

A blush spreads across her grinning face. "That's not really an incentive to behave, Hayes."

I drag my hand down my face, thinking of missed goals and extra killers across the rink. "Don't get me all worked up in these unforgiving pants," I grumble as I give her yet another quick kiss on the lips.

"Why? Do you have a Zamboner?" she teases as we both laugh again. I disrupt her laugh by pressing my lips to hers, my heart beating faster than it does on a breakaway on open ice. Our tongues collide as we collapse in bed and her arms wrap around me tightly, making it more difficult to leave. *The team won't miss me, will they? I'm sure Coach will understand.* Her hands trail down my chest, and I gently grab her wrist, finally pulling back and giving her one last kiss.

"See you later, siren. I'll text you when we get to Dallas."

"Bye Hayes. I lo-" she stops herself. "I ...loved the time we got to spend together yesterday."

I fight back a smile, tightening my jaw to keep it in check. Her brows narrow as she bites her lip, glancing away. *Did she almost say the words I've been wanting to say to her?* It hasn't been long since that night at Walt's, but damn it feels like a lifetime. *Is she feeling the same thing I am?* I've always been told it's going to feel wrong until it feels right, and in every relationship I've ever had, there's always been something nagging at me. Even in the early 'honeymoon' phase, something has felt...*off.* But this? Somehow this just feels right. More than right, this feels perfect. This feels like home.

28
olivia

"Okay, girl. Spill it," Maggie says as she pours the first of our brunch bottomless mimosas. "I need to hear all the details because I know something happened. You are *glow-ing* Liv."

She's not wrong. I feel like I am glowing, flying, or dreaming. Maybe all three.

"Maggie...it was the best day of my life. I don't know what's happening to me." A smile so big my cheeks hurt stretches across my face. "I took him to lunch, we went to an arcade bar, then Grant Park Beach, and, somehow, I ended up in his bed this morning with a spare key to his apartment."

Maggie stops mid-sip, the glass still at her mouth, staring at me with her eyes almost bulging out of her head. She chugs her entire drink in one swallow and pours another, downing that one too.

"Ummm...what?! I'm sorry; who are you, and what have you done with my dear, sweet, innocent best friend Olivia?" she screeches. "I'm going to need you to fill in some of the details between the start and the end of this literal day date. I assume we can call it a date now?"

"Well, since he said, 'you're mine' to me last night in a sultry voice after he got me off, I guess we can call it a date," I say with a smirk as I hide my face behind my own glass.

"OLIVIA! WHAT?" Her mouth opens and closes without any words coming out, and I'm a little concerned her eyes may never close again. "Oh my God! This is better than any of my romance novels. He actually said, 'you're mine'? Holy. Shit. Does he have any friends?"

"I mean, he has a whole team of hockey players, but I think most of them are married. Who knows, maybe he has a brother, a cousin, or a neighbor. We didn't get too into family details last night."

"Well, of course not; he was too busy getting all up in your business. I have never been more jealous in my entire life. Wait a minute. Did you say he got you off? As in, *he* got you *off* off. You didn't have to act your way out?"

"Yes, he did, and no, I didn't," I say very seriously as I tip my glass toward her.

"Oh my God. Wow." Maggie leans in closer, glancing around before eyeing me with a salacious smirk. "Tell me about Hayes Jr. What's it like?"

"Maggie!" I gasp, heat flaring in my cheeks, doing a quick check of the brunch crowd around us, thankful no one is looking our way. "*No.* I am not going into detail about the monster residing between his legs."

"I knew it! Your smile is too big for him to have had a teeny weenie," she says, leaning back as we both cackle as the mimosas hit our empty stomachs.

"We just had a great time. The conversation flowed so easily. It's like he gave me this gift of not having to be anything but myself around him. He's nothing like Cayden. I had to work so hard to feel like I was living up to his standards and not upsetting him. But with Hayes? He keeps telling me to be myself. To be confident. To be proud of my voice and my songs. He even laughs at my jokes." I swirl my glass, watching the bubbles dance. "I bet he would let me do the dance to the power play song at the games."

"Liv, I am so glad Cayden is out of your life. Have you heard from him at all?" she asks, sounding concerned.

"No, I haven't heard from him. Honestly, I'm…relieved. I thought I would be more upset about it, but I felt like something was up with him too. Cayden was a different person near the end, and now Hayes has come along and literally swept me off my feet, and I'm like…teenie weenie who?" I say, and we both cackle again, both of us shaking and holding our sides as we gasp for air between fits of laughter.

"I'm so happy for you, Liv." She finishes her drink, glancing at me through her lashes. "No offense, but Cayden was a Grade A prick. I never liked the way he treated you," she says with a regretful look on her face. "I should have spoken up before now, but I wanted to support you as your friend, and I didn't know how."

Reaching across the table, I squeeze her hand with mine. "It's okay, Mags. It's not your fault. When you're in a bad relationship, it's hard to see the things that are wrong from the inside. It's always easier to see the red flags from the outside. I would have blown it off had you said something anyway. Too caught up in his toxic chaos. We should make a pact to tell each other when someone is dating a giant douche. Maybe we have a code word we can say to let the other one know there might be some red flags."

"Oh my God, that's perfect! We are totally doing this. What should the word be?" she says, bouncing in her seat a little too excitedly.

"It has to be something we don't use very often. If we used the word mimosa, we'd never be able to date anyone," I snort, taking another sip.

"True. How about dongle?" she suggests, and we both burst into a fit of laughter again.

I raise my glass to hers. "A toast to never having to use the word dongle!" We cheers and knock back another round of mimosas.

As we continue to enjoy brunch, I fill her in on some more of the details. She doesn't need to know every single second of our 'sordid' yet romantic day, but I do want to get her opinion about one thing. I can't shake the fear crawling through me every time it pops into my head.

"Mags…when Hayes was leaving this morning, I almost said… it," I painfully admit, scrunching my face, nervously tapping my fingers on my glass. *She's going to think I'm a complete lunatic.*

"Wait, what?" she blinks, "Like *it* it? Like 'the L word' it?" she asks stunned.

"Yep. I recovered and said, 'I loved spending time with you yesterday,' but now I'm panicking. I think I may have freaked him out. It's way too soon to say that, right? Cayden would have left me the moment I even hinted at that."

"Well, he's not Cayden, that's for sure." Crossing her arms over her chest, she bites her lip, not meeting my eye. "Did he act weird after you said that? Do you think he picked up on it?" she asks.

I rub my hands down my thighs, shifting in my seat. "I mean, he seemed okay. I think? He just smiled and said, 'me too,' then told me goodbye and left. He said he'd text me when he got to Dallas, but I'm not exactly sure when that is. So, I'm sure I'll be in 'Olivia freak out mode' until I hear from him," I reply. "I just hope he doesn't pick up on the clingy thing."

"Olivia Marie Brooks. You are *not* clingy. A boyfriend who doesn't want to spend time with you does not make you clingy. That is the stupidest term ever created and should only refer to plastic wrap food covering. Whatever frat boy douchebag made that up should hang by his testicles until he apologizes," she says, and we laugh at the mention of testicles. *Maybe we should slow down a little on the champagne.*

I shrug my shoulders looking down at my fingers tapping out a rhythm on the table. "I know. It's just hard to shake after hearing it for so long."

"Liv, let me ask you a quession…quesssstion?….ques-tion," she slurs. *I think it's time to cut her off from the mimosas.* "You almost said it, so my *question* is, is it true? Do you think you love him?"

Do I love him? *Is it possible to love someone I barely know?* This man has done nothing but treat me with kindness and respect and seemed so genuinely bummed to leave me this morning. This man who left me a freaking *spare key* to his apartment after spending one day with me.

"I think so…" I say, almost like a question, with a cringy smile on my face. "Am I crazy? How can I love someone I've only known for a short period of time?" My heart is racing, the sound of silverware clanging filling the restaurant. It's not that I need her validation to be with Hayes, but God am I an approval whore.

"First of all, he seems awesome, Liv, and from the look on your face, I'd say you *are* madly in love with him. I, for one, am over the moon happy for you. You deserve the world, and you finally have someone willing to give it to you. Second, as to how this can happen so fast. You are *amazing*, Liv. Cayden never knew what he had, and it seems like Hayes does. Shit, if you had a dick, I'd marry you!" Her cheeks flush as she pushes her glass away. "Damn, these mimosas are strong…" Maggie refocuses on me, her face softening with a smile. "Sometimes the stars just align. Who are we to question it? You're so lucky, Liv. It's beyond time you got someone good to love you."

"You are the best bestie a girl could have," I say as I raise my glass to her again.

"To besties!" she says, lifting her water as I finish the last of my mimosa.

I jolt as my phone buzzes on the table. "It's Hayes," I say, looking up, my eyes as wide as can be. *Holy shit, he's actually texting me when he said he would.*

"Fuck yes! This is great! I am *so* glad he texted you while we are still at brunch. What does it say?!" she says in a loud *'I've had a lot of champagne'* kind of way.

"Shhhhh. Mags keep it down!" I say, darting my eyes around to see several people glaring at us. *Guess we won't be coming back here for brunch.* I read the text out loud to Maggie, my heart in my throat.

HAYES

> Hey gorgeous. Just got to Dallas. Miss you already.

Maggie snatches my phone out of my hand, her thumbs flying across the screen before she passes it back with a smug smirk.

OLIVIA

> Hey handsome! Glad you made it safely. Miss you too.

I huff, opening my mouth to chastise Maggie when another text comes through.

HAYES

> You get out of the apartment okay? Steal anything good?

OLIVIA

Just your giant TV. You didn't need that, right?

HAYES

Lol. Did you take the TV to brunch with you?

OLIVIA

Yeah, I paid a creepy old guy in the parking lot to watch it for a couple hours. He told me I had nice legs.

HAYES

Good move. And he's not wrong. 😊 But tell him to stay away from what's mine.

Olivia, I wanted to tell you something…

"What's he saying now?" Maggie asks, interrupting my happy Hayes bubble.

"I don't know!" I scream back at her, the blood draining from my face. "It's the little typing dots; they keep starting and stopping!!" We both wait with bated breath, Maggie's nails clicking along the table as she drums her fingers. I slap my hand over my mouth as the text comes through. Tears blur my vision and my pulse races as I read the text over and over. *Does this mean what I think it does?*

"What did he say, Liv?! I'm dying over here!"

HAYES

I wanted to tell you I loved the time I got to spend with you yesterday too. 😊

OLIVIA

😭😭😭

156

HAYES

We're on the bus to the hotel now. I'll call you later once I get settled in my room for the night.

OLIVIA

Okay. Loved getting these texts from you.

HAYES

Love getting texts from you too, sweet girl

"Ohhhhhhhh, this man has it *bad* for you, Liv! He totally loves you too!" she reaches across the table to give my hand a squeeze. I squeeze it back, so grateful she's here to share this moment.

He heard me almost say it. *And he's not running away.* He's not scared. He's not afraid to commit. I know we both got out of complicated relationships, but what if all that bad stuff led to where we are right now? What if we needed to get our hearts broken to truly find the person who would cherish it? If that's truly the case, then it's not too fast at all. I cradle my phone to my chest, blinking away the moisture in my eyes as I look at Maggie. *I think I am seriously falling in love with this man.* Thursday cannot get here soon enough.

29
olivia

Binge-watching TV in bed is my go-to for winding down after a long day, but I have no clue what's happening in this crime documentary. *Wait…did he just kill her or kidnap her?* I can't seem to peel my eyes away from my phone. Stalking it. Waiting for it to ring. Hayes said he'd call when he was settled in for the night. *What time is settled?*

Sighing loudly, I drop my phone on my chest, tapping out a fast rhythm on the case with my nails. I should just text him. *That's not clingy, right?* My fingers still. *Nope. Olivia Marie, we are not going down that road again.* Shaking my head back and forth, I remind myself he's not a runner. He's a skater…they glide, right? This is simply me being impatient to hear the voice of the man who took *amazing* care of me in every way possible last night.

I unlock my phone, staring blankly at the empty text field. *How do I ask him when he's going to call me without sounding like a weirdo?* Maybe I am a weirdo, but there's no time to get a new personality. *Maybe I just text hello?*

"Why is this so difficult?" I grumble, letting out a frustrated groan.

I can do this. I type a quick text and hit send before I chicken out.

OLIVIA

No emergencies yet tonight? 😉

I throw my phone, too scared to watch for a reply. *Yep, he's definitely going to think I'm a weirdo.* Out of the corner of my eye, I see the screen of my phone light up like a glow stick buried in my comforter. I snatch it up, the corners of my lips spreading up my face. *He's calling me.* I stare at the phone, almost afraid to touch it as if it will disappear. My shaky fingers finally swipe across the screen to answer it.

"Hello?"

"Olivia," he says with a deep rumble. My thighs squeeze together at hearing him say my name, his voice full of promises and pleasure. "You know you can just call me if you want to talk, right? I don't bite…well," he chuckles darkly, "we haven't gotten to that yet anyway."

My God, why does the thought of that have me already dripping wet? Concentrate Olivia; speak a response to the sexy voice on the other end of the line.

"I didn't know if you were still busy with the team; I didn't want to bother you," I say, squinting my eyes and biting the inside of my cheek.

"I actually just got to my room after our team dinner. You need to know you are never bothering me. Ever. If you call and I can't answer, I'll call you back the second I can. I need you to understand there is *nothing* I want more than to hear from you, siren. I'm going to have to punish you when I get back home; I need to make sure I get my point across."

My fingers grip my phone tighter, my pulse racing at the thought of him spanking me again. "Promise?"

He lets out a loud groan, the sound rumbling through every inch of me. "You are beyond incredible, Olivia. And here I am, thousands of miles away from you, when all I want is to have you in every way possible."

Beaming from ear to ear, I reply, "You're incredible too. I wish you were here. I know it's not been long, but...I feel like I've known you forever."

"Me too. I wish I'd met you a long time ago. But sometimes I think you have to go through a lot of shit to find the diamond in the rough."

"Did you just quote *Aladdin*?" I tease with a raised eyebrow.

"I mean..." he says with a laugh. "You are a diamond in the rough, but I didn't need a genie or a lamp to find you. Just a long day of unpacking and a beer at Walt's."

"Funny, I thought you would have rubbed your magic lamp at some point." I slap my hand over my mouth to cover my gasp. *Shit, did I just say that* out loud?

"Every night since we met and sometimes in the morning. I can't get you out of my mind, siren...and I don't want to."

Holy mother of pearl. Warmth races between my legs, my back arching off the bed at the thought of Hayes getting off while thinking about me. "Seriously?"

"Dead serious. And what about you, Miss Filthy Mouth?"

I freeze, my mouth dropping open. *I did not expect the conversation to shift in this direction.* I clear my throat. "M-me? We are talking about *you* here."

"Oh, no, no, no. You started this. You have a magic lamp you can rub too." His voice drops down to a growl. "So, Olivia, my question is...have you touched yourself thinking about me?"

I am trying not to let my eyes bug out any further as my heart races. I've never talked about the 'm word' with anyone I've ever been with. That's always been done by each involved party in private. Tapping my fingers against my forehead, my body tenses. I honestly don't know why I even made the comment about Hayes rubbing one out. *What was I thinking?*

I sigh, staring up at the ceiling, hyperaware of the growing arousal between my legs. Maybe, deep down, I need to talk about it. This man, and everything about him, is like a freaking truth serum. His presence alone makes me want to confess all of my deepest, darkest secrets.

"I...maybe. Like...you know...maybe once. Or twice," I mumble, my voice barely above a whisper.

"Once or twice? Oh, sweet girl...you are a *terrible* liar. I can just picture your pretty face blushing right now." *Well, he's not wrong.* "I've told you, there's nothing to be embarrassed about with me. So, tell me...how often do you touch yourself thinking of me? My cock. My mouth."

Holy shit, am I talking about this? You can do this, Liv. I swallow back my fear. "If I'm being honest, it's more like...every day since I met you."

From the growl Hayes releases, I have a hunch he's holding onto more than just his phone right now, and my toes curl into the sheets at the thought. "Olivia, have you ever had phone sex?"

My body shivers as goosebumps cover me and every drop of blood races below my waist. "No," I finally find my voice to shakily reply, "I've always felt like I would be awkward."

"You have never been awkward with me once, Olivia." I hear fabric rustling in the background, my heart pounding as I picture what Hayes could be doing. "What makes you afraid?"

"It's not that I'm afraid now...I don't ever feel afraid with you, Hayes. There's something about you that makes me want to try things I've never done before," I admit. And it's the truth. Heat rushes through my body. The things I would let this man talk me into are endless.

"Good. I don't want you to ever feel awkward with me. We can work up to full-on phone sex another time. I have an idea that I think you'll like; something to make it easier when the time comes."

"Are you sure?" I ask, guilt already creeping in.

"Positive. But I have an idea for tonight, too, if you're up for it." My breath catches in my throat, my heart pounding as my legs open voluntarily. "What if I do all the talking? You just lay back, slip your hand inside your panties that I know are soaked by now, and I'll talk us both through it. Would that be okay?"

"Yes," the response flies out of my mouth so quickly, that I'm surprised at my boldness.

"Good. I assume you're in bed and wearing next to nothing?"

I put the phone on speaker, set it next to me, and turn off the TV. "I'm wearing a Riders t-shirt and some black lace panties."

"*Fuck* me," he groans, and I can picture his eyes rolling back in his head with pleasure. "Don't say another word. I want to hear every little sound you make until we're ready to hang up. Got it?"

My hands tremble with anticipation. *I'm going to explode before I even touch myself.*

"Yes, sir."

"Goddammit siren, you know how to push my buttons," he rumbles, and I can't help but smile knowing how turned on he is. "Take your hands and slide them up under your shirt for me like a good girl. Palm those gorgeous tits of yours. Imagine me rubbing your nipples between my fingers, pinching them just enough that it hurts but brings you almost more pleasure than you can handle."

I groan, my chest pushing further into my hands, my nipples hardening as I obey his commands. *This is unbelievably hot. I want more.*

"That's my good girl. Don't hide your moans from me. You know I love to hear your little gasps of pleasure. Just hearing them has my dick twitching. You are perfect." *Dear Lord, I did not know I had a praise kink, but every word has me writhing for more.* "Now lower your hand down and slide it inside those soaked panties. Feel how wet you are for me, Olivia. My cock is so fucking hard right now picturing your dripping wet cunt. I can't keep my hand off myself, wishing it were you here instead. I love the way you grip my dick with those tiny hands of yours, the way you fist my fucking balls as you finish, the way your wet pussy drips on me before I even slide inside you."

I gasp at his words, my toes curling deeper into my sheets. His breaths are faster, panting between every word as the slapping sound of him jerking off echoes faintly through the phone.

"Slide a finger inside that pussy of yours. I want you to feel what my dick feels every time I press inside you. That soft, sweet core is my own heaven on earth."

My finger curling up inside me to hit that spot has feral sounds coming out of me I didn't even know I could make. I am feverish, aching for his touch.

"Did I ever tell you, that first night we met at Walt's, I came home and couldn't get you out of my mind? Even before I had a real taste of you, I knew I couldn't live without you. I tried thinking of anything else to get my mind off of you, but I couldn't escape the mark you left on my thoughts after you wrapped that damn gorgeous body around me. I pumped my fucking dick so hard I saw stars just imagining having you. And now that I've had a taste of the real thing? You've made me a hungry man, siren. The only thing that will ever satisfy me is you."

I let out a loud moan, my heart and my pussy somehow melting simultaneously, and it's the hottest thing I've ever experienced.

"Be a good girl and take that finger, covered in sweet lube from your cunt, and rub it on that sensitive clit for me. God, I want to taste your sweet pussy right now, licking up every bit of your wetness knowing it's for me and me alone."

Crying out, I desperately follow his orders, wishing it were his tongue on me. Touching myself while imagining Hayes doing the same in his hotel room…hell, for weeks now…brings me almost over the edge.

Hayes pants again, barely able to speak. "I'm getting close, siren, and I want you to come with me. I want to hear you scream my name as your body shakes from teasing your sweet pussy. I'm stroking my cock so fast, but nothing compares to the feeling of being inside your cunt. Do you know how tight you are? How wet you are? How the walls of your pussy choke my dick when I'm inside you? I want to fill you up until my cum leaks out of you, dripping down those gorgeous legs, begging me to fill it once more." His heavy breaths become more intense, growing louder as if he's right here with me, ready to explode. "Oh *fuck*, Olivia…be a good girl and come with me." He screams my name from deep in his chest as I cry out his, both of us finding our release together despite being so far apart. My entire body trembles, my back arching so high I feel as if I'm levitating over the bed. Aftershocks roll through me, my soul still basking in the wake of his praise. I'm not one to cry after sex, but tears burn in my eyes, my heart soothed by the way Hayes makes me feel so unbelievably wanted.

My entire body goes limp, my arms and legs shaky even though I'm lying in bed. "Hayes. That was insane. Crazy hot. I'll just be over here sleeping for the next week. Wake me up once you're home."

He lets out a low rumble. "I'm glad you enjoyed it. I'm assuming you'd be up for doing that again sometime?'

"Jury's still out, but I have a good feeling about their decision."

30
hayes

Something about knowing Olivia is watching me while wearing my jersey gives me an extra level of fuel for tonight's game against Dallas. As I listened to the anthem tonight, their singer was good, but nothing compared to *my* song siren. I shift on my skates, glancing at the camera with a knowing smile. If she doesn't realize she's going to be a part of my life for a long time, I'm going to do everything in my power to help her see I'm in this for the long haul.

But for now, I have to focus on hockey. It's early in the season, and we've started to find our groove as a team. Dallas always has a great team, and this year is no exception. They made some good trades during the off season and re-signed some of their big name players, but so did Milwaukee. I can't hide the feral grin twisting my face. *Tonight's matchup is going to be a battle.*

Deep into the third period, the score is still zero for both teams. My line-mates and I have done a better job getting through the neutral zone this period, which is something we've been working to improve, but we haven't gotten anything to convert yet. We've had some amazing scoring chances, but their goalie, one of the best in the league, is playing out of his mind. *We've got to keep pushing to get the win tonight.* I stare at the scoreboard, the massive zero taunting me. We can't take our foot off the gas now.

Skating off the ice, I slide into my seat on the bench out of breath. "Fuck! 15 has been slamming me into the boards all night. I can't get a fucking shot off."

"I got your back, Larsy," Bougie says as he slides down the bench until he settles next to me taking a breather between shifts. "That motherfucker is not going to know what hit him next time he gets near you. He's been out for blood this entire game, and I'm gonna give it to him. It's just going to be his blood instead of ours."

"Fuck yeah," I say, fist bumping him.

Looking down the ice, I see Vladi standing calmly in his crease, one arm raised as the puck flies to the side of his goalpost. *How is that motherfucker* always *relaxed?* The whistle blows. Dallas iced the puck. *Perfect timing.* We get a fresh line on the ice while Dallas has to keep their tired line on, and we face off directly to the left of their goalie. *Game fucking on.* Adrenaline pumps through my veins and sweat drips down my face. I take a swig from my water bottle, adjust my gloves, and take in a deep breath. *Let's win this damn game.* My line is up for the next shift, and we hop over the boards back onto the ice. The ref stands with the puck as 15 faces off against Johansen. My hands flex around my stick as I brace against the Dallas player covering me. The puck drops and all hell breaks loose. We win the draw, and EJ kicks it behind him to our defenseman Colton Taylor. I see 15 head my way, but as promised, Bougie's got my back and gets a great hit on him.

Tay quickly passes it to me for a one-timer. I fire the puck off with all the strength I have left this far into the third period, watching it fly through the air. Dallas' goalie dives to block it. I smirk. He's not fast enough. The puck sails right above his glove and into the net. A deadly smile twists my face. My teammates surround me, screaming my name. "Fuck yeah, Larsy!"

We win again, 1-0. Vladi got his first shutout of the season, and I got the game-winning goal. *This is going to be my fucking year.*

As I get off the ice, I do a couple of media interviews, then I shed the multiple layers of equipment to shower, dress, and board the bus back to the airport. This is the first time since before the game I've gotten a chance to check my phone. My heart rate has calmed down from the game, but amps back up when I see I have texts from Olivia. She sent a picture a few hours ago of her wearing my jersey while watching the game and telling me good luck. Then another congratulating me on the win and my goal tonight. I keep my phone close to my chest, away from my nosy as fuck teammates, but I can't help the smile spreading across my face. *I miss her so fucking much.* I text her back even though it's late, not knowing if I'll wake her but desperate to talk to her.

HAYES

Thank you. It was a great game, only outdone by how beautiful you look in my jersey. What about a picture of you wearing only the jersey? 😉

I see the little typing bubbles starting and stopping, furiously tapping my foot on the charter bus floor. *Shit, is this too much for her?* My stomach clenches at the thought of scaring her off, but my gut still tells me my siren will deliver. *Please, let me be right.* My phone vibrates with another text, my dick lifting against my slacks.

OLIVIA

(sends photo wearing only the jersey)

A shot of arousal goes straight to my dick as I stare wide-eyed at the photo, angling my phone so I can see it, but Vladi, sitting next to me, can't. Luckily, he's basking in his shutout with our team-mates, bottles being passed around the bus through a chorus of whoops and cheers, not paying much attention to me. *Thank fuck I got the window seat.* I know my jersey hangs well past her knees, but she's lying in bed with *my* game-worn sweater draped over her legs, barely covering that sweet cunt of hers. I tuck my cock into the waistband of my suit, briefly closing my eyes as I fight to get myself under control before I reply.

HAYES

Fuck, Olivia. I do not want to get on a plane with a bunch of guys right now.

OLIVIA

You're making me blush.

HAYES

I'd like to be making you do more than blush right now. Fuck this damn hockey travel. I need my dick between your sexy legs, filling up that sweet pussy of yours and watching it drip out of you.

I'm feral for her right now and a thousand miles away. This is fucking torture. The little bubbles keep starting and stopping on my phone as the bus takes off from the arena. Vladi is now in his seat, and I shift away from his nosy-ass a little more. My screen lights up again with her reply.

OLIVIA

These legs and this cunt are anxiously awaiting your return. When do you get home again? 😉

Holy shit. I fucking hit the jackpot with this woman.

HAYES

Not soon enough. lol

We're almost to the airport. I won't get into the hotel until probably around 1AM. Guessing you'll be asleep by then.

OLIVIA

Yeah, I don't think I'll still be awake lol. But can't wait to chat more tomorrow. Goodnight Hayes. 🩶

HAYES

Sweet dreams, beautiful girl. 😘

Once I get seated on the plane, I see Bougie drop a coffee off in the cockpit. *Who the fuck does he know up there? Probably one of his millions of social media followers.* I roll my eyes as he walks through the cabin stripping off his clothes like he's on the set of Magic Mike, throwing his shirt and dress pants around the cabin, as usual. Vladi walks down the aisle to claim his seat next to Bougie, giving me an evil glare as he passes. Since we're on a winning streak, his superstitious ass has to sit next to Bougie, and he fucking hates it. I smile back with a devilish grin, shooting him a wink. *This has been the best prank and motivator for that grumpy ass goalie.*

"Larsy…hell of a game," Zack Reeves says as he takes a seat beside me on the plane. This is his first road trip with the team this season since he's been rehabbing his injury. He's a legend, and we're all anxious for him to get back on the ice.

"Thanks; it's a great start to the season so far," I say. "How are you healing up?"

"Doing good," he says as he lightly taps his knee. "Doc says I should be good to go by the next home game back in Milwaukee."

"No shit! Excited to finally hit the ice together. Happy for you, Z."

"Appreciate it. I hate being off the ice, but it's helped me spend a little more time at home with the fam and learn to relax a bit," he replies with a grin. "How are you adjusting, Larsy? You seem like you're in an awfully good mood tonight. You've been all smiles since we left the arena."

"I didn't realize I was being watched," I say, shooting him side-eye. *Apparently, Vladi's not the only nosy-asshole on this team.* "I'm just happy to get the win and a goal tonight. Nice start to the road trip."

"Sure, Larsy. Keep telling yourself that. That's not a 'goal and a win' smile. You look like a boy who just got a date to the prom," he razzes me, giving me a knowing look and glancing at my phone.

I laugh, not the least bit upset at getting called out about Olivia. "Guess I'm not very good at hiding my emotions." I hesitate, my knee bouncing a hundred miles an hour. I don't want this gossip spreading like wildfire among this group of motherfuckers. But Zack's onto me, and as team captain, he's legally bound to keep it quiet. "I'm…sort of seeing someone. It's new."

"I figured as much," he says. "Glad to see you happy, man. When I first met my wife, she had me in the palm of her hands from the moment she smiled at me. Three kids later, and a fourth one on the way, Kara still has me following her like a little puppy dog."

I smile, listening to him talk about how in love he is with his wife. *That's what I've wanted my entire life.* Obviously, hockey has always been my dream. But I think I've always wanted to have someone to share it with. Maybe it's because I didn't have that growing up. My parents were divorced, and my dad wasn't in the picture. It was just me and my mom. I've always wanted to have kids and be a good dad to them. A better dad than what I had. And if they wanted, teach them to play hockey.

And as crazy as it sounds, Olivia is that person. It's been so quick, but she just does something to me. I've always been cautious with relationships, especially being a professional athlete with girls who just want fame and my paycheck. I've never wanted to jump in or commit to anything too quickly, but when I'm with Olivia, all my hesitation fades away. One would think I would be even more reserved about getting into a serious relationship so fast. But Olivia just makes everything…right.

"How long did you two date before you got married?" I ask.

Zack flashes me a knowing smile. "Six months. With the crazy travel, I wanted her to be there when I got home at night, and I wanted her to know I was committed. Shit, I probably would have married her on our first date if she asked me. I was at a point where I knew what I wanted, and she knew what she wanted, so we went for it. And I've never regretted it a day in my life."

"When you know, you know."

"Exactly. So, this mystery girl you're seeing, is it serious?"

"We met pretty quick after I moved into town, shared a moment, and then didn't see each other again until the home opener when she was standing on the ice singing the national anthem."

"Holy shit. Our singer? The Weapon?" he says a little louder than I would like.

"Shhhh!! Keep your loud ass voice down!" I hiss, putting my hand over his mouth, my eyes darting around the plane, scanning for signs anyone heard. "Nothing is *official,* and I don't want it all over the locker room just yet. But yes, it's Olivia, our national anthem singer." I cringe, remembering all the bullshit over the past week. "Former anthem singer. She got fired."

"She got *fired*? What? Why? She's fucking amazing. And when she sings, we win." He looks at me, worry tainting his face.

"It's kind of a long story, but she was dating a guy who, apparently, got you to sign some pucks at the home opener. They aren't supposed to do that, so they let her go."

"You are fucking kidding me. I know exactly who you're talking about. That motherfucker wouldn't leave me alone; he kept calling me 'Z' like he was my best friend. I signed his damn pucks to get him off my back so I could head to the locker room. She got fired for *that*? It wasn't her fault at all!"

"I know," I shake my head, clenching my fists thinking about that stupid asshat ex of hers. "I asked her if I could talk to the entertainment guy - David, I think his name is? - but she said that would probably make it worse." I sigh, dragging a hand through my hair.

"Well, she didn't tell *me* no. Shit. I just realized she didn't sing at the last home game we lost. Fuck! As soon as we get back to Milwaukee, I'll talk to David. As team captain, I am not losing games because we have some rando-subpar anthem singer throwing off the energy in the arena because the asshole she was dating broke the rules," he grumbles before sitting up straight, a concerned look on his face. "Okay, wait. She was dating that guy? But now you're seeing her?"

"I told you. *Long* story. After he got her fired, he dumped her."

"And that's when Hayes Larson swooped in to sweep her off of her feet?" he says with a smirk.

"I guess you could say that."

"Well, you found yourself quite the catch there. I've never actually met her, but she is gorgeous, and from what I hear, everyone on the Riders staff loves her. And obviously, she's got a killer voice." Zack glances around, letting the chaos of the celebration wash over us. "We've got another two hours on this flight, so tell me the details...I'm a sucker for a good story."

Zack and I spend the rest of the flight talking. He's the captain for a reason. Even rehabbing an injury, he made sure I felt at home here in Milwaukee before the season started. And now he's sitting here letting me go on and on about Olivia and agreeing that if Cayden Banks ever steps foot in our arena, he will be slammed into the boards with a head and leave the ice without one.

"Larsy, can I give you some advice?"

"I would expect nothing less from you, Cap."

"If you think you love this girl, and from the look on your face, you do, tell her. Don't live in fear of what might be. Sometimes things don't work out, and we have to deal with the consequences. But in my experience, we learn to play without fear, might as well love without it too."

"Damn, Z. Do they teach you to say this shit in Captain School?" I nudge him with my elbow with a smile. And fuck. He's right. About all of it. *My* only *fear is being without her.* Just then, the pilot comes over the intercom and lets us know we're about to land, so the team starts to shuffle with movement as people put away their video games, laptops, and decks of cards, throwing drinks in the trash as the attendants come through.

"What makes you think I love her?" I ask as we descend toward the airport.

He smiles with a look that says he's about to drop another truth bomb on me. My fingers tap furiously on my thigh, waiting for his response. "Hayes, I feel like I'm looking into a mirror as you're talking to me. I remember having a similar conversation with a teammate back when I met Kara. He gave me some advice I will pass along to you." He waits until I meet his eye, unable to hide from the reality he's about to share. "Hockey is the best sport. We are so damn lucky to get to play it and make a living doing it. But hockey doesn't last forever. We get older. We get injured. We retire. Eventually, it will end. But love and family? That is what lasts. That's what really matters."

I wake up the next morning and immediately grab my phone to see if I've heard from Olivia. Knowing her, I'm guessing she didn't text me good morning because she didn't want to bother me. I'm right. Shaking my head, I roll my eyes as I send her a good morning text. I need to get through to her that she is never an inconvenience to me, no matter what time of day, even if I have to spank it out of her. I want her to understand I will *always* have time for her.

I laid in bed last night thinking about everything Zack said. Maybe I'm not as crazy as I think I am. *What if the notion of falling in love at first sight isn't that crazy after all?* I'm sure it's not common these days, but one thing I know about rarities is their scarceness makes them even more precious. We both seem to have talents we quickly excelled at. Maybe our brains are just wired that way - picking up on things we are destined for. I guess that could be the reason this relationship is propelling forward so quickly. My bed feels so empty without her. I need to see this girl. I need to tell her how I feel and feel her on me. Tomorrow's game cannot get here fast enough. I smile as my phone dings with a new text. I'm pretty sure this woman is my fucking destiny, and I need the rest of eternity to begin.

31
olivia

"Thank *God* the Bayview Bourbon campaign got sent to the client last night," I grumble to Maggie, slouching deep in my chair. "I am so glad to have that off my plate. Now I can finally get Bill off my back about it."

"Ditto. He's been extra annoying lately. He came over yesterday and asked if I could put a drop shadow on a photo. A *drop shadow.* I had to find a polite way to explain that we no longer use graphic design elements from 1996."

I roll my eyes. "I don't know how we would survive without each other. Also," I straighten in my chair, leaning across our shared desks, "what's for lunch today?"

"Olivia, it's 8:45."

"And what better time is there to plot out where we are going for lunch today?"

"I brought my lunch. I *should* eat that," Maggie says hesitantly. "But...I *could* be persuaded to go out."

"I was kind of thinking that new make-your-own-salad place

down on Broadway. I could use a blueberry muffin...*or* four from their bread bar," I say with a glimmer in my eye, hoping she agrees.

"I love how that place comes across as being healthy with fresh greens and kale, and then once you pay, you have access to a smorgasbord of super carb-heavy breads, soups, and desserts. I transform into Templeton from *Charlotte's Web* once I pass that cash register."

"But it's basically salad...with a side of cornbread, asiago cheese breadsticks, and ice cream sundaes. It's called *balance.*"

"Hell yeah, it is. I'm in."

"Sweet! Only two more hours to plot out our attack on the bread station," I say as I turn back toward my monitor, my phone lighting up with a text.

HAYES

Hello, is this my emergency contact Olivia Brooks? I have another emergency.

OLIVIA

Another one? Do I need to wrap you in bubble wrap?

Can you provide me with the details of your emergency, sir?

HAYES

I had a dream last night about this girl, but I'm worried she's not real. She was beautiful with long auburn hair, blue eyes, and sexy legs. Do you know anyone that matches that description?

I can't hold back the giddy smile forming on my face, warmth creeping across my cheeks. *God, this man is everything.*

OLIVIA

How is this an emergency?

HAYES

If she's not real, I'll die.

OLIVIA

Hmm…interesting. How can I help you prove she exists?

HAYES

Well, I gave her a spare key to my apartment. I thought maybe, she could use it on Wednesday night and stay at my place. That way, when I get home from my road trip, I could crawl into bed with her.

OLIVIA

I think that is a fantastic idea. But…what if she is fake, and you end up going home alone?

I really love egging this man on…and I love that he eats it up.

HAYES

I'm 99% sure she's real, and I'm pretty sure she'll show up.

OLIVIA

I think you're right.

HAYES

So, it's a date?

OLIVIA

A date in your bed? Sir, I would NEVER!

HAYES

You can call me sir then too

Holy shit. My thighs squeeze together as I do a quick scan around the office. Maggie is giving me serious side-eye while she's on a call, but I breathe a sigh of relief seeing everyone else staring blankly into their monitors. *Thank God no one can see the wetness building between my thighs.*

OLIVIA

Okay, in all seriousness, I'm at my desk at work right now, and this conversation is causing me all kinds of issues lol

HAYES

My plan is working then😈

OLIVIA

But I'll be there Wednesday night. 😏🔥

HAYES

Feel free to put on my jersey again, just the jersey, and watch the game from my bed. In case you see anything on TV that excites you 😎🏒

OLIVIA

Nothing more exciting than watching 22 skating past the blue line and shooting the puck toward the goal.

HAYES

Why does you saying 'blue line' get me all worked up like when you knew what a deke was? I'm pretty sure you're perfect.

Did he call me perfect? My heart is pounding in my chest as I try and calm my shaking hands enough to respond to the text. But how do I stay calm when the most perfect man in the world just called *me* perfect? *No big deal, right? Oh my God, this is such a big deal.*

OLIVIA

It's one of my many skills

HAYES

You do have some amazing skills 😌. I gotta get up and get going for the day. I'll call you later. 😴

OLIVIA

Can't wait to talk to you again. And can't wait to see you later this week. 🧊

"Excuse me, Miss 'I'm too busy to talk to my work bestie but can text for five minutes'…I'm assuming Larsy said good morning over there?" Maggie asks, hovering over me as I hold my phone close to my chest and away from her.

"Yes," I reply, trying to play it cool. "He wants me to go over to his place and watch the game so I can be there when he gets home."

"*Girl*. I swear you won the man lottery."

"I certainly feel like I hit the jackpot with Hayes. Cayden would have asked me to avoid him for three days if he got back from a road trip. Ugh…I have to stop comparing them. But…Cayden was just so…so…"

"Douchey? Selfish? Narcissistic? Egotistical?" Maggie suggests, offering several options as she ticks down her fingers.

"All of the above?" I say as we laugh. "Hayes just makes me so comfortable in my own skin. I've never had anyone make me feel this special. I mean, he probably has ulterior motives for asking me to come over, but…I can't say I'm mad about it," I say as we exchange a high-five.

"Liv, I'm so freaking happy for you! When can I meet him?" Maggie asks, walking backward back to her desk.

"The team schedule is so crazy right now, but I promise I'll find a time to introduce you. Just, you know, not Wednesday night."

"Yeah, so I love you, Liv, but I don't love you enough to be there when your hot hockey player beau comes over to slam you into the headboard."

Okay, now I am having a problem thinking about Hayes slamming me into the headboard while I scream his name until my throat is hoarse.

How is it possible I am in Hayes Larson's bed, watching him on TV, in his jersey, knowing in a few hours he will be flying home to be with me? He was joking about making sure I was real, but I'm the one wondering how this isn't a dream. I bite the inside of my cheek, the pain reminding me this *is* real.

The deepest corners of my mind keep whispering this is too perfect to last and that, one day, I'll wake up to the same recurring nightmare of being alone. I'm a thirty-one-year-old woman from the Midwest, and he is an insanely hot hockey god. What would it even be like to be married to a hockey player who is on the road a lot? *Am I capable of handling that?* He's got to have girls coming out of the woodwork to be with him. Ladies handing him hotel room keys at all the away games. Women much prettier, thinner, and more famous clinging to him as he walks down the street. *Why would he want to stay with me?*

I flop back on the bed, rubbing my eyes until I see stars. *Geez, Olivia, calm your tits.* I'm acting like I'm already engaged to this guy, and we haven't even defined this relationship…or whatever this is. *Take a breath and relax.* Sitting up, I settle against the headboard. I should simply enjoy this and see where it goes. Although now that I think about it…Olivia Larson does have a nice ring to it.

My stomach twists into knots, and my nerves are a hot mess. Hayes is playing great tonight, but we are still down 2-1 with two minutes left at the end of the third. Hayes is flying down the ice with the puck, passing it to Johansen, who is waiting in the slot. He takes the shot, but Columbus' goalie blocks it. The rebound comes out, and Hayes is right there to grab the puck again. He's surrounded by the opposing players, all of them pushing and shoving, trying to get the puck away. Hayes thrashes around, and suddenly this has turned into a full-on brawl between him and two of the Columbus players. I pop up to my knees in the bed, my hands flying to cover my face. My heart is pounding. *Oh my God, please don't get hurt, Hayes.* One of the officials blows his whistle, trying to separate all the players and figure out who started what. My heart freezes as they skate Hayes over to the penalty box for instigating.

"What kind of bullshit call is that?! No penalty for the other team?" I scream at the TV. *Fuck!* Now Columbus is on the power play for the last minute and a half. Hayes slams his helmet and stick inside the penalty box. Shit, he's *clearly* pissed. I jump out of bed, pacing in front of the TV. The teams face off, and we spend the last minute and a half trying to keep the other team from scoring instead of pulling our goalie to try and tie it up. The game clock ticks down to zero, and the horn sounds. I collapse back on the bed, a weight pressing into my chest. Milwaukee suffers another loss.

I run my fingers along the seam on the sheets, a dull ache in my heart for Hayes and his team. Hockey is a long season. You can't win every game, and I've seen our team lose plenty of times. But… it's different now.

Cayden was horrible when one of his teams lost. It was like he went into a depression, and he wasn't even playing.

Olivia, I force a deep breath; *Hayes is* not *Cayden.* Hayes is a professional athlete. He can handle a loss. Cayden is a fucking tool who acted like he had a stake in the game. Hayes is different. Cayden's entire personality depended on something outside of his control. Hayes' doesn't. Hayes is better.

For now, I shoot him a quick text…

OLIVIA

> You played great tonight! Sorry for the loss. Refs are blind 😎 🐴. I'll probably be asleep when you get home, but wake me up when you get in. Can't wait to see you

Normally, I have a hard time sleeping in a strange place by myself. But it's been such a long week. My head hits the pillow, the nicest, most expensive pillow I've ever slept on in my life, and I quickly pass out.

I stir in my sleep as warm hands wrap around me, my neck tingling from soft kisses as a spicy, musky scent washes over me.

"I missed you, Olivia," a deep voice whispers in my ear.

"Hayes," I say with a super groggy smile, trying to wake myself up. "I missed you too." I turn my head to kiss him, pleased when his lips effortlessly find mine. "What time is it?"

"1:45. Go back to sleep, siren. I'm exhausted." He kisses me again. "I can't believe I came home to you in my bed. I missed you; I just need to hold you."

"Me too. I'm sorry you guys lost. Does snuggling help you get over a loss?"

"Olivia, I've been dealing with being outplayed for most of my life. Losses suck, but they happen. Losing is just part of the game." He drops his forehead to my shoulder, the warmth of his breath spreading goosebumps across my skin. "I know your mind is wheeling with thoughts of me being upset and standoffish, but that's not me," Hayes says as I start to wake a little more, his voice thrumming through me. "And whether or not it helps me get over a loss is yet to be determined," he says as he cozies up closer. "But there is nothing I would rather be doing than snuggling with you."

"Are you sure?" I tease, wiggling into him. "Because, from what I'm feeling, you'd like to do more than snuggle."

He lets out a soft laugh. "I really want to let you get some rest, but seeing you in my bed, my name across your back, has me fucking hard as a rock."

"Well, we can't have you trying to get a good night's sleep like that, now, can we." I turn over to face him as I grasp his length. He moans as a warmth settles deep within me. "Fun fact. I told my boss I needed to work from home tomorrow. He thinks I need to let a repair man in my house, so I can sleep in and have a lazy morning with you."

"Olivia Brooks, you sneaky liar." He drops his head into the crook of my neck, his lips lifting into a smile against my skin. "I love your ploy to spend more time with me."

I roll over to face him. "Oh, you love it, do you?"

Hayes gazes at me quietly, the burning heat in his eyes melting me to my core. He cups my cheek with his hand, my breath catching at the look on his face. "Olivia, I love you."

My heart is beating in my throat, my pulse racing so fast I can't breathe. "You...you..." I can't form the words. "You love me?" I blink, trying to convince myself this is real. "Already?"

His brows draw together, a tentative smile on his face. "I do. I don't know how this happened so fast," he admits as I lean into his hand. "But I know I don't want to spend another minute of my life without telling you how I feel. After Walt's, when I thought I may never see you again, was the longest I ever want to be without you."

My pulse races, and tears of joy flood my eyes at his words.

This man is everything.

"I almost said it when you left for your trip. I was so worried it would freak you out and you'd leave."

"I know," he says as he flashes that damn gorgeous smile at me. "I haven't taken enough hits to be that dense, and it didn't scare me one bit. Honestly, I wish you had said it so I could say it back. And now, I don't ever want to not say it." His thumb traces my cheek, more goosebumps erupting across my body. "I am madly in love with you."

I pause, cherishing how vulnerable he is. I take in a deep breath, filling my lungs with newfound confidence. I don't have to hold back my feelings anymore. "I love you too."

He presses his lips to mine with a fierce passion, melting all of my worries about him being on the road, trusting his actions, and my paranoia of not being enough. As he claims me, I'm reminded of the good and selfless man he is. This all seems fast, but it also feels right. I don't know what I've done in my life to deserve this man, but the one thing I know is that I'm never letting go.

32
hayes

I love sleeping in my own bed. I paid premium for this mattress, and it's been worth every penny. I need to sleep well, without any extra stress on my back, and hotel beds can be killer. Waking up feeling like I slept on a big, fluffy cloud always makes me feel glad to be home. Especially when I wake up with my siren curled into me. Her auburn hair is splayed across my white pillowcase and is more beautiful than the view of the sunrise coming up over the lake.

I hop out of bed, throwing on a pair of boxer briefs, to make us some coffee and breakfast. Thankfully, I have today off. No game. No practice. I need to fuel up and get in a quick run, but that's it.

"How are you up earlier than me?" Olivia groggily mumbles rubbing the sleep from her eyes, her adorable self walking into my kitchen as I'm filling the water in the coffee maker.

"I've always been an early riser."

"Oh, I almost forgot! I made you something," she says, springing to the kitchen island grabbing a pie plate. "I found a market that had some decent peaches this late in the season, so I made you a pie. It's from scratch. Even the crust."

My stomach groans, lusting at the sight of my absolute favorite dessert. *She made me a pie.* "Oh my God. We are fucking eating this for breakfast."

"You want to eat it for breakfast?"

"Why the hell not? First of all, you know I have zero problem eating dessert before a meal. Second, you can't just wave a pie in my face and expect me to not eat it immediately. And third, it's fruit. And pie crust is basically bread. It's the same as eating toast, part of a healthy, well-balanced meal."

Her face lights up like a Christmas tree, her eyes beaming with excitement. "I like the way you think Larsy. Toast and fruit it is. I'm still sad you got up before me though. You got in so late last night, I thought for sure you'd sleep in. I was going to make you coffee, but you beat me to it," she says with a tired pout.

"Well, you'll have to get up earlier to beat me to the coffee," I say as I pull her close and kiss her. "Would you like to know my secret?"

"I'd like to know *all* of your secrets, Hayes."

"Naps. Lots of naps. That's how hockey players survive, especially during crazy travel weeks. We eat lunch, then we nap to get some energy back before the game. It's all very choreographed actually."

"Wow, choreographed is a big word for a tough jock hockey player to use," she taunts, tilting her head with a smirk.

"You sure are a feisty siren in the morning, aren't you? You want to get punished before the coffee is even brewed?"

"Well, sir, we do have some time while the coffee is percolating, and, wouldn't you know, there is a countertop right next to the coffee pot."

I swear to all things Gretzky this woman is damn perfect. She fucking loves me being in control, and I love having her. My heart is furiously pumping blood straight to my dick at her words. *God I have so many things I want to do to her.*

"I have a better idea," I say taking a step toward Olivia and throwing her over my shoulder. She squeals as I walk her over and toss her on the couch. She's still wearing my jersey. With nothing on underneath. Seeing my name on her back gets me so turned on. But right now, I need to see every inch of her body. I lean her up and strip her, leaving her naked before me. *Fuck she's so damn sexy.*

I kneel in front of her, slowly kissing my way up her irresistible legs. She pushes her hands through my hair, goosebumps covering my skin as she massages my scalp, making my dick jump inside my boxer briefs. Nerves tingle up my spine as she lightly tugs at the strands, pulling a grunt from my chest as I move my lips closer to the top of her thighs.

She stiffens, sitting up to look me in the eyes. "Hayes, you really don't have to do this. Let me do something for you."

"You're right, Olivia," I level my eyes at her with a stern, disappointed look, "I don't have to do this. I fucking *want* to. I want to taste you. I want to please you. I want to make you scream my name so loud my neighbors call to complain. You are not, and you never will be, a burden or an inconvenience to me. Got it?"

She pauses for a moment, but a shy smile creeps up on her face as she replies. "Yes."

I pause for a moment …my cock tenting my boxer briefs, wondering if she's up for a little more.

I grip her chin, tilting it toward me, forcing her to look me in the eye. "Yes, what?"

She looks at me with wide, wondering eyes, swallowing before she shyly replies, "Yes, sir."

My heart pounds at the sound of her calling me sir. *Fuck. I knew this girl would be fun, but she is my every dream come to life.*

"Better. Now, are you going to be a good girl for me and sit here while I put my tongue on this gorgeous body of yours and make you come?"

"Yes, sir."

"That's my siren," I purr as she moans at the praise. I lean down again, parting her thighs to get a full view of her. "This cunt is mine." I place my lips on her inner thigh, sinking my teeth in just the tiniest bit, and sucking her delicious skin until she's crying out again.

"Oh my God, wow. What…what are you doing?" she looks at me with her brows narrowed, but a glimmer of excitement.

"You belong to me, siren. I'm marking you so there's no doubt in your mind that I will ever want *anyone* else in this world but you."

She arches her back with a moan as I part her lips, keeping her right on the edge, finally giving in and circling my tongue on her sensitive clit. *She is so wet for me already.*

"That feels unreal," she gasps with broken breaths.

I devour her, taking my time. Once again, paying attention to her every sound, every movement she makes to ensure I'm working her in just the right spots. Her body quivers as she grinds herself against my mouth. Pride swells within me as I feel her enjoying this. Her pleasure fills an empty space in my heart I didn't realize existed. *I've got my girl right where I want her.*

Looking up as I taste her, I see her palming her gorgeous tits. "What a good fucking girl you are, squeezing those tits for me," I growl as she lets out a sultry moan. "You like being a good girl for me?"

"Shit…. Yes. I love being your good girl."

My eyes roll back in my head as I let out a loud growl. I fucking *knew* she had a praise kink. Holy shit I love this woman.

"Good. Next time, you'll ask before you put your hands on

yourself like that, or you'll receive a punishment. Do you understand?"

"Yes."

I place my hand around her throat with just the slightest pressure. "Yes *what*, Olivia?"

Her stunned gaze bores into my eyes,

"Yes, sir."

I release my grip and focus back on the beautiful pussy before me. She moans again, my tongue teasing her sensitive clit.

"Fuck, Hayes, I'm…I'm close," she whimpers, barely able to speak. I've noticed she has one little spot near her clit, and I unleash my tongue right on the target. She writhes against me, arching her back and screaming my name in ecstasy as she finds her release. I smile, letting out an almost villainous laugh, feeling a sense of accomplishment, like I just scored a game winning goal. *I love making this woman feel good*. The glow on her face is sexy as fuck. Her entire body shivers from the aftershocks of the mind-blowing orgasm I just gave her. Knowing I did that makes my heart, and my cock, swell.

"Hayes, oh my God. That was…. That was….."

"Is Olivia Brooks at a loss for words? Why, I never thought I'd see the day," I say as I place more kisses on her thighs.

She lets out a sigh, slumping against the couch. "It was fucking unbelievable. How are you so good at that?"

"You know my job is to anticipate other people. I have to feel, watch, and listen to what's going on around me if I want any success on the ice. Luckily, I found a way to translate those skills into something that benefits us both."

"Well, I'm certainly not going to complain about that." She looks down contemplatively, her gaze tracing my face before her eyes narrow, revealing a deep internal debate I'm desperate to be invited to.

"Hayes," she says in a stern, commanding tone, "stand up."

My eyebrows raise, but I remain on my knees.

She huffs, pushing half-heartedly against my shoulder. "Listen. I like it when you're bossy. I like it a *lot*. But you…you've unlocked something inside me," she whispers in a declaration of new-found confidence. "I don't feel like I need to be anything other than myself. You let me be whatever I want. You do so much to make me feel good; I want to make you feel good. I want to tell *you* what to do. So…I'm going to ask you again, and this time you're going to comply. Stand. The fuck. Up."

Well, ho-ly shit.

I jump to my feet as fast as humanly possible, my heart beating in my throat. Olivia sits fully upright on the couch, grabs my ass and pulls me toward her. She slides my boxer briefs past my hips, letting them fall to the floor, my stiff dick springing free before her. She grabs my cock, gripping it like it's a prize she's won and ready to claim.

"I've been wanting to taste this for days. And you're going to let me. And when you're close, you are going to tell me." Her eyes find mine, dark and full of promise. "I want you to come all over my tits. Do you understand?"

Holy fucking shit. What kind of alternate sex dimension have I fallen into? This woman is abso-fucking-lutely perfect. I tighten my jaw, raising my eyebrow at her confidently asking for what she wants.

"I understand."

"Good," she says, dragging her thumb through the bead of precum leaking from me. She stares up at me, licking my cock from bottom to top, a fiery heat spreading across my body with every stroke of her tongue. A rumble builds deep in my chest. I'm desperate to feel her lips fully around me. Desperate for my hardness to feel the heat of her mouth. Desperate for her. I take in a sharp breath as she places her soft lips on the head of my cock, teasing me with her lips pursed together. Finally, mercifully, she parts her lips to take me in, gripping my cock in her hand like it's her goddamn microphone. Seeing her mouth wrapped around me sends my eyes rolling into the back of my head. *I'm never going to be able to watch her sing into a mic the same way again.*

Gently grasping her hair, I push her to take me deeper. I don't know what kind of witchcraft she's using but somehow, she's licking the bottom ridge of my head at the same time she's moving her mouth up and down me. "I've been imagining your lips around me for so long, siren, and you are better than I could have ever dreamed. You take my cock in your mouth so damn perfectly."

She moans around my girth, her hand moving in a rhythmic motion and creating a wet suction pulling my cock into her mouth. I shiver at the unbelievable feeling of her teeth barely scraping my cock. Her other hand grips my balls, squeezing them with the fucking perfect amount of pressure as she takes my cock as far back into her mouth as she can, nearly choking on me.

I groan, my head tilting toward the ceiling as stars dance in my vision. I am barely holding on. I don't know if there is an Olympic medal for giving a perfect blowjob, but she would be getting a perfect ten from Judge 22. "*Fuck,* the things you do to me. You're gonna make me come."

She pulls her mouth away with a quiet pop, and I immediately stroke my cock, feeling the instant withdrawal of her lips on me. Sitting on the couch, she grabs her tits, pushing them together, holding them out like a present she's gift wrapped just for me.

She bats her eyes at me with a dirty smile on her face. "Fucking stroke your cock for me, Hayes. Watching you touch yourself like that, all for me, makes me so wet. So ready. So needy. I need your cum on me. *Now.*"

Fuck, if this woman being in control isn't the hottest thing I've ever seen. My hand may be on my cock, but she's the one with me wrapped around her goddamn finger. My balls tighten, and my entire body tenses as I cry out, my hips thrusting and spilling my release over her bare chest as directed. Silence blankets us, our heavy breaths beating a steady rhythm as we both calm down from our high. This gorgeous woman continues to surprise me every day, and I can't wait to be there for every new discovery she makes.

"Would you like to come to the game Saturday night? I know a guy with tickets." I smirk as we finally sit down to breakfast.

She snorts as we enjoy a bite of the fucking best pie I've ever eaten. *The only thing that tastes better than this is Olivia.* "I would love to. But…is it weird if I come? I mean, I want to see *you*, for sure, and I guess it's a big arena, so I hopefully wouldn't see all the Riders staff I know." She rubs her hands down her thighs as she scrunches her face. "I'm sure they have one of the backups lined up to sing. Ugh… this is all so weird now."

"No pressure. I can imagine it would feel awkward. If it helps, I can get you tickets with the WAGs. Normally, they have tickets on the glass, but it's Zack's first game back this season, so they have a suite. Then you wouldn't have to be so close to the ice."

"The WAGs? As in wives and girlfriends? Does this mean I fall into that category now?" she asks, scrunching up her nose. I can't help but smile, my heart calming at her look.

"I was thinking we could even go steady," I joke. "Actually… wait here; I'll be right back."

Jumping up from the kitchen table, I grab a notepad and pen from the drawer with the apartment complex logo on it. Jotting down a note, I fold it in half and pass it across the table.

Olivia's laughter fills the kitchen, a smile stretching ear to ear across her face as she opens the paper and picks up the pen to write her reply before sliding it back.

I stare down at the note, my pulse racing and my fingers pounding out a rhythm on my coffee mug. I read her response and a giant, dumbass grin spreads across my face.

OLIVIA, WILL YOU BE MY GIRLFRIEND?
X YES
_ NO

"Oh, thank God. If you said no, breakfast might have gotten really awkward," I say grabbing the note and holding it in my hand. *I'm saving this for later.* "Why does this make me feel like I'm in high school again? Except way less nerdy."

She snorts, rolling her eyes and sipping her coffee. "Hayes, there is no way you were nerdy in high school."

"Oh, I was a *total* nerd, Olivia. Scouts honor," I swear, holding up two fingers in the universal scout hand signal. "I'll get my yearbooks from my mom sometime and show you. I was a certified nerd. Glasses, dorky clothes, and braces. Acne from all the sweat under my chin strap was no joke."

"I didn't know there was such a thing as hockey acne."

"Oh, it's real. Thankfully, my skin got used to it as I got older and I learned about facial cleansers. But I was not the fine specimen of sexiness you see before you today," I say as I wave my hand across my face like a game show hostess.

She eyes me with a smile, blushing as her tongue wets her bottom lip.

"I would have loved nerdy Hayes. He sounds like my type," she said with a shy smile. "For some reason, you make me feel like I'm back in high school too. Especially since you asked me to wear your jersey. No one ever asked me to wear one in school. You're my first."

"Wait...you're telling me I got your jersey v-card? I'm the only guy who's ever given you a jersey?"

"Yep. Only you."

I lean across the table pressing my lips against hers. "I am so fucking thankful to have you as my girlfriend and honored to be your first jersey."

What I hold back from telling her is I hope I'm her last.

33
olivia

I've been to a lot of hockey games in my life, but never in a suite like this. There are huge TVs on the wall, photos of famous Riders players from the past, a fully stocked bar, a buffet that's already making my mouth water, and a dessert display that Hayes and his sweet tooth would demolish. *Damn, I could get used to this.* I knew the players' wives were up here for some of the games, but I never really paid attention, too focused on everything I have to do before the game. Seeing them all here, cheering on their men, is a different experience. I take a deep breath, rubbing my hands down my thighs. I want to make a good impression. I am normally one of the coldest people in America, but tonight sweat is pooling under my jersey from my damn nerves. *How am I sweating in an ice arena?* It's funny how I can sing in front of the entire crowd but being in a suite with less than thirty people has me sweating bullets.

Every woman here is in 'show makeup.' I have work makeup, which is a quick morning foundation, blush, and eyeliner, then I have my show makeup, which is a long process with lashes, bronzer, highlighter, curled hair, hair extensions, and all my fancy jewelry. Every woman here seems to have on their show makeup. *Are they like this every game?* I'm suddenly glad I went the extra mile tonight with my hair and makeup.

I asked Hayes if I could bring Maggie along since I didn't know anyone, and I'm so glad she was able to come. Especially because I wasn't sure if these women would be nice, catty, cliquey, or just flat out mean. At least I'd have a friend to help me navigate potentially shark infested waters.

"Liv, this is a *sick* suite. Except every girl in here is a perfect ten." Maggie steps behind me, dropping her head on my shoulder as she glances around again. "I'm over here looking like a five in my nicest jeans and Riders t-shirt."

"Whatever," I scoff, forcing her to stand next to me. "We are both *solid* eights, and you know it." We both laugh, the tension in my shoulders melting away.

"Olivia!" a gorgeous blonde woman, with a very pregnant belly and holding a toddler on her hip, says. "I'm Kara Reeves, Zack's wife. Welcome to the WAG suite." Her smile is super friendly and welcoming, helping the rest of my anxiety disappear.

"Thank you. It's nice to meet you, Kara, I'm Olivia Brooks, and this is my friend, Maggie James."

"Nice to meet you, Maggie. Olivia, we all know who you are. We love hearing you sing the anthem." Wait…*the WAGS know who I am?* Kara drops her voice, leaning closer as she glances at the ice. "Listen, Zack told me what happened. We're going to get you back out there singing. I don't know who else they have lined up, but we need our weapon back." She winks with a conspiratory look, straightening and gently bouncing the toddler in her arms.

My face heats as I rub my palms down my thighs. "I appreciate the kind words. Sometimes things happen beyond our control, and this was one of them. I'll live," I say, shaking off the disappointment of not being down on the ice tonight, motioning to the toddler hiding his face in her chest. "Who is this little cutie?"

"This is Jackson," her face softens, "And the two littles running around like heathens are Sophia and Molly. Another boy - yet to be named - is on the way," she says, rubbing her belly. "That's Zack's mom and dad over there with the girls," she nods with her chin, "They are excited to see Zack back on the ice after his injury, and, of course, to see their grandkids. To tell you the truth, I'm ecstatic to have extra hands at the game with these three wonderful, high-energy children," she says as we all laugh. "Come on, I'll introduce you around, then we'll find some seats."

Kara walks us around to meet the other wives and girlfriends, and I relax even more when I realize everyone is actually nice. *Not the shark fest I was expecting at all.* Some are very young, and I immediately feel old around them. I forget some of the rookies are just barely in their twenties. Kara seems like she's at least closer to my age. Not that any of that matters. More than anything, I'm blown away that here I am, at thirty-one, and some of these girls are not even legal to drink and are dating high-profile NHL players. When I was twenty, I was still stumbling my way through life, nowhere near being in a relationship with a pro-athlete.

We find our seats and get ready for the starting line ups. Everyone cheers as the players are announced, being the loudest for their man on the ice. Kara is so gracious and has gotten us three seats together. She stands beside me as we rise for the anthem, *of course it's the Singing Grannies,* and puts her hand on my back.

"Just know that while we all love America, even though most of us are Canadian, we love it more when you're singing." I give her a warm smile, thankful for all her help in breaking the anxiety of someone else performing tonight.

———

As we head into the third period, both Hayes and Zack are having great games. They are playing on the first line tonight, Hayes has a goal while Zack has an assist, but the Riders are still down by one. Before play starts up, Kara and I talk more about our guys while Maggie wanders off, refilling her drink and talking with some of the other ladies in the suite.

"If you don't mind me asking, what's it like being married to a player? How do you handle all the travel and odd schedules?" I ask twisting my fingers in my lap.

"Well, it's not always as easy as it looks from the outside," she sighs, "but there is nothing I wouldn't do to help Zack live out his dream. It can be tough when he's on the road, especially when the kids are having a bad day throwing tantrums and missing daddy. Thankfully, we can pay for a housekeeper, so at least I'm not taking care of the kids and trying to keep the house in order. But the amazing thing is that when he's home, he really picks up the slack. He helps get the kids fed, plays with them, and helps put them to bed every night." A warm smile lights up her face. "And seeing Zack out there on the ice, I'm just so proud of him. You can see the passion he plays with. He has that same passion for our family, and it makes me love him more every day. Just don't tell him I said that," she winks, absentmindedly rubbing her belly. "Four kids are going to be a handful, and if he hears that, we'll have ten before you know it."

"Your secret is safe with me," I promise, pretending to zip my lips and throw away the key.

"And this group of girls here helps too," she gestures around the room, "We all know what the other is going through when they are on the road, so we reach out if we need something."

I glance around, finding it surprisingly easy to picture myself connecting with the women surrounding me. *Maybe it wouldn't be so hard to fit into this group after all.*

"So, Olivia, tell me about you and Hayes," Kara smirks, "I mean, Zack told me a little about you two, but I'd love to hear it from your perspective. That man's game has been on fire this season, and my instincts tell me that's no coincidence."

Warmth fills my heart at the thought of Hayes talking to anyone about me. I rub my hands on my thighs, "Oh…did Hayes talk to Zack about me?"

"Honey, let me tell you something about Zack. He can get anyone to spill their guts, especially about their feelings, in an instant. He had me telling him my life story and deepest secrets on our first date." A wicked smile sharpens her features, her eyes focused on mine. "Also…my guess is Hayes likes to talk about you, and he doesn't know many people here yet."

"Good point," I murmur, biting my lip. "We haven't known each other that long actually. It's all so new and so fast, but…it feels as if some force put us in the same place at the same time to be together. Ugh…that sounds cheesy saying it out loud."

"Olivia, it's not cheesy at all. I know exactly what you mean. Sometimes it doesn't take long to figure out life has brought you exactly where you're meant to be."

Her words hit me like a truth tidal wave to the heart. I do feel like everything I've been through has led to me being here tonight. My heart races as I watch my boyfriend, out on the ice, putting his heart and soul into the game, just as he has with me these past few weeks.

Molly tugs on my leg and asks if she can sit in my lap with her little tablet, bored with the game and watching a show. Picking her up, I sit her in the seat with me. Glancing around the tablet, I see Hayes flying across the ice. *Does he want a wife? Kids? Would he want me to be that wife?* My heart swells at the thought, but I try to calm myself down. We just made it official with a note, but here I am already dreaming of walking down the aisle with a baby on the way.

Snuggling the little munchkin close, I watch the Riders speed around the ice, leaving the other team in their dust. With everything I went through with Cayden, I never felt like this. I always hoped it would get to this point, but if I'm being honest, I never actually saw it happening. I think in the back of my mind I knew he wasn't in this for the long haul. A hint of regret brushes through me, but I quickly shake it off. As awful as that was, I can't regret what brought me to where I am today, to Hayes. He seems to be in this with no fear, no concerns, no doubts, and melting my heart along the way. And I'm starting to think I may be feeling that way myself.

Despite Zack and Hayes both having a stellar game, the Riders lose 3-2. Afterward, Kara walks us all to the hallway outside the players locker room, and I can't help but constantly glance around. I've been in lots of different areas of this arena, but never here.

"Wow, Kara, that locker room smell is…potent," I say as she lets out a roaring laugh.

"I almost forgot what it's like to *not* smell that. I swear, I'm desensitized at this point. You'll get used to it. Just wait until the playoffs," she scrunches her nose, "it will be way worse with the superstitious guys not washing various clothing items."

"Okay Kara, what's the scoop on the single players here?" Maggie asks. "The tea I got from the other WAGs is that Volkov, Johansen, and Boucher are all eligible bachelors."

"Yes, I believe they are single. You sure you're up for the hockey wife life Maggie? All of those guys are great. But emotionally? Some of them are tough nuts to crack."

"Well, they do call me the nutcracker," Maggie smirks, leaning back against the wall as we come to a stop in the tunnel.

"Since when has anyone called *you* the nutcracker?" I snap back with one eyebrow raised.

"Since now."

"DADDY!" Kara's daughters scream in unison as they race toward Zack.

"Hi babies! Did you have fun with grandma and grandpa?" Zack asks as he wraps them up in a big hug, reaching over to wiggle his fingers toward Jackson and leaning in to give Kara a quick kiss.

"Daddy, we had *so* much fun! We got snacks and I drew on the wall with one of my crayons and sorry the bad guys won the game and Miss Olivia let me sit on her lap and I saw you on the ice. Wait, are we going home now?" Molly says in one run-on sentence.

"Wow, that was a lot of information there, pumpkin. You drew on the wall in the suite with your crayons?" He looks up at Kara who just shrugs. "Yes, baby, we are headed home now. Do you girls want to ride home with me?"

"YES!!! We get to ride in Daddy's truck!" the girls shout, dancing around the hallway.

"Oh! Zack, this is Olivia Brooks, Hayes' *girlfriend*," Kara says, introducing us. "And this is her friend, Maggie James." He reaches out to shake Maggie's hand first, then mine.

"Olivia, it's so nice to finally meet The Weapon in person. I see you here at all the games, but never had a chance to tell you how beautiful of a voice you have," he says. "For what it's worth, I'm sorry me signing those pucks got you in trouble. No offense, but I was trying to get that guy away from me."

"Nice to meet you too. Honestly, I should have been trying to get away from that guy a long time ago, so I get it." We both chuckle, each with our own sour memories of Cayden and his selfish heart.

"Hayes should be out in a minute." He glances behind me, leaning in a little closer, and whispers. "If you tell him I said this, he'll kill me, but that man has it bad for you." He smiles and winks at us as he walks away.

I cannot imagine how red my cheeks must be at this moment, and from the look on Maggie's face she's about to explode with excitement.

"I told you, Olivia! Hayes has it bad for you. Even the captain agrees!" Maggie shouts as she pats my arm in excitement.

"Okay, yes...you were right, Mags. Just be cool about it, okay?"

"When have I ever been anything but the epitome of cool?"

I roll my eyes, the back of my neck prickling. Looking over, I see Hayes heading our way. I swear to all things holy, this man in a suit has my knees weak and he's not even touching me. It's like a slow-motion scene in a movie, and he's walking towards me with the song *Let's Get It On* playing in the background. When he's finally close enough, he pulls me into a hug. His hair is still wet, and whatever shampoo he has in the locker room smells like mint and cedar. *God, that smell is intoxicating.* He pulls back from our embrace, giving me a quick kiss. The sound of a fake cough pulls me out of my trance.

Okay, maybe it wasn't a quick kiss.

"Hayes, this is my best friend, Maggie, who apparently needs a cough drop," I snark giving Maggie some serious side-eye. "And Maggie, this is Hayes," I say introducing them, my cheeks hot.

"I have heard so much about you, Hayes; it's nice to finally put a face with a name."

"Nice to meet you too," Hayes smiles, shaking her hand.

"But just know, if you hurt Olivia, I will literally murder you."

"*Maggie,* oh my God, stop it," I shout, punching her arm.

"I see your friend watches a lot of true crime shows too." Hayes laughs giving me a wicked side-eye. "Don't worry, Maggie. We're on the same team here. No one will hurt Olivia *ever* again." Warmth surrounds my heart, my thighs squeezing tight as he pulls me closer, his arm wrapped around my waist. I'm not a damsel in distress by any means, but the thought of him being protective over me is surprisingly hot. *I would totally bail this man out of jail for defending me.*

"I like this guy, Liv," Maggie says with a wink. "One hell of an improvement compared to the last one; I can't wait to get to know you better. But I need to be going, so I'll leave you two love birds alone."

"Thanks for the ride to the game, Mags, and for helping me brave the WAGs." I hug her goodbye, thankful to have someone like her in my life.

"Anytime I get to help you with something that involves free food and alcohol, you have my number. Love you, girl! Don't do anything I wouldn't do!" Hayes and I wave goodbye to Maggie as she walks away.

"Let's get out of here," he says, taking my hand and walking me toward the players' parking lot.

"Sorry you lost. That last goal for the other team was such a fluke," I say, bumping into him with my shoulder. "But you looked great out there. Thanks for inviting me; I loved watching you play."

"Thanks, sweet girl. Losing always sucks, but I feel like I played my game tonight. I wished we could have pulled out the win for you."

"Do you want to know what my favorite part of the game was?"

"Harley throwing free t-shirts?"

"No," I say with a laugh, rolling my eyes. "My favorite part was watching you slide down the bench between shifts."

Hayes gasps, a baffled look on his face. "*That* was your favorite part of the game? Not watching me sprint down the ice trying to beat a guy to the puck? Or slamming someone into the boards? Or my assist? My goal?"

"I mean…those were all great, but watching you slide down the bench is the most adorable thing I've ever seen in my life. You scoot your butt down first, then shift your upper body to meet it. All the other guys slide down in one motion. But you go ass first. And for some reason, I couldn't wait for you to get off the ice so I could see this little moment only I was noticing."

As we reach his spot, he crowds me against his car and tucks a curl of my hair behind my ear, giving me another one of his smoldering smiles. "I never realized I scooted differently than my teammates, but I'm glad you enjoyed it." He brushes his thumb across my lip, tingles racing across my body and pooling in my core. "My favorite part of the game was knowing you were in the stands watching. Wearing my jersey. Screaming my name. I felt like I was on fire knowing you were here."

"I'm glad I could help. You were a force to be reckoned with tonight."

Leaning down, he growls, "I'm going to be an even bigger force to be reckoned with once I get you home, just you wait, siren. You haven't seen anything yet."

34

hayes

The energy I have after a game is hard to get rid of. My adrenaline runs at full speed for hours during the game, then it's over. I shower and rest, but my mind is wide awake, replaying every moment of the game, and my body jitters as if I just shotgunned three energy drinks. It's a high that's hard to come down from. The team nutritionists give us supplements for better sleep, but with just a short practice tomorrow, I'm not taking any of those tonight. *I want this energy for Olivia.* I don't think she has any idea what she's in for with post-game Hayes Larson at the helm.

We arrive back at my apartment and, once again, barely get in the door before our hands are all over each other. I pick her up mid-kiss and walk her to the bedroom, already imagining what I'm going to do once we get there.

"Are you tired from your game?" she asks, "I certainly don't want to exhaust you any further."

I curl a piece of her long hair around my finger. "Olivia, there is nothing you could do to exhaust me."

She stares back at me with heat in her eyes, my body aching for more. More of her. All of her.

"I want to take care of you tonight, Hayes. Watching you fly up and down the ice, racing to the puck, being there for your teammates, sliding down the bench, you were incredible. You take care of everyone around you, especially me. Tonight, I want to help you relax, unwind, and not worry about a thing," she purrs, slipping her hands beneath the lapels of my suit jacket and sliding it off my arms, letting it drop to the floor with a delicate swish of fabric. Her eyes don't leave mine as she reaches for my shirt, undoing the buttons one at a time. Fire courses through every vein in my body as she slips my shirt off my shoulders, gently running her hands over my chest. Her wandering touch grazes lower to unbuckle my belt and my cock twitches beneath her touch as she undoes my pants. I slip my shoes off, flipping them across the room, stepping out of my pants and standing bare before her.

"My, my, Hayes," she lifts a delicate brow, her eyes dancing as they slowly lift to mine. "Commando after the game?"

I flash her a wicked smile. "After being locked down in gear all night, I need some breathing room down there. And...I didn't think I'd be wearing them long anyway," I say with a wink.

"Well, isn't that presumptuous of you," she smirks, her eyes filled with hunger.

"Lie back on the bed," she orders, and I immediately obey her sultry command. She stands at the end of the bed, slowly disrobing herself, taking her time and teasing me with every inch of skin she reveals. I ache for her touch. I can't help but slowly stroke myself as I watch her strip. Once she's shed her clothing, all except her sexy set of black lace undergarments, she lowers herself onto the bed, crawling towards me. *Holy mother of hockey, my siren is* crawling *to me like the good girl she is.* I may never recover from this. Death from a sexy siren is the way I want to go.

"I have a question for you, Hayesy-poo. Do you like being a Milwaukee Rider?"

"*Fuck* yes. Especially if it involves you in this town with me," I grunt as she slowly licks my cock from the base all the way to the tip. My pulse races, tightness building in my fucking balls. I am about to come unglued as she teases the fuck out of me. She takes her time, licking me and placing delicate kisses along my length as she rubs my tight thigh muscles.

"Do you think I could be a Milwaukee Rider?" she asks, looking up at me with those fucking expressive eyes, her tongue still teasing me between her words. "Because I want you to lie back and let me ride this crotch rocket all night long."

"*Holy fucking shit.* Your dirty little mouth is going to be the death of me," I say, straining to keep my composure. This sexy woman makes it so hard to last long. She climbs up to kiss me, positioning herself so her soaking wet entrance coats my cock without being inside her. Wait, how is my cock drenched but she's still wearing...*oh fuck me.* I can't control my hips thrusting up from the bed at the realization. "Olivia, are you wearing crotchless panties?"

The corners of her mouth lift, forming a mischievous grin. "They were a late night internet purchase after I had a little too much wine. You like?"

Pulling her hips toward me, I press my hardness against her entrance. "Feel that, siren? That's how much I like it." Her head tilts back, her tits spilling out of her bra. She finally leans back and sinks down, taking me deep inside her. "You are so fucking tight. I love watching you take me."

Olivia pauses, a slight wince on her face, letting herself adjust. "It's like you were made to fill up my cunt."

My thoughts exactly.

Olivia slowly starts to move, her voluptuous tits right in my face. I reach up to grab her hips as we find our rhythm, our bodies crashing together in violent perfection. She leans forward a bit, and *...fuck, that angle is heavenly.* "Siren, just like that. You feel amazing on my cock, riding me like such a good girl." Her thighs squeeze my hips as she slides up and down on top of me.

"Hayes, give it to me. Fill up my cunt," she begs, and I'm done. I raise my hips and explode into her, shaking and screaming her name. She leans forward, kissing me as she climbs off and lies beside me, her head on my chest.

"I don't know what I ever did to deserve you," I say kissing her again. "You make me feel so good, not just here in bed, but every day. This just feels-"

"Right." she says, interrupting me.

"So right. Why does it feel so right?"

"I don't know. But I don't want this to end. Ever. This seems too good to be true, and I...I keep waiting for the hammer to drop."

"I feel the same way. Is there a way to destroy hammers? Like, all of them? Except maybe Thor's hammer, that thing's pretty badass."

"I wish I knew, but for now, I think we just enjoy this moment." She props herself up on her elbow, her lip trapped between her teeth. "How about you reach down, lube me up with what you just shot inside me, and get me off."

"*Fuck.* Are you *sure* your ex was a real human man? Who in their right mind would not want to fuck you every day? Multiple times a day. Cancel your plans for the week, we're not leaving this room," I say as we both laugh.

"Hayes, I've never been like this with anyone else. You just...do something to me. You make me feel safe. Like I can be anything or anyone I want, and you'll still love me. I've never felt this with anyone before."

I brush a stray piece of hair from her face. "I want you to always be comfortable with me. You make me feel things I've never felt before too." I lean down and kiss her with fire and passion, telling her without words I never want this to end.

I don't know what is happening, but I know I would give up my own life for this woman. She is my every dream, my every want, and my future. I feel the same way she does, like the hammer is going to drop and this will all be gone in an instant. We can't predict the future, but I swear on my life, I will never let her go. *Especially now that I know she's up for a little cum play.*

"Now," I growl, "let's see if I can help you out with your little request." I slowly reach down between her thighs, using the remnants of my release to help her find hers.

We lie in bed, basking in the euphoria of being well taken care of. But now I've recovered a bit, I'm still wide awake and hungry for more.

"Olivia," I sing song, stilling her fingers as they glide through my chest hair, "are you up for some more excitement this evening?"

"What did you have in mind, sir?" *Fuck me, the sound of that word coming out of her mouth could take over cities.*

"I have a gift for you."

Her eyes widen, staring back at me, lighting up in the dark room at the mention of a gift.

"You got me a present?"

"Yep. Wait right here," I say, quickly hopping out of bed and grabbing a small bag from my closet.

"What is it?" she asks almost giddy, smiling from ear to ear. I love making her smile. *God I can't wait to shower her with gifts.* Every holiday, birthday, anniversary, and even the fake ones invented by greeting card companies.

"Remember when we talked about phone sex, and I said I had an idea?" Her eyes widen and her fingers tighten around the sheets, her embarrassment starting to creep up. Sitting on the bed beside her, I place my arm around her shoulders as I hand her my gift.

Olivia opens the bag, her eyes still wide and unable to speak as she pulls the pink toy out and stares at me.

"There's an app that goes with it and I have it downloaded on my phone. That way, when I'm out of town, even if you don't want to talk or video chat with me, I can still help you get off. I have a similar one, too, I'll pack on my road trips."

Her cheeks flush as she darts her glaze between me and the toy. "Hayes. This is…. wow…it's…"

"Is this okay? Do you have many sex toys?"

"Yeah. I have a couple. They are super old school…nothing with Bluetooth!" she giggles as I throw my head back with laughter.

Sobering, I gently kiss along her neck, whispering each word in her ear. "I thought we could test it out tonight, so we know what we're doing the next time I'm out of town."

She flashes me a warm smile, "I think that's a wonderful idea."

"Lie back, sweet girl," I say as I gently lean her back onto the bed. I've already gotten the toy synced with my phone, and I'm already hard picturing Olivia using this. I open the app and turn it on to the lowest setting, the toy vibrating in Olivia's hand.

"Oh my God…. Wow. This is…. *powerful,*" she says.

"I think you can handle it," I say with a wink, stroking her face with my hand. "Want to show me how you'll use that next time I'm out of town?"

Olivia looks at me with trepidation. *Has she never played with toys with another man before?*

"Listen, if this is too much right now, it's okay. Use the 'z' word if you need to. But, please know you have nothing to be embarrassed about. I love every part of your heart and every inch of your body. I only want to make you feel good, never embarrassed. Okay?"

A small tear forms as she nods, her chin dropping to her chest as she looks at me through her lashes.

"Hayes, I fucking love you so much. You've given me so much power, confidence, and freedom to be myself. But this is all foreign to me, and sometimes Old Olivia is going to rear her ugly head. It's not that I've never used a vibrator before, it was just always on my own. I felt like I had to keep it a secret from anyone I was with. I never could have used toys with any of my former partners. I was always too self-conscious and worried it would be awkward." She lifts her head, leaning forward until her forehead rests against mine. "I don't feel that way with you. It's just...new for me."

My heart breaks at the vulnerability in her voice; my body desperate to take away her fear and self-doubt. "I have so many new things I want us to do together. This is just the start. Here," I take the toy out of her hand, "why don't I help you get started?"

I slowly rub the toy down her chest, taking extra time over her sensitive, peaked nipples, holding it there until Olivia moans, writhing beneath me. I continue moving the vibrator down her stomach, hovering above the apex of her thighs. I spread her legs wide to give me better access to that sweet, sweet, wetness I am certain is still there and building once more. Slowly moving the toy across her pink center, I lightly press it against her entrance, watching Olivia begin to moan. Her singing may be a siren song, but her moaning makes me lose control.

"Fuck, that's amazing," she whimpers, her hips grinding against the toy, slowly move it toward her most sensitive part. Reaching up, I grab her hand and pull it down to grip the vibrator along with me. Slowly, gently, teasing it up and down her soaking slit.

Leaning down, I whisper, "Olivia, can you hold this for a

minute while I adjust the settings on the app to see what drives you wild?"

"Fuck, yes Hayes," she says with shattered breaths.

I smile proudly at her braveness, and I feel like my heart has just learned to beat knowing she's comfortable with me. Nothing brings me more joy than witnessing her growing self-confidence and knowing I had even the slightest part to play in it.

Pressing my mouth against her sensitive neck, I suck hard enough to bruise before sitting up and taking out my phone. I run through a few settings as she pleasures herself with the toy. She moans through several of the patterns I hit.

I should have made a 'moan scale' for the different ways she's whimpering.

"Oh my God…Hayes. Stop! Stop on that one. Holy *fuck*, that feels amazing."

"What a good girl you are, getting yourself off in front of me," I praise, drawing another loud moan from her chest. "Is this what you're going to do when I'm on the road? Call me up, let me adjust the settings on this app, then finish once we hit 8?"

Olivia arches off the bed, the vibrator causing tremors throughout her body. "Yes. Oh God, I'm so close…"

Witnessing her gain the confidence to pleasure herself in front of me makes my heart and my dick swell. *I love watching her come undone.* "Be a good girl and make yourself come for me. Hold that toy right on your fucking clit and come so hard for me. I want you to see stars, siren."

That's all it takes for Olivia to explode, her arousal trickling out of her beautiful pussy. I turn the toy off, setting it on the nightstand, and climb on top of her, my cock pressing against her.

"That's my good girl," I groan, gazing deep into her heavy-lidded eyes. She's still having aftershocks from her colossal orgasm, her mind trying to process the pleasure flowing within it. I tuck a strand of hair behind her ear, giving her a few seconds to catch her breath. "Olivia, you are exquisite. I cannot wait to use that next time I'm out of town, sweet girl," I say as she flashes that stunning smile at me, "but right now, I'm going to fuck you hard until you beg me to stop."

Her eyes roll back in her head as she whimpers with need, pushing me deeper as she lifts her hips. I know she wants me on her, in her, around her, I want that too, and I'm going to give this girl every-fucking-thing she wants.

35
olivia

Tonight is the big Bayview Bourbon party for their new Black Tie label campaign. Maggie and I spent months hunched over our desks like little trolls working to prepare for this launch, and now that it's here, I finally get a chance to rest. Everyone from Lakeshore Creative will be here as well as some local Milwaukee celebrities, the local media, and several of the Riders. Maggie, God bless her gossipy self, told our client rep I was bringing Hayes as my date. So, they asked if we could get more of the Riders to help promote the brand. I was so hesitant to ask Hayes to invite all of his teammates, but his response was simply, "Hockey players and free bourbon? How many can the venue accommodate?" I secretly think Maggie did this as an excuse to be around more hockey players.

"Holy shit, Liv, this place looks unreal!" Maggie gasps as we walk into the event space at the art museum.

"Right? This is amazing."

Maggie and I are here a little early to make sure everything is in place, and thankfully it looks fantastic. We hired an event planner to create a black-tie theme for the gala, and their attention to detail is unmatched. Black chiffon fabric, adorned with fairy lights, cascades across the ceiling while a stunning crystal chandelier hangs in the center of the ballroom. There are multiple bars featuring samples of the new Black Tie label along with cocktails highlighting the new line. The dessert display boasts a variety of black and white colored sweets and the most adorable little tuxedo cake pops. Hanging throughout the space are various graphics Maggie designed, art boards showcasing the ads that will soon hit magazines, billboards, and commercials across the country. She even worked with our printing company to create giant cutouts of the bourbon bottles for guests to take photos with. *I don't think she realizes how talented she is.*

"Mags, I still can't believe we get to come to events like this."

"Given the shit we put up with from people like Bill and the demanding clients we work with, we'd better get invited to these things." She rolls her eyes, slowly spinning in a circle and taking it all in, a satisfied smile on her face. "It's one of the few perks we get, and I, for one, am drinking my weight in top-shelf Black Tie Bourbon tonight."

"Let's hit the bar while we wait for guests to show up."

As we wait for our drinks, I see five gentlemen in tuxedos walking into the gala in a 'Flying V' formation. The Milwaukee Steel Riders have arrived, and it's as if they are walking in slow motion as nearly every head in the room turns to watch. I am stunned to see the most dapper one, the one I've been waiting for all night, is in the center, his eyes focused only on me.

Hayes. I swallow, my hand trembling as I straighten from the bar. *Holy mother of pearl.*

I've seen Hayes in a suit, and it's a *nice* view, but Hayes in a tux? *I'm going to need one of those old-timey southern lady fans to cool myself down.* Especially since we are in an art museum and not a building full of ice. The way his pants hug his muscular thighs and highlight the fuck out of his juicy ass has me praying for this event to be over quickly. Not to mention that bowtie. *Why does he look so hot in a bowtie?* He's going to need to walk behind me the rest of the night. This man looks like he stepped off the red carpet at a fancy awards ceremony surrounded by screaming fans. But he didn't. He's here. With me. As *my* date.

What world am I living in?

"Hey gorgeous," Hayes says, placing a gentle kiss on my lips, his scent entrancing me.

"Hey handsome…you are wearing the hell out of that tux."

"Me? You look absolutely stunning. Let me get a better look at you." Hayes takes a step back, as I twirl around for him. As a short girl, I don't typically wear floor-length dresses, but this canary yellow gown just spoke to me. I feel like a movie star from the 1920s.

"You like?"

Hayes pulls me close, whispering into my ear with a deep, dark tone, "There's only one problem with this dress, Olivia…I can't see your gorgeous legs, and it's making me want to rip it off and fuck you senseless in the janitor's closet."

Heat crawls into my face, surging deep into my belly at the thought of Hayes and I fooling around at this event.

"I think that's two problems," I sass back, leaning closer into him.

"You're looking for a punishment tonight, aren't you, sweet girl?"

"I have no idea what you're talking about." I smile, his hand snaking around me to give me a pinch on the ass.

"That's a preview for later," he says as I gasp and give him a little smack on the arm.

He's such a troublemaker, but God, do I love it.

Late into the evening, the room is packed with guests as I stand crowded around one of the larger high-top tables with Maggie, Hayes, and a few of his teammates. Boucher, Johansen, Taylor, and Volkov are here tonight, and I notice Maggie sizing them all up like a snake deciding which mouse will be her first victim. I give her a not-so-subtle *'be chill'* look, and she proceeds to scratch her face with just her middle finger in retort. I roll my eyes back at her. *Way to be mature, Mags.*

I lean over to Hayes. "I'll grab us some more drinks...keep an eye on Maggie while I'm gone. Make sure she doesn't kidnap any of your friends."

He chuckles, side-eyeing my friend and kissing my temple. "I don't think that's physically possible, but I'll keep an eye on her."

"You don't know Maggie like I do," I say, kissing his cheek as he laughs, not wanting to let go of my hand as I walk away. "I'll be right back, Haysey-poo"

"Haysey-poo, huh?" I hear Bougie gasp, his teammates immediately razzing him about this little nickname. Smirking, I know my job is clearly done.

I am sooo *getting punished later...and I can't wait.*

I check my phone while I'm waiting for our drinks when I hear someone talking beside me.

"Well, well, well; look who it is."

My skin prickles at the familiar voice. *What in the actual fuck?*

"What the hell are you doing here, Cayden?" I glance over my shoulder, refusing to give the douchebag my full attention. "This party was invite only."

"Enjoying some delicious bourbon, Livy." He leans against the bar, crowding me as he shoots me what he assumes to be a megawatt smile.

It falls short, and my lips thin. "Don't call me Livy."

"And I have an invite. My roommate's dad is a liquor distributor, and he couldn't make it, so he gave us his tickets."

Fucking fantastic.

Glancing back towards our table, I desperately try to use some sort of telekinesis to get Hayes' attention to come and rescue me. *Why can humans not speak to their fated mate through their minds like in my books?* Out of the corner of my eye, I notice a skinny blonde with ginormous boobs, overly injected lips, and a head that seems way too big for her body approaching. Her extremely short dress gives off slutty Halloween vibes rather than the classy gala attire everyone else is wearing. She stops in front of me and places her arm around Cayden's waist, who of course is wearing jeans and a blazer, and no tie to a freaking black-tie event.

"Cay-Cay," she whines, "How long do we have to stay here? This is boring."

Cay-Cay? Barf.

"Not much longer, Shay-Shay," he replies, leaning over to grotesquely kiss her.

Cay-Cay and Shay-Shay? Double barf. I can't hide the sneer twisting my lips. *What did I ever see in this guy?*

"Cayden, who is your friend?"

"Oh, this is Shay. We work together. She just started a few months ago."

My eyes well with tears, rage coursing through my veins as the puzzle pieces fall into place. I'm guessing I've just met his distraction during the last crumbling bits of our relationship.

"Hi! I'm Shay; I work with Cay, and I'm also a personal trainer on the side," she says, smiling brightly and reaching her hand out to shake mine.

I blink at her hand, my own curling into a fist. *She has no fucking clue who I am.*

"Olivia," I say, forcing the words through my teeth and quickly shaking her hand.

"How do you two know each other, Cay-Cay?" Shay asks, glancing between the two of us.

"Oh, Livy's just someone I used to hang out with, sweetheart."

"Someone you used to hang out with?" I scoff, my eyes like ice as I stare the two of them down. "Not your former girlfriend? Real classy, Cayden. I wouldn't expect anything more from you anyway."

I'm about to turn and walk away, when warmth radiates behind me and an arm gently wraps around my shoulders. A calmness washes over me as I lean into his touch.

Hayes.

"What the fuck are you doing here, Cayden?" Hayes snaps, his voice deadly in my ear as his arm tightens across my chest. "Stay away from Olivia."

"Larsy! This is awesome!" Cayden looks around, standing on his tiptoes to try and see over the crowd. "Are there other Riders players here?"

Hayes is in Cayden's face so fast, his heat is still cocooned around me. I grab his arm to make sure we aren't going to have an incident, especially with my bosses and a big client here.

"You don't fucking listen, do you? I warned you that if you ever called me Larsy again, it would be the last words you ever spoke. Yet here you are, ignoring my request and ruining the evening my beautiful, talented girlfriend has been working on for months."

"Wait, wait, wait...your *girlfriend*? Olivia?" Cayden's laughter causes a few heads to turn towards us, while Shay is currently taking selfies on her phone. "You're seriously dating Olivia? The clingiest girl there ever was? Dude, I warned you. You'll see for yourself. Good thing you have a lot of away games this season, otherwise you wouldn't get any time alone."

Oh fuck. I can actually hear my heart racing. This is not going to end well. The look in Hayes' eyes is feral. And not in the 'I want to bang my girl and make her mine' way, but in the 'I'm going to murder this guy' way. His hands are tightly clenched by his sides, his face a deep shade of red I've never seen before. Not even on the ice. I am still holding him back. He's not fighting my hold on him, but I need some backup. I miraculously make eye contact with Maggie, who sees what's happening with wide eyes and a panic-stricken face. She quickly wrangles up the guys and heads my way.

"Hayes, he's not worth it," I beg, trying to calm him down. "He's a jerk and we all know it. Let it go."

"NO," Hayes barks. "Olivia, I will not have this fucking asshole, or anyone else, talk about my woman like that."

Well, now *I kind of want to let him beat the shit out of Cayden.*

Finally, the cavalry arrives. Maggie approaches with Hayes' teammates who stand beside us, helping me keep Hayes from doing something stupid. Thankfully they walk him back a few steps from Cayden.

"I'm good," he says ripping his arm out of Vladi's. "I'm not going to do anything stupid. This fucking waste of space is not worth it," he sneers, his eyes never leaving Cayden. "But you should know you are dead wrong about Olivia. She is *the* most amazing girl I've ever met in my entire life. What you see as *clingy*, I see as the most gorgeous, warm, and sexy woman pressing her sexy-as-fuck body up against mine. And if she's considered clingy, so am I, because I don't want to be away from her for one day, let alone an hour or a minute. You treated her like shit. Like she was a bother. Like you didn't actually give a damn how she was. But there is no one in this world I would rather have cling to me than this woman."

Oh.

My.

Fucking.

God.

Hayes letting Cayden have it is the sexiest thing I've ever witnessed in my entire thirty-one years of life. Shock, heat, joy, and a feral rage course through my body, setting me on fire in a way I've never experienced before.

Cayden's face is a mixture of fear, embarrassment, and anger. And 'Shay-Shay' seems oblivious to whatever the hell is going on using her phone to check her makeup. I glance over at Maggie, a giant-ass grin on her face at the sight of Cayden getting verbally dismantled in front of her. *I'm surprised she's not chiming in.*

Hayes continues, "If you ever come near her again, I will *not* hold back." He looks back at me, and firmly says, "We're leaving… if that's okay."

"Yeah, let's get out of here," I whisper, my shoulders relaxing knowing I'm completely under Hayes protection.

Hayes turns back once more to speak to Cayden, taking a step toward him and bumping shoulders with Bougie and EJ. "I almost forgot. Do you want to know the best part about 'clingy' Olivia? The way her pussy clings to my dick while she screams my name. Something she never did with you."

Hayes pulls me into his body, mercilessly slamming his lips on mine with a fierceness I've only seen when he's trying to score the winning goal.

Holy shit this man is the fucking king of my world.

He breaks our kiss, leading me towards the door. "Wait… Hayes," he turns, his eyes softening as he looks at me, "I drove Maggie here. I need to make sure she gets home okay."

"Vladi, Bougie, EJ...Make sure Maggie makes it home safely," he says firmly, as if he's commanding his army.

"You got it, Larsy; anything for you." Bougie shouts as Vladi gives Hayes a quick nod.

I see Maggie's eyes light up at the thought of one of these guys taking her home before Hayes whisks me away.

"Wait...you dated her?" Shay asks, her voice shrill as she's just now catching up on the situation.

I follow him toward the exit, and we head to the car, neither of us saying a word. Cayden, I'm sure, *I hope,* is still standing stunned with his jaw on the floor.

Good riddance, motherfucker.

36
hayes

The ride is quiet as I hold Olivia's hand. I tell her to just relax, close her eyes, and we'll work all of this out at home. And, like a good girl, she does just that. She just witnessed her ex spewing hate toward her, me hurling hate back in her defense, and I don't know how she's dealing with this. Shit...I don't know how *I'm* dealing with it. I still have adrenaline running through me, like I just finished a playoff game that ended in double OT. I wanted to punch that fucker so bad, but I held back for Olivia. I quickly shake off the hint of worry that crosses my mind at Olivia seeing Cayden. I remind myself that she has no desire to go back to that trainwreck, and I know she's mine. I trust her completely; she's not Chelsea. So, I just hold her hand and let us both process. As we walk into my apartment, I turn around and pull Olivia into a tight embrace. Immediately, she begins to sob and my heart fractures in my chest.

"Siren, my sweet Olivia. That was a lot to take in. You okay, sweet girl?" I kiss the top of her head, my hand stroking her back.

She nods and sniffs as I lead her to the couch. We sit next to one another, and I gently pull her legs over mine, drawing her as close as possible. I want to hold her, but I also want to look into her sorrowful eyes as we talk.

"Olivia, talk to me. What's going through that head of yours?"

She stares at me for a moment, her eyes full of tears and her expression full of worry and unease. Finally, she opens her mouth and rasps out some words.

"It is a lot to process. Before you walked over, Cayden basically confirmed he was cheating on me with the Triple B, big-boobed blonde, he was with tonight. I knew that's what he was probably doing, but it still hurt to have it thrown in my face like that. I feel so *stupid*. How did I not see what a horrible person he was? I'm such a fool. How did I not see..." She freezes, her mouth snapping shut with an audible click. "Oh my God, Hayes. This is probably awkward as hell for you. I shouldn't be telling you any of this. I'll call Magg-"

"Olivia," I interrupt, holding her face gently with my palm. "I'm here for you. I want you to tell me anything and everything. Just because you don't want to be with someone anymore, doesn't mean the hurt of them cheating is any less painful. I've been there, remember?"

She nods and sniffles back more tears, her fingers curling into the lapel of my tux.

"Olivia, you are not a fool. The only fool is the one who thought that Triple B was anything remotely close to the wonderful, amazing, thoughtful, kind person you are inside and out. I'm sorry if my emotions got the best of me tonight, but I have been wanting to punch that guy since Walt's, and I got damn close to doing it tonight."

She huffs a slight laugh, then narrows her eyes toward me. "What did he mean when he said he warned you I was clingy?"

Oh fuck. My stomach sinks with the realization I never told her about that conversation. "That night at Walt's, when he sat next to me at the bar, he said some very unkind things about you. They are honestly not worth repeating, but the gist of it was you were so clingy he needed to go play 'puck' with his friends or something. I'm sorry," I say scratching the back of my head, "I forgot about it until he brought it up tonight. If you want, I can tell you everything I remember about our conversation. But from what you've told me about your relationship, it's nothing you don't already know."

"Yeah," she scrunches her nose, resting her head against my shoulder, "that's okay. I am ready to forget about that fucking douche." She laughs, some of the tension finally leaving her body. "Hayes...thank you."

I cock my head to the side, raising an eyebrow. "Thank you for what?"

It's her turn to cup my cheek, her eyes tracing every inch of my face. "Oh, I don't know, defending my honor, telling Cayden off, making it seem like you would flat out murder him if he ever looked my way again. And for somehow finding a way to flip the word clingy to be something positive."

"Olivia, there is nothing more in this world I want than for us to cling to one another. That's how we get through this crazy life... together."

Her stunning eyes, tainted with streaks of red, stare up at me, her long lashes still holding the remnants of her tears. "I don't deserve you, Hayes."

"I don't deserve you either, my sweet girl. But here we are, two people who don't deserve one another, fighting to show the other how worthy they truly are."

Olivia leans her head on my shoulder, and I wrap my arms around her as tight as I can. "What do you need tonight? I can run you a hot bath. We can cuddle on the couch. I didn't make it home with the gift bag full of bourbon, but I do have some alcohol and some top-shelf vanilla ice cream. We could eat some dessert and watch a crime show where someone gets murdered."

Olivia laughs, the sound filling my heart with warmth knowing I made her feel even one percent better.

"Ice cream and a murder show sounds perfect." She settles back against me, a contented sigh relaxing her body. "I am sorry all this went down tonight, Hayes. I really wanted you to take me in that janitor's closet or punish me when we got home. Now I just look like a puffy, crying hot mess."

"There is no need to be sorry. I love your puffy, crying face as much as I do all your faces. The laughing one, the smart ass one, the one when you're looking at me like you want to fuck me in the janitor's closet, or the one you have right now where you're trying not to laugh. It's been a long night, and we both could use a little relaxing. But…don't think that tomorrow morning won't hold some consequences for calling me Haysey-poo in front of my teammates." Olivia's smile beams. "I can't believe I forgot your 'I'm in so much trouble but I'm not mad about it' face."

"I love you, Hayes."

"Love you too," I say, placing a kiss on her forehead. "Let's change into comfy clothes and then we can relax. I'll get the ice cream, you pick out the murder."

37
olivia

It's been a week since the gala, and things with Hayes have been nothing short of amazing. He's always sending me texts during the day, and he always gets back to mine as soon as he can when he's busy. Even when we are thousands of miles apart, I feel closer to him than I did being with someone who never left my zip code. Not to mention the fun we've had with the app-controlled toy during his road trip earlier this week.

Here in my house, I'm doing some laundry and sorting through the mail I haven't checked in a couple days. It's mostly junk that is destined to hit the recycle bin, a couple of bills, and a letter about my upcoming lease renewal. I bite my lip. *I need to let my landlord know soon if I'll be staying or leaving.*

I love this place. I love the cool breeze coming off the lake. I love having historic charm while still having modern updates. I love having a music room. Why would I even hesitate to renew my lease?

Hayes. Hayes is why. The tall, handsome man who defended my honor, takes care of me, and lets me be myself.

I wish my lease was a little longer so I would have more time to decide. *Surely, Hayes will not want me to move in with him this soon.* Tapping the letter against my palm, I glance around my rental house. *I would be out of my mind to think that, right?* But it was so nice to be in his bed when he came home. Maybe I'll just ask my landlord if I can get an extension instead of renewing.

I can't tell Hayes. I want to move in with him because he wants me to, not because of a timeline set by my landlord. *Calm your tits, Olivia. He said he loves you, not that he wants to move in with you.*

My phone rings. *Who is calling me?* Hayes is still at practice. I look down to see a familiar name on the screen, my brows lifting in surprise.

"Hi David," I say, confusion coloring my voice.

"Hey Olivia. Listen, I was calling to apologize." He sighs, sounding embarrassed. "Zack Reeves talked to me and said you had nothing to do with him signing those pucks. You weren't even there. And you aren't together with that guy anymore. So...if you'd still like to be the Riders anthem singer, we'd love to have you back."

I grin from ear to ear like an idiot. *Zack talked to David?* I'm sure Hayes had something to do with this and I can't wait to give him a hard time about it later. "Oh, wow. That's...that's great, David; thank you!"

"It would be on a probationary period for the rest of the season, but as long as there are no more incidents, you should be fine."

My breath catches in my throat. "Incidents?" I croak.

"Just the usual rules, Olivia. No fraternizing with the players or any other inappropriate behavior. Represent the Riders franchise with pride and decorum."

"Right. Got it. No fraternizing with the players." *Shit, shit, shit.* Fraternizing is the understatement of the year for what Hayes and I have been doing.

"I already lined up some singers for the next few games, but as long as we're on the same page, I'll email you the details with the next open slot. I'll have your credentials and tickets at security as usual. Can't wait to have you back! The Riders need their weapon."

"Um, yeah. Thanks so much, David; I…I can't wait to be back either," I say with a shaky voice, my fingers fidgeting with my sleeve.

And there it is.

The mother-fucking hammer.

Shit.

"He said *what*?" Maggie screeches over the phone.

"He said no fraternizing with players. Which, in case you need a recap, I am currently dating, and super in love with, a very hot Rider. What the fuck am I going to do?"

"You have to tell Hayes," she says authoritatively. "He can pull some strings, right?"

"Mags, I cannot ask him to talk to the team he just signed with to make an exception for his girlfriend of less than a month. I don't think people will understand I'm not just some puck bunny, flavor of the month for the new guy on the team."

"Olivia Marie Brooks. You are *not* a puck bunny! Do not say that about yourself. This is different. What you guys have is special, and people will see that. I mean, *I* see it, and I'm jealous as hell! Sure, people are going to talk. But you're dating a professional athlete. People are going to talk no matter what you do."

"I guess you have a point. I just…I can't ask Hayes to do that. It's just…not me."

"Liv. Tell Hayes. You go on and on about how he lets you be yourself, that you feel safe with him. *Tell him* what's going on; let him help you decide what to do. Or, even better, decide together. He seems like such a great, level-headed guy, and he is so crazy in love with you. You two will figure it out."

I shake my head. *Dammit.* "Mags, I *really* hate it when you're right."

"So, you hate me a lot then, huh?" she teases. "Trust me, Olivia. This guy would burn down a building for you. Just talk to him. *And...*I better be your plus one at the games since your boyfriend is, you know, *playing.*"

"Of course, Maggie. Let me deal with this crisis first, then I'll see what I can do about tickets."

"You're the best, Liv!" she says as I roll my eyes.

She *is* right. If this will ever work, I have to tell him what's going on. I have to be honest. Hayes isn't Cayden; he isn't going to bolt because I'm being vulnerable and sharing a fear. *Fuck,* I groan, dropping my face into my hands, *I hate this.*

Hayes calls as he's leaving the Riders' practice facility to let me know he's running a couple of errands and will be at my place around five for dinner. I force a smile and nod, even though he can't see me, telling him that's great, drive safe, and I'll make something for us to eat.

"Are you okay?" he asks. "You sound like something's got you worried."

Shit. This man can read me like a book, even over the phone.

"Yeah, I'm okay," I lie. I'm kind of *not* okay.

"Olivia. Don't lie to me. I haven't known you long, but I can already tell when something's up."

I sigh, pacing back and forth in my living room. *Here goes nothing.*

"Okay…so, I got a call from David Green today. He said Zack talked to him and explained everything. They…they are giving me my anthem job back."

Hayes gasps, and I can hear his smile through the phone. "Olivia, that's great! I'm so happy for you! Wait…why is this bad news?" he asks, both excited and confused.

"Well, because I would be back in an official capacity with the Riders, I would no longer be able to *fraternize* with the players. Which would mean-"

"Which would mean no fraternizing with me," he says, finishing my sentence.

My heart drops into my stomach, and I wonder if his is doing the same. There's a long silence, not even the sound of the road is breaking it. I want him to say something. But he doesn't. I bite my lip, trying to hold back the tears threatening to fall.

"Are you still there?" I finally ask, my voice barely above a whisper.

"Yeah, I'm here. Just…thinking…I don't know what to say. I don't want to lose you, but I can't ask you to give this up for me."

"I know. I…I don't know what to do either. I love you. Like, *love you*, love you," I pause for a moment, tears burning my eyes. "Listen, I will tell David I'm not coming back. I can still sing at Walt's. I can still sing other places and keep writing songs. What I can't do is let you go."

"No, I can't let you do that," he says with a sigh. "Listen to me, okay? We're going to figure this out. I feel horrible you're in this position; you shouldn't have to choose. I'm going to go run my errands super-fast, and I'll be there as soon as I can. We'll come up with a plan. Together. Okay?"

"Okay," I say, choking back tears.

"Do you want me to come over now? I can get this stuff done later," he asks.

"No, no. I'll be fine for a couple of hours. I need to get dinner started anyway."

"Okay. I'll pick up some ice cream. I think better with high quality vanilla ice cream," he says, and for some reason, that makes me smile through the disappointment of this situation. "I'll be there in a couple of hours, then we'll come up with the best plan in the history of plans. I love you, Olivia."

"I love you too."

And I do. I really do love this man.

As I take the chicken out of the oven, I realize it's almost six o'clock and a knot forms in my stomach. Hayes still isn't here. He said he'd be here at five after stopping to get ice cream. *Maybe that took longer than he expected*? I don't actually know what his other errands were. I bite my lip, rubbing my palms down my thighs. *Maybe he got caught up at one of those.* Glancing at the clock, my chest tightens. Surely that's it. It's not because he doesn't want to be with me anymore. *He said he loved me, right?* Maybe I imagined that. The pause he had was really long. *Did he just say what he said after that to placate me?* Oh God, I'm fucking spiraling here. *I should call Maggie;* she can always talk me down from a spiral.

As I pick up the phone, there is a knock on the door. *Finally.* My muscles relax, my body able to take its first deep breath in minutes. *Thank God he's here.* I open the door with a smile, which quickly fades into shock and annoyance. Standing at my door with a bouquet of flowers is not Hayes.

"Cayden, what the hell are you doing here?"

"Hi Olivia. Can I come in?"

What in the actual the fuck is he doing here?

"No. You cannot come in. This is not a good time," I say sternly.

"I just wanted to come here and tell you I miss you. Things didn't work out with Shay, and I wanted to apologize for leaving you at the game and for breaking up with you and for the shitty things I said at the gala. Honestly, I haven't been happy since we broke up and I realized I don't want to lose you."

"What the hell, Cayden? You barely wanted to spend time with me, you got me fired from my anthem job, and *now* you say you miss me? You called me clingy in front of my boyfriend and a lot of my co-workers. And now that you don't have access to my hockey tickets, you suddenly miss me? This is too much. I can't handle this right now." *The fucking audacity of this guy.*

"Please Olivia, just let me come inside," he says again, almost pushing his way through the door.

"NO," I snap, pulling the door shut fully stepping out onto the porch. "You are not coming in here. I told you, this is not a good time. And there will never *be* a good time."

"What, is Hayes Larson here?" he grunts a little too pissy for my taste. I can tell he's getting angry, and I've finally reached a point where I. Don't. Fucking. Care.

"No, *Cayden*, there is no one else here, but I am expecting company soon. And, not that it's any of your business, it is Hayes Larson, my *boyfriend*. Someone who treats me with respect and wants to spend time with me. Someone who realizes my talent is *mine* and appreciates me as much as I appreciate him."

I hear my phone going off on my kitchen table and realize it's probably Hayes calling to tell me he's running late. *Thank God.* "You need to go. My boyfriend is on his way and, in case you've forgotten, he will not be happy if he arrives and you are standing on my porch. So, I suggest you get the fuck out of here. Right now. Because if he does show up while you're here, I'll be bailing him out of jail for the beating he will give you. And he *will* beat the shit out of you. I will not hold him back a second time."

His face turns a dark shade of red as his nostrils flare. "I can take anyone in a fight. You're such a slut, Olivia. You found the first guy who paid any attention to you after we broke up and jumped straight into bed with him. Does he know how impossible you are to please? You know he will realize you're a clingy bitch sooner rather than later. Probably a good thing I was cheating on you, you fucking whore. You couldn't get my dick hard if you tried!" he yells as he throws the flowers in the grass and storms off to his car.

"Hope you know whoever you date next is going to realize you're a lazy fucking douche with a micro-penis!" I shout as he gets in his car and drives away.

Good fucking riddance.

I take a deep breath, my hands still shaking from that interaction as I rage walk back inside, slamming the door to my house, to that asshole, and to that phase of my life. *I cannot wait for Hayes to get here.* I need the world's biggest hug and to tell him how I was a badass woman and stood up to Cayden.

My phone keeps ringing, immediately starting again once it times out. I start to answer my phone, but it's not Hayes. It says "Maybe: Milwaukee Memorial Hospital." *That's odd.*

My hands shake as I swipe to answer, a sudden panic weighing on my chest. "Hello?"

"Hi, is this Olivia Brooks?"

"Yes, this is she."

"Hi, Ms. Brooks, my name is Mary, and I'm calling from the Trauma Team at Milwaukee Memorial. I'm calling because Hayes Larson was involved in an accident, and you're listed in his phone as the emergency contact."

The room starts to spin, and my knees can't hold up my weight as I collapse on the floor trying not to drop my phone.

"W-w-what? Hayes was in an accident?" I mumble, choking back tears and fighting to stay calm. "Is he…is he okay?"

"They are running some tests now, ma'am, but it would be a good idea for you to come down as soon as possible."

"Okay; I'll be right there," I say, hanging up the phone.

I can't breathe. I can't see straight. I certainly can't drive. I need to know if Hayes is okay. *Please be okay. Please be okay.* I don't need to sing; I don't need anything but him.

I quickly dial Maggie's number, thankful she picks up on the first ring. "Mags...can you come pick me up?"

38
olivia

Maggie drops me off outside the emergency room and speeds away to find a parking space. I rub my hands up and down my thighs, the weight in my chest feeling like it's collapsing in on me. I'm still not sure what's happening, but I know I don't want to be here alone. I glance towards the parking lot, not seeing Maggie or her car anywhere. She said she'd stay with me as long as I needed her.

Hospital waiting rooms are the worst. The sterile beige walls with cheesy artwork from the 1980s is the farthest thing from a comforting environment. It's depressing seeing the room filled with people here for a variety of reasons. Some are here for something simple - a broken arm, a bad cough, or a kidney stone. Some may be here for a more serious reason like a heart attack, a stroke, trauma, or even a death. I don't even know what camp I fall into right now. I don't even know what's happened. *Please, God, don't let it be bad.* I head toward the reception desk and the middle-aged woman sitting at the computer.

Please be nice. I can't deal with not nice today.

"Hi; I'm here for Hayes Larson. I got a phone call that he was in an accident," I mumble, my voice still shaky as tears well in my eyes, my throat struggling against the giant lump in it.

"Hi Ms. Brooks. I'm Mary, the one who called you. Let me see if I can get you an update," she says with a warm but concerned smile. "Wait right here."

Wait right here? Mary, I'm not fucking going anywhere. I'm not leaving until I can see Hayes. *My* Hayes. I'm not the most religious person, but I say another prayer. Probably the thousandth one I've said since I got Mary's phone call. Please let him be okay. I just found him; I can't lose him.

"Ms. Brooks?" Mary says, walking my way.

"Please, call me Olivia."

She smiles, her eyes guarded. "He just got back from CT. I can take you to him now." Mary leads me down a hallway in the emergency room. It's not that big of an area, but this is the longest walk I've ever taken in my life. Every muscle in my body tenses with fear and anticipation as we pass room after room, dreading what might be waiting for me when I finally reach Hayes. *Is he okay? Is he hurt bad enough to miss hockey? What if he can't play again?* We continue walking by what seems like a hundred more rooms, then around a corner and down another long hall.

How many rooms are in this fucking place?!?!

Finally, we stop at room 22. *Well, that's ironic.* A nurse is walking out as I stumble toward it.

"You must be Olivia," the nurse smiles. "He's been asking for you."

My heart in my throat I can barely stand, let alone speak as I stare blankly at her hoping she has good news. "Is he…is he okay?"

"He's going to be fine. Someone side swiped him, and he's most likely got a concussion, but he's going to be okay. We're still waiting on all the results from his scans, but he's awake. Just in pain and a little groggy. You can go in and see him now."

Tears threaten to spill down my cheeks, relief making my knees weak. "Thank you." I glance over my shoulder at Mary. "Can you tell my friend Maggie he's okay and I'll keep her posted? She was parking the car and is probably out in the waiting room now."

Mary smiles. "Sure will. If you want, just let the nurse know and I can bring her back if you need me too." I thank her as she walks back to her desk, and I place my hand on the door to Hayes' room.

Walking in, my heart drops. There he is. Lying on a bed not made for a professional athlete full of muscle. Cuts and bruises litter his face. Machines beep, and there's a slow dripping IV hooked into his arm. But he's okay. He's okay.

"Hayes?" I whisper as I inch toward him on the hospital gurney.

"Olivia. Come here," he slurs, and I full-on ugly cry. I lean over, kissing his battered face and gently embrace him as if he's a Fabergé egg that will break if held the wrong way. I want to hold him and never let go just to reassure myself he's here and breathing and okay.

Hayes tries to make room for me to sit beside him, but the hospital gurney is smaller than Rose's floating door in *Titanic*. Instead, I pull up a chair and sit beside him, refusing to let go of his hand.

"Oh my God, Hayes, they called me, and…I-I was so scared. I don't know what I would have done." I gently squeeze his fingers, kissing his knuckles. "Are you okay? What happened?"

"I think the ice cream is going to be melted," he says, and I laugh through my tears.

"Hayes Larson don't make jokes with me right now. I thought you were dead!"

"Thank God you put yourself in my phone as my emergency contact. I had no clue what your phone number was. Someone kept asking who they could call, and I could picture your face, but I couldn't think of your name. I was fucking freaking out. Thank fuck my phone survived the crash because finally, someone said, 'Is it Olivia? She's listed in here as your I.C.E. contact'. The minute they said your name, it all came flooding back, and I cried. I fucking cried," he says, choking back tears as he gently turns his head toward me. "How could I forget 'Olivia'? The most beautiful name for the most beautiful girl I've ever seen." A tear streaks down his cheek, disappearing into the tangled mess of his hair. "How could some asshole sideswipe me and knock that out of my head? I'm getting it tattooed on me tomorrow," he vows, making me laugh again.

"You cried? For me?" I say, tears still streaming down my face.

"Olivia, how could I not? I love you, and I was freaking the fuck out, convinced I had amnesia and wasn't going to remember who you were. I couldn't even remember my own name."

I sniffle as I tell him, "That's the plot of *Muppets Take Manhattan*. Kermit gets hit by a car and gets amnesia. He can't remember who he is, but Piggy karate chops him, he gets his memory back, and it all works out in the end. Just like now." I kiss his knuckles again. "I'm glad you don't have amnesia but know that I would gladly karate chop you if it helped. Seriously, how have you not seen this movie?" I say to him with a little chuckle as I sit rubbing his hand with my thumb.

"I can't wait to watch it," he looks at me as he winces out a smile.

"Don't smile! It looks like it hurts," I chastise, quickly dropping another kiss to his forehead.

"I fucking hurt everywhere. I feel like I got slammed into the boards, only a million times worse."

I squeeze his hand tighter, my heart aching for my tough guy, my protector, in such a fragile state. "I bet. Do you remember what happened?"

Hayes tells me he finished his errands and was headed over to my place when some idiot was speeding and blew through a stop sign right into the side of his car. Luckily, it hit behind the driver's seat, so he just got the blowback, whacking his head hard against the window.

"Hayes, I was so scared. You are the most important thing in the world to me, and when you weren't at my house when you said you would be, I felt like something was wrong. Then I spiraled thinking it was because of the whole anthem thing, and I felt so bad. *And then* Cayden showed up at my door..."

"WHAT?!" Hayes says as his heart rate monitor goes crazy.

"Oh God, calm down. I opened the door, thinking it was you, only to find it was Cayden instead. Apparently, things didn't work out with Shay-Shay, and he wanted to get back together with me. I told him to fuck off and that my boyfriend was on the way, ready beat the shit out of him if he didn't get off my porch."

He grimaces at me with pride. "I so would have beat the shit out of him. Then you'd be bailing me out of jail instead of visiting me in the hospital. I don't know which is better honestly," he says, and we both laugh.

"Mr. Larson?" a voice says from behind, as I turn to see a physician walking in the door. "I'm Dr. Knight. Your scans all came back clean. You do have a pretty nasty concussion, which I'm sure you're familiar with as a hockey player. Everything else looks good though. You'll just be sore for a few days."

"Thank God," Hayes sighs, sinking back into the scratchy sheets, "When can I get back to playing?"

"I'll send everything over to Dr. Gregory with the Riders; he'll make that determination. As long as your concussion heals up quickly, you won't be out of the game too long. We're glad to have you here in Milwaukee. You're a good addition to the team. I'm sorry this is your introduction to the town."

We both chuckle. "Not the welcome I wanted, but outside of this, I've had a great time here in the city. Not sure what your schedule is like, but I'll have the Riders reach out and we'll get you and your staff some tickets for taking good care of me. And for getting my girlfriend here so quickly."

"We are all huge Riders fans here, so we'd love that. I'll have the nurse come back and get your paperwork, so you should be good to go home in a bit. Do you have someone to stay with you tonight?"

"Yes, he does," I say before Hayes gets the chance. "I will not be leaving his side."

I'm not leaving his side tonight, tomorrow, or next week. Whether he likes it or not, Hayes Larson is stuck with me. I don't want to leave his side ever again.

39

hayes

I've had concussions before, they *always* suck, but this one is especially bad. In addition to the brain fog, every beam of light and smallest noise make me want to puke. At least I'm home in my very expensive bed, with a sleep mask on trying to rest. But I can't. I'm fucking beyond pissed some idiot hit me; now I'm basically on bed rest. And to make things worse, the doctor said no screens for forty-eight hours, then another forty-eight hours of limited screens and rest. So I can't even check my texts, scroll social media, or watch TV. It's like a fucking prison sentence but I'm stuck in an episode of Little House on the Prairie. I'm used to being on the go. Always traveling. Always practicing. Always working out. I don't sit around all day. I kick my legs and pound my fist on the bed in frustration. This is the worst form of torture.

The one bright spot is Olivia. She took off work and has been waiting on me hand and foot, making sure I have what I need. She helped me puke into the airline type barf bag the hospital sent home. She even helped me call Dr. Gregory, Coach Cal, and my agent.

It's such a stark contrast to relationships I've had in the past. Last summer I had the flu while dating Chelsea. She refused to come near me for fear she would get sick too. She actually opened the door to our room, threw a box of tissues at me, and told me to get well soon. Then she left and went to stay with her friend until I was better. *I wonder if Spam Risk Brian is helping her puke through her morning sickness or if he doesn't want to risk getting pregnant.* With the combined brain power of the two of them, I don't doubt he would believe he could catch a pregnancy like the flu.

But Olivia? My body calms, finally finding peace in my compromised state. She has not left my side once. I don't know how she's dealt with my crabby, frustrated ass, but I know one thing…

I fucking love this woman so much. She's it. My future. My present. My everything.

My phone buzzes next to me, and I ask Olivia who it is.

"It's your mom; want me to answer? She's actually FaceTiming you."

"Yeah. I'd better let her see I'm okay," I groan, throwing an arm across my eyes and squeezing my lips together to keep the nausea at bay.

"I'll um…. I'll swipe to answer, then let you have some privacy to talk to her." I hear the shakiness in her voice, but I want my siren here with me.

"No. Stay. I want my mom to meet you. Even over the phone."

I can't see her smile, but I can hear it in her soft voice as she says, "Okay."

I know I'm not supposed to, but I take my eye mask off to let my mom see me and that I'm alive. And that I still have eyes. "Hi Mom."

"Hayes, oh my God your poor face! How are you feeling, honey? Who's there taking care of you? I can't get a flight out until this afternoon, but I'll be there as soon as I can. My car is in the shop, otherwise I'd already be on my way."

"Mom, it's okay. I want you to meet Olivia. My girlfriend." I see a wide smile stretch across her face on the phone, a similar one appearing on mine. "She hasn't left my side and is giving me the full Kristi Larson treatment. She won't even let me listen to the TV, let alone watch it," I grumble as my mom laughs in approval.

"Hi Ms. Larson, it's nice to meet you. I wish it wasn't under these circumstances, but Hayes talks about you all the time. It's nice to put a face with a name," Olivia says.

"It's nice to meet you too, Olivia. Hayes hasn't *mentioned* you yet," she says somehow giving me her evil side-eye over the phone, "but I know he's been busy with a new team, so I'll let it slide just this once. I'm glad to hear he's bragging on me when I'm not around. I *did* dedicate my entire life to raising him and taking him to all his hockey games, so he better be saying nice things."

Olivia laughs. "Only good things, Ms. Larson, I promise."

"Oh, for Pete's sake, dear, call me Kristi."

"Okay, Kristi, if you're sure. Hayes is doing well; the doctor said he needs at least forty-eight hours with no screen time and plenty of rest, so I'm making sure he keeps to that. He's not even supposed to have his mask off right now," she says as she gives me a mean side-eye and a smirk.

"Well, Olivia, it sounds like you've got Hayes under control, and believe me, I know what a challenge that is." She laughs, some of the worry leaving her face. "Thank you for being there for him when I'm so far away."

"There's nowhere I'd rather be."

"Olivia, would you mind terribly if I had just a quick minute to talk to my son alone? You can come back in just a moment."

"Of course; no problem at all. I'll refill his water and take the trash out, so you two can have a minute."

"Olivia," I say, reaching for her hand as she walks away, "Do *not* take the trash out. I can do that later."

"Hayes Michael Larson, you let that girl help you if she wants to. You need your rest," my mom scolds over the phone. I see Olivia laughing as she waves and closes the door. *Great, now I have two women telling me what to do.* But for some crazy reason, I'm okay with it.

"Okay, Mom. What did you need to tell me?"

"I want to make sure you're actually okay, and I need more details about you and Olivia," she says, wiggling her eyebrows, and I can't help but laugh.

"I think you are more interested in the second part of that question than the first."

"Listen, I am old. I live alone. Other people's relationships are my livelihood. So *yes,* I want to know how it's going."

"She is amazing, Mom. I don't know what else to say. She's gorgeous, funny. She's an unbelievably talented singer, and she *loves* hockey. And when I give her shit, she gives it right back to me. She has not left my side since she arrived at the hospital. She helped me call and text everyone, helped me walk to the bathroom when I got a little dizzy this morning…Mom, she even started my laundry. I don't know what I did to deserve her."

"You are a good man, that's what you did to deserve her. You take care of everyone around you all the time. You paid off my house, for Pete's sake. You deserve someone to take care of you like you take care of the world." She pauses, a faraway look in her eye. "I know I've only met her over the phone, but…I like her." My mom winks at me with a giant grin on her face. *Holy shit. She has never said she liked anyone I've dated.* She for sure did not like Chelsea, always referring to her as *Gold Digger* or *Cheating Gold Digger* once the truth came out.

"I like her too. A lot. I've never loved anything like this outside of hockey." *Wow...I just said that out loud.* My heart is pounding in my chest. "Mom, she's the one. I knew it from the moment I first saw her."

"I'm so happy for you, honey. I really am," she says wiping a tear from her eye. "I may take that flight just to meet her in person."

"Not to see your only son and make sure he's okay?!" I raise an eyebrow at her and give her a wincing smile, my body still in pain but my heart so fucking happy that my amazing mom gets me. But that doesn't mean I can't give her the same shit I've given her my whole life.

"Well, that too," she laughs, "But I can see you're in good hands, so that helps."

"Actually, Mom, why don't you hold off on booking that flight. I have an idea, and I may need your help."

My in-home prison sentence is finally over, which means I have my screens back and the first thing I'm going to do is watch that Muppets movie. Despite feeling like shit for days, I've enjoyed spending time with Olivia. She's been my saving grace through this entire shitty ordeal. My heart swells at the way she's taken care of me. Even in the little things like making sure I took my meds on time and reading to me in bed. Everything from sports scores, league news, and even a few chapters from what she calls her smut books. *Who knew women were reading this word porn, and why has it been kept a secret from us men?!*

We also talked about a lot of real things while holed up in my apartment. Our family dynamics growing up, the fact we both want to start a family someday, the sometimes-shitty nature of being in the league and having to pack up and move your entire life at the drop of a hat. Luckily, I have a no-trade clause for the next three years in my contract, but three years will be up before you know it.

Today though, Olivia is dropping me off at the practice facility to get evaluated by our doctors and trainers before running to her house to grab some of her things and catch up on work. I feel like a kid getting dropped off and picked up, but I don't mind another excuse to be with Olivia for a few more minutes of the day.

"What's the word, Doc? I'm feeling great. Fog is gone. No more headaches or light sensitivity. I'm ready to play."

"I know you're itching to get back out there, Larsy, but these things take time," Dr. Gregory says, glancing down at my chart before eyeing me warily. "I'm going to clear you to skate *for now*, and we'll re-evaluate after you get a couple of sessions under your belt."

"I'll take it." I sigh, dropping my head back to stare at the ceiling. "Better than nothing. You know, I actually skate better than I walk."

"I'm sure that's true, but it's my job to make sure you can do both and stay healthy. So, you're cleared to skate for tomorrow's practice only, and we'll take the rest of the week day-to-day. Deal?"

"Deal. Thanks Doc!" I shout, literally racing toward the locker room. The first thing I do is grab my phone and text Olivia the good news.

HAYES

Cleared to skate tomorrow! No games yet, but skating is a big win. 😊

OLIVIA

YESSS!!! So happy for you! 😊

Let's celebrate tonight!

HAYES

And how do you propose we celebrate?

A wicked grin spreads across my face. *I am so ready to get my hands on every inch of my siren.*

OLIVIA

Well…what else are you cleared to do? 😏

HAYES

Olivia Brooks, what are you implying?

OLIVIA

I wasn't implying anything, sir. Just a concerned caretaker asking what all you're cleared for. That's all. 😇

HAYES

Sure. 😈

OLIVIA

What time should I pick you up?

HAYES

I want to do a quick workout since I've been laying around for the past few days, so give me a couple hours.

OLIVIA

I love how a 'quick workout' for you is two hours. A quick workout for me is walking up the one flight of stairs to my office. And that's only if there are super judgy people there telling me not to take the elevator up one floor.

As if I'm not proud enough of everything she does, *I fucking love that my girl is so damn funny.*

Lol. I'll see you in a bit.

"Larsy!!!!! They cleared you?" Zack asks.

"What's up, Z?" I laugh as I shake his hand. "I'm cleared to skate, then day-to-day."

"Can't wait to have you back out on the ice, man. I'm so glad you're okay." He cringes, his face warping with fear and pain. "I saw the pics of your car. Thank God you got hit where you did, or you'd be out for the season."

"No shit. I'm glad I don't remember much of it or I'd be scared to even get in a car. I don't know who was watching out for me, but I'm glad they were. Thanks for sending food over to me and Olivia. She would not leave my side, so it was nice to have dinner show up unannounced."

"That's what we do. We take care of our team. All part of my Captain duties." He winks as he gives me a captain salute. "Also, Kara made me, but I was going to do it anyway."

I laugh, thankful to have the whole Reeves family looking out for mine. "How are you feeling after being back a few games now?"

"Feeling great. If anyone knows how bad it sucks to be out, it's me. Hopefully we'll get our line back on the ice soon."

"Dude, I can't wait," I groan, already itching to be back in uniform during a game. "Hey, I wanted to thank you for talking to David Green about Olivia. The day of the accident he called and offered her the anthem job back."

"Oh, thank fuck. I mean, the other singers are okay, but Olivia is the fucking shit. The Riders need their weapon."

"I'm glad you think so. I don't think I've ever heard you swear this much about the national anthem," I snort, pulling my clothes off to change into my workout gear.

"I gotta get my swearing out here, 'cause I can't at home around the kids. Fuck. Shit. Cocksucker!"

Man, have I missed the chaos of the locker room.

"Who's a cocksucker?" Bougie yells as he saunters into the locker room after practice. Vladi shuffles in behind him rolling his eyes, the usual irritation on his face from any time spent around his favorite rookie and good luck charm.

"Bougie…always so classy entering a room," I snark, as he comes over to bring me in for a quick bro hug.

"Larsy! Damn good to see ya! Are the rumors true? We getting The Weapon back?'

I glance over to Zack shaking his head, raising his hands saying he had nothing to do with this. I look back to Bougie with one eyebrow raised. "How did you hear about that?"

"When are you going to learn that I know everything?"

"Ignore him," Vladi growls, as he smacks Bougie on the back of the head. "We saw David in the hallway and I asked if we could get The Weapon back. We have not won a home game since she's been gone. He said it was in the works. You know how it goes, brother. Now that Olivia is yours, she's part of the Rider family. And we look after our own."

How the hell does my grumpy-as-fuck best friend say the most profound words and why is my chest so damn tight right now.

"Fuck, Vladi. You're like…Russian Yoda," Bougie pipes up. "So Larsy, is it true? Is she back?"

"Well…there's more to the story. Apparently, they are not allowed to date the players. So, we're in a bit of a situation now. I don't want her to give up this singing gig. She loves it so much. But I'm sure as hell not ending things with her."

Zack looks up from unlacing his skates, his brows furrowed with worry. "Oh, shit. I didn't think about that."

"I didn't either. I don't want to get her in trouble or fired, and I don't know what the organization will do."

"Well, you won't go anywhere. Milwaukee isn't going to trade their new star center because he's dating the anthem singer. Her on the other hand…" Zack glances at me with a sad look in his eyes.

I look to Vladi, needing some more of his Yoda-like wisdom. He pauses for a moment, his eyes narrowed, deep in thought. "You know Larsy…there is a way to fix this situation."

My heart races faster than me flying down the ice on a break-away and I can't help the dumbass smile forming at what he's implying. "Yeah…I do. You guys down to help me with it?"

Bougie walks over, putting his arm around my shoulder. "That's what teammates are for."

40
olivia

"We still haven't talked about it yet," I groan to Maggie over FaceTime. "We haven't talked about the *amazing plan* we were going to come up with to keep dating while keeping my anthem job. Avoiding it is best, Mags, I cannot possibly talk to him about this while he's *concussed*."

She glares at me like I'm about to be sent to my room. "Olivia! You *need* to talk to him. You have to work this out."

"I know," I mumble, flopping my head back on the couch in defeat. "But...if we talk then it becomes...real. And real means something bad is going to happen."

"Okay, that doesn't mean something bad is going to happen. You love him, don't you?" she asks, her voice guarded. "And he loves you?"

"More than anything." My trembling heart flutters thinking about just how crazy in love I am with this man.

"Then what is the problem here? I know you two haven't been together long, but you've overcome a douchey ex-boyfriend, getting fired, and a car accident. If you can deal with all that, you can surely work through this. If I didn't know better, it sounds like you're talking about a conversation with Cayden, who *would* have berated you, instead of Hayes, who does nothing but support you. He thinks you walk on water, Liv."

"Mags...why do you have to drop a truth bomb like that?" I whine, punching a throw pillow and pouting like a toddler. "I just want you to tell me to bottle up my feelings, eat an entire pint of ice cream, and sit on the couch and cry."

"I'm dropping this truth on you because I think you actually found a guy you can talk to about your truths."

Damn her. Why does she have to be right? When you've been living in the dark cave of fear for so long it's hard to walk into the light, allowing yourself to be out in the open where you're all exposed. While I may love being physically naked around Hayes, my emotions are still shy, bruised, and slow to heal from my past.

I wish I had the confidence in relationships that I have singing. When I'm on stage I know exactly what I'm doing. There is no fear. No hesitation. Nothing but the deep seeded feeling of belonging. In relationships, I'm a scared baby bird trying to get the courage to flap my wings and leave the nest.

"I guess you're right," I groan, spinning on my heel. "I'm headed over to pick him up, but just so you know I *so* hate you for being logical."

"Hate you too, Liv!! Be fearless and logical!" she exclaims with a wave before I end the call.

Maybe I should be fearless and logical. Grunting, I jam my phone into my pocket. *Damn best friends and their advice.*

Pulling up at the practice facility, Hayes is waiting outside like a little kid being picked up from school, his face splitting into a giant grin once he spots my car. *He's so freaking adorable.* He hops in the car, leaning over to give me a kiss before buckling in.

Okay, Olivia you can do this.

Putting the car in drive, I head toward the parking lot exit. *Just talk to him about this…later…after dinner. Yeah. Perfect. After dinner.*

"How was your workout? Still feeling okay?" I ask as we drive back home.

"Workout was great! Just the tiniest smidge of a headache, but nothing like the first day after the accident. I just did light weights and some cardio. And before you say anything, no I did not overdo it," he promises with a smile I can hear in his voice.

"Good. Don't make me call Mama Kristi and report you for overdoing it."

"You wouldn't dare," he snarls with horror.

"Oh, I *would* dare. Now that I have her number, we are besties. And she said to let her know if you were doing too much, too fast. She swore she would be on the next flight here to, how did she put it, 'smack you upside the head.' I, for one, would pay big money to see that," I muse with a laugh.

"Oh my God, what have I done to my life?" Hayes says, dropping his face in his hands, equally annoyed as he is smitten.

I open my mouth to tease him more when my phone rings and comes through the speakerphone in the car. It's my landlord.

Shit. I haven't decided what to do about that yet either.

"You can answer that if you want," Hayes says.

A knot twists in my stomach as I try my best to focus on the traffic ahead of us. "Oh, no, it's fine. It's just my landlord; I can call him back."

"Your landlord? Is everything okay with your house?" His worry fills the car. "You can totally answer, Liv."

He just called me Liv. My heart is literally melting like an ice cream cone inside my chest. I love it when he calls me Olivia, but the fact that he's calling me Liv as if he's known me forever makes my pulse race in a whole new way like it found a rhythm it's never beaten to before. *Focus Liv. Your phone is still ringing and Hayes probably thinks your place is on fire.*

"My house is fine," I say as I swallow back a huge lump in my throat. "My…my lease is up, and he wants to know if I am renewing. I have to let him know soon."

"How soon?" Hayes asks, his voice quiet and inquisitive.

"Next week."

"I see."

We are both silent as the call goes to voicemail. I hate that I'm driving and can't see his facial expression. My heart pounds, my chest aching from the tension. *I'm sure he's freaking out.* Spots dance across my vision. *Oh shit…now* I'm *freaking out.* I don't know if I can grip the steering wheel any tighter with the sweat coating my palms. *Breathe, Olivia, calm your tits and breathe. Just tell him you're renewing your lease, then it will all be fine.*

"Olivia," Hayes says with a serious tone. "Can you pull the car over?"

"What?" I gasp, "…sure. Are you okay? Do you need to go to the hospital? Is the concussion bad again? Oh God, Hayes, do we need to call 911?"

"Olivia," he says again very calmly, "I'm fine. Just pull the car over up there in the parking lot." My shaky hand flips the turn signal, my stomach churning. *What is happening?*

My gut twisting and my hands shaky, I pull over into a nearby grocery store, putting the car in park. I turn in my seat to face Hayes who has a serious, contemplative look on his face.

"Hayes, listen, I am just going to-"

"No." He stops me mid-sentence, holding his hand up between us. "I know what is about to come out of your mouth, and the answer is one-hundred percent no."

Oh God, he doesn't want me to move in with him. It's okay. I can handle this. It's only been a few weeks. It's irrational to think we'd be moving in together so soon. Who knows what a year will bring. Or shit...maybe he's decided he can't do this anymore. *I am such a fucking idiot.*

"Before you get too deep into your spiral, which I know you are already doing-" *damn, this guy can read me like a book,* "-the answer is no. You are not going to renew your lease."

"What?" I breathe, shocked and confused.

"I said, you are not going to renew your lease. Unless you want to, of course. But...I'd much rather you move in with me."

"You...you want me to move in with you?"

"Olivia, I cannot breathe without you near me. You make me feel alive. You make me laugh. You bring so much joy into my life. You're the best thing that's ever happened to me. And I happen to have a cool, but travel-heavy job. I want to share every moment with you. I want to have all of our things under the same roof, so you don't have to go grab stuff all the time."

My vision blurs, tears welling up, fears melting away. "You do?"

"I do," he says.

Oh my God he just said 'I do' and that has me feeling a whole other set of feelings.

Hayes reaches forward to the touch screen and hits the 'missed calls' button. He hovers his finger over the last number, looking at me out of the corner of his eye. "Move in with me, siren? We can call him back right now and tell him your decision."

I start to ask him if he's sure, but I know I don't have to ask. This man loves me. I love him. And there is only one answer to this question.

"I would love to move in with you. These last few weeks, and especially the last few days, made me realize I don't want to be without you either."

He places his hand on my cheek and leans in to kiss me. He's so gentle at first, our lips teasing one another, then our passion heats up. *If it weren't for the console between us, this probably would become a very voyeuristic incident.* Hayes pulls back and takes my hand, giving my palm a gentle kiss as well.

"But, Hayes, what about-"

"Shhhhh," he says, interrupting me again. "No buts. I actually have another question for you."

"You do?" I say, my eyes wide, biting my lower lip.

"Olivia Marie Brooks, would you make me the happiest man alive and…go on a date with me tomorrow night?"

I laugh at his fake proposal, a smidge sad it wasn't real, but also relieved we aren't getting engaged in a parking lot. "Of course, Hayes Michael Larson, I will go on a date with you. Where are we going?"

"It's a surprise. But I think, hope, you'll like it," he says, grinning from ear to ear with his smoldering eyes staring me down. "Now, let's get back to the task at hand." Hayes gestures to the number on the touchscreen, and with a deep breath, and a lot of courage, I push it.

"Hello, Mr. Lochmueller? This is Olivia Brooks. I'm just calling to let you know I won't be renewing my lease."

41
olivia

I asked Hayes what to wear for this surprise date, but he said nothing. Not one hint. Not even a teeny-tiny suggestion of where we might be going or what we'd be doing. And now I'm trying to steady my shaking hands as I apply my eyeliner. *Why am I so damn nervous about this date?* I decided on a mid-thigh black dress with knee high black velvet boots. We've had a warm fall this year, so my bare legs don't mind the open air. Unless we're doing anything related to ice, then I'll be freezing my ass off. *Oh well…at least Hayes will be there to keep me warm.* I do a half spin in the mirror, checking my outfit one final time. I texted Maggie a photo and she assured me I look hot. But I can't shake the feeling that something is different about tonight.

Stepping onto the porch, I see Hayes pull up in his rental car. This is his first full day driving on his own since the accident. At least he's been cleared to do that. My heart races when I think about him driving again, but he's never let anything stop him. This won't either. He jogs around to the passenger side to open my door. I can't help but smile at the gesture, admiring the man who never fails to put me first. He's wearing a fitted pair of grey dress pants and a white button-down shirt. *Holy fucking hotness.* This man in tailored dress clothes, especially those tight-fitting pants where the outline of his cell phone, and other things, makes it hard to breathe. I bite my lip, rubbing my palms down my thighs. *Well, maybe it's not the outline of the phone getting me worked up.*

"Hey beautiful," Hayes whispers, grabbing me by the waist and pulling me into him, nuzzling his face into the sensitive crook of my neck. His slight stubble sends a shiver through my entire body. "You look so hot in that dress and those sexy-as-fuck boots. Dammit! Why did I suggest going out? Let's just go back inside," he says as he jokingly starts to walk me backward.

I laugh as I lean in to kiss him. "This was all *your* idea, mister. No take backs. Plus, I'm way too intrigued as to where you are taking me on this date."

"Okay, *fine,* we'll go out. But just know that outfit is going to have me *very* distracted and I can't wait to see it on my floor later tonight."

"Mission accomplished," I say with a wink. "Although, your dress pants may have me a little distracted as well. I would like to personally thank whoever it was that decided hockey players had to wear suits, because you wear the hell out of those slacks."

"You're not helping, siren," he chuckles. "I think you're going to need a punishment for all of this teasing."

"Then I'll say it again…mission accomplished."

"Alright, Miss Sassy…get in the car before I throw you over my shoulder and do unspeakable things to you," he says as he helps me into my seat, shutting the door behind me. I'm already blushing at the mention of unspeakable things, more than ready to find out what he has planned.

"Can you tell me where we are going yet?" I ask as he slides into the driver's seat.

"Nope. Like I said, it's a surprise."

I cross my arms, pretending to pout. "And what if I don't like surprises?"

"Oh, but I think you do."

"I guess we'll see. Jury's still out."

We pull up to an old brick building with a cool historic feel to it. Walking up to the entrance, Hayes opens the giant glass doors and gestures for me to head inside.

"What is this place?" I ask, taking in the interior of the building. Brick walls line the corridor, highlighting the brass art deco lighting. I see several tenant spaces for everything from a café to jewelry store to a spa as we walk through the long hallway, only heightening my curiosity. At the end, I see *Milwaukee Sound Studio* and a gentleman waiting on the other side of the glass door to welcome us. I feel like a swarm of butterflies are flying around in my stomach, my nerves and excitement surging like a wave of electricity.

"Mr. Larson, welcome to Milwaukee Sound! And you must be Olivia," he says as he extends his hand to introduce himself. "I'm Dan, the owner of the studio space here. Follow me; I'll take you to where you'll be for the evening."

"Hayes, what is this?" I ask, my heart racing and my mouth bone dry.

That damn smile and those damn eyes smolder at me again as Hayes says, "You'll see."

Dan leads us down another hallway and into a room marked *Studio 1*. As he opens the door, I see a single table with a white tablecloth in the middle of the room, set with two chairs side-by-side, place settings, and a dozen roses. There are no overhead lights on, just the soft glow of candles of varying heights lit throughout the space. Turning slightly, I notice the most stunning grand piano across the room. Pressure builds in my eyes as I see a glass wall overlooking a control booth.

"Hayes..." I whisper, too scared to talk any louder, "what is this? Why are we here?"

He takes my hand, his soothing touch always a calming force, his soft gaze filled with anticipation. "We're here for a few reasons. First, remember the errands I was running a few days ago? This was one of them. I came to check out this space for you. This is yours to use to record in whenever you like. Just call Dan up; it's all paid for."

Dan walks over, extending his business card to me. "Here's my info. Just call or shoot me a text and we'll get you on the books. We can set you up with studio musicians, recording engineers, mixing, mastering, you name it, we do just about everything here in house. I've heard you sing at Riders games and at Walt's. I can't wait to work with someone as talented as you."

"Thanks for setting this all up, Dan," Hayes says, shaking his hand.

"Anything for Hayes Larson. We're so excited to have you here in Milwaukee. My kids can't wait to go to the game next week. Appreciate the tickets! I'll leave you two to enjoy your dinner; holler if you need me." Dan nods as he leaves the room, a small smile on his face.

"Hayes, you can't do this. When did you have the time to even arrange all this? It's too much. I...I don't even know what to say. I mean, obviously thank you, but seriously, this is way too mu-"

"Olivia," Hayes soothes, cutting me off. "Nothing is too much for you. You deserve every good thing in this world, and I'm going to do my damnedest to make sure you get it."

It's impossible to hold back my tears, my sobs catching in my throat. I'm overwhelmed by the love and boundless care this man pours out to me every single day. I reach up to grab behind his neck, pulling him close for a kiss.

God, I love this man.

"Have a seat," he says as he leads me over to the table and pulls out one of the chairs. The minute we are both seated, his arm around my shoulders, a waiter comes in to pour wine as another server comes in with our food.

I eye the plate in shock, my mouth watering at the smell. "Hayes, is this the same salmon meal we had at The Harbor?"

"Called in another favor. You'd be amazed what people will do for free hockey tickets and a pre-game ride on the Zamboni," he says with a wink.

"When do I get to ride the Zamboni?"

I gasp as he grabs my hand placing it between his legs. *He wasn't kidding when he said he liked this outfit.* Leaning in, he whispers in my ear, "Olivia, I think we've determined what you like to ride, and it's not an ice resurfacing truck."

Heat courses through me at feeling his hardness, my thighs involuntarily squeezing together. *I love the way he always makes me feel wanted.* A wicked smile creeps across my face. "Well, you're not wrong. I'm all about fulfilling some fantasies, especially on top of that grand piano, but there also seem to be a lot of windows and security cameras in here."

"Good point," he says raising an eyebrow with a pouty look. "We'll revisit this topic later tonight when your legs are wrapped around my shoulders. Now, excuse me while I order a piano for rush delivery to the apartment," Hayes says as he leans in to press his lips to mine, silencing my laughter. *This man.* "Now let's eat this salmon before it gets cold."

The only sound for the next few minutes is the clinking of silverware against our plates, as we reminisce about our first meal together. "This is without a doubt, the best date I've ever been on in my life. I still can't believe I get to record in here. I don't know how I'll ever be able to properly thank you for this."

"You are so talented, siren, I want you to share your music with anyone and everyone who wants to hear it. Whatever I can do to help you achieve your dreams, I'm going to do. And there's something else I've been thinking about," Hayes says, silence filling the air around us. I rub my hands up and down my thighs, unsure of what is going on. "I want you to sing for the Riders again, and I know we haven't talked about it since the accident." He hesitates again, his throat bobbing with a heavy swallow. "Do you remember what I said to you that day? That we were going to come up with a plan and it was going to be the best plan there ever was?"

"Yeah," I say, choking back more tears. "I remember. But I'm okay giving that up if I can be with you. When I got that call from the hospital, and I thought you were…" I stop, not able to finish. Not able to go back to that terrifying moment. "I don't ever want to lose you. Never. I couldn't survive it. I love you so much."

He reaches over to grab my hand, his touch always a calming presence. "I love you too. More than I thought I could love another person," he says. "I did some thinking, and I came up with a plan. What if…what if you could have both?"

"I mean, that would be great, but I don't think the Riders will allow it. You can't socialize with or date a player, and there's no way they'd bend the rules for me after everything that happened with Cayden."

Hayes stands up, scooting his chair back, reaching into his back pocket for something. Bending down to get on one knee in front of me, making my breath catch in my chest.

"Hayes, what are you doing?"

"You're right, Olivia. You can't date a player," his eyes catch mine, something I don't allow myself to hope for shining in their depths. "But I did some investigating, and it turns out you *can* sing if you're married to a player."

My throat tightens, my pulse racing. *Did he just say married?*

Hayes holds a black jewelry box before me and opens it, revealing a little light shining brightly to highlight what's sparkling inside. I stare down at the most breathtaking, giant square cut pink diamond in a white gold setting I've ever seen in my life. My eyes go wide, and I pull my hand up to cover my mouth.

"Oh my God, Hayes," I whisper as I begin full-on ugly crying.

"Olivia, I know it's not been long, but I know what I want. I want you. I want to marry you. I want to live my life with you. I want to start a family with you. I want it all. I know this seems so fast, but when you know it's right, you know it's right. And there is nothing in this world that has ever felt more right to me than being with you. Olivia Marie Brooks, will you be my forever emergency contact and marry me?"

"You're proposing? You…you want to marry me?"

"Remember how I don't offer things up I don't want to do?"

I laugh, blinking to see the man I'm going to marry. "I remember," I say nodding, probably looking like a bobblehead shaking my head erratically through my tears.

"This is definitely something I would not offer up if I didn't mean it," he says, his gaze matching mine, as if he can see right through me. "So, you haven't given me an answer yet. Is the jury still out on this question?"

My heart beats faster than if I was running a race. Not because I'm nervous - something about Hayes makes me feel safe and calm. Nothing has ever felt more right, but the words about to come out of my mouth are going to change the rest of my life. That's the reason for the speeding freight train in my chest.

"No jury needed for this. I'm in. My answer is yes."

42
hayes

My hands are shaky as fuck as I slip the ring on her finger, feeling like a nervous teenager about to grab a girl's boobs for the first time. My heart skips a beat, staring at her finger with *my* ring on it. I still cannot believe she said yes. My gorgeous, caring, soulmate is going to be my wife. My *wife*. I give her a moment to look at the ring, admiring the way her soft eyes sparkle as tears stream down her cheeks, reaching all the way down to her jawline and dripping down the length of her neck. I stand, taking Olivia's hand and pulling her up so I can wrap her in my arms and kiss her gorgeous lips. She opens her mouth and our tongues collide, heat and passion building between us. This woman has me weak in the knees just at the thought of spending the rest of my life with her. *I cannot wait for her to have my last name and officially be mine forever.* She is *my* Olivia.

As we pull back, I reach up to wipe the tears from her skin and place one last peck on her mouth. "I have one more surprise for you tonight."

"What? There *cannot* be more," she insists with a smile. "You've given me a cart blanche account at a recording studio and a ring that cost God knows how much with your fancy hockey salary. Please tell me we are going to get dollar tacos or something."

I let out a roaring laugh, pulling her in close once more. "We are not getting dollar tacos, although that does sound tempting even after the salmon. But, I was thinking, since there's a home game next week, what do you say we just get married tonight?"

"Tonight?" she looks up at me with wide eyes, telling me she's not sure if I'm joking or not. "Like, *tonight,* tonight? I know you're new in town, but this isn't Vegas. There aren't many late-night wedding chapels here in Milwaukee."

"What if I told you I had that covered?"

"Hayes…are you serious? You want to get married *tonight*?"

"If you want to, it's all set up. If not, what I have arranged can just be an engagement celebration. But, I'd love for you to be my wife. Tonight. What do you say?" I ask, my voice shaking with a hint of nervousness. I don't want to pressure her, but my heart tells me she wants this just as much as I do.

"Hayes, I love you…I love you so much. But, if I'm being honest…" she pauses for what seems like the longest span of time of my entire life, my hands nervously rubbing her back as I hold her tight to my chest. "…If I'm being honest, I would have married you the first night we met. This has been the longest few weeks of my life waiting." She smiles, leaning into me with a grin that makes my heart skip a beat. "Let's go get married."

43
olivia

"What are we doing here?" I whisper, confused by what we are doing at Button Bashers. "The sign on the door says they are closed for a private event."

Hayes pulls open the door, his hand on the small of my back guiding me inside. "They are closed for a private event. *Our* private event."

We take a few steps in the door, the lights flashing on the pinball machines around the room. My eyes dart around the room, beyond confused as to what the hell we are doing here. *He said we were getting married tonight, right? Why are we at an arcade bar?*

"Surprise!"

As I look around, I see all of our friends, family, and half the Milwaukee Steel Riders team clapping and shouting with huge smiles on their faces.

"Surprise, Liv!" Maggie yells as she tackles me with a hug. "Congrats! Welcome to your engagement/wedding party!"

"Maggie!" I scream, crying *again*. "Oh my gosh. How did all of this happen?!"

Hayes plants a quick kiss on my forehead, "I'll let you two catch up for a minute. I'm gonna go say hi to the guys. Thanks for all your help Maggie," he says with a sly smile as he saunters away towards his teammates.

"You snagged a hell of a guy, Liv. Hayes *kind of* stole my number out of your phone, and we've been working on this secretly for a few days. Along with some help from his mom, the Reeves, Boucher, and um…Vladi," her voice trailing off as her gaze falls to the floor, before her eye catches on my new accessory. "He wanted to surprise you with a grand gesture. And this," she grabs my left hand and brings it toward her face, "this *giant* pink rock is a grand fucking gesture. Holy shit, Liv, this ring is gorgeous!" She dances and jumps around as she hugs me again, her joy only adding to my own. I would have married Hayes with just he and I at an altar, but the fact that he arranged for my best friend to be here makes it even better. My breath catches, my chest tight as I realize the lengths everyone went to make this happen. For me. For Hayes. For us.

"There's some other folks you may want to say hi to as well," Maggie says as I turn to see two familiar faces.

"Walt? Johnny?!!! What are you doing here?" Tears continue to track lines down my cheeks. "Who's manning the bar?"

"We decided to close up for the special occasion," Johnny says as he leans in to hug me. My throat tightens, my lungs struggling for air at the kindness of their gesture. "Plus, we haven't had a night off in damn-near twenty-years."

Walt comes in to hug me next, shooting Johnny a look full of love. "I don't know how I let this one convince me to close up shop, but I do know you're worth it, honey. You found yourself a good one; we couldn't be happier for you."

"What about you, Maggie?" Johnny pipes up, wrapping an arm around her shoulders. "There's quite a few Riders here tonight. Got your eye on any of 'em? Thanks to Hayes and Liv, they've been hanging out at Walt's and bringing in a lot of business. Good men; I'm happy to put in a good word for ya," he says with a wink.

I look to Maggie with a smile, but she doesn't return it. Instead, there is a horrified look on her face, like someone just told her unicorns aren't real. *What is that about?*

"Olivia!!" I hear a female voice calling my name from deep within the crowd somewhere.

"That's my cue to get Walt and Johnny seated!" Maggie says, whisking the two gentlemen away, seemingly relieved to end this conversation. "Olivia, go greet your future mother-in-law!" I watch Maggie disappear into the crowd, unsure of what I just witnessed. *I'll be investigating this when I'm not about to walk down the aisle.* Rolling my eyes at her dramatic exit, I'm quickly distracted by the sight of a sixty-something-year-old blonde woman barreling towards me.

"Kristi! Oh my God it's so nice to meet you in person finally," I say as Hayes' mom pulls me in for a giant bear hug.

"Oh, my goodness. You are a good hugger! No wonder my son fell for you so fast," she says with a smile, holding me at arm's length. "And look at you. You are *gorgeous*. Nothing like that other girl he dated." Her lip curls, a frown marring her face. "I could tell from the minute I met her she was no good for him. You, on the other hand, are perfect."

Familiar arms wrap around my waist, Hayes' presence surrounding me with a warmth I never want to be without. "I see you two found each other. This is not going to end well for me, is it?"

"Oh, for Pete's sake, we just both love you and are worriers. Deal with it!" Kristi chastises him, hugging her son. "You did good, Hayes. She's a keeper; I can tell."

Warmth fills my heart seeing the sweet relationship these two have. I'm beyond excited to make Hayes my family. But with the non-existent relationship I have with my parents, my heart swells at the idea of having Kristi in my life as well. Standing here with them makes everything feel…complete.

"I should hope so; we are about to get married," he gazes down at me. I swear his look makes me tingle in places I didn't even know had the ability to tingle. "Well, fiancée, would you like to get married now?"

Heat blooms in my cheeks, my muscles aching from how big my smile has been since the studio. Hayes and I talked in the car on the way over. We're going to have a more formal celebration during the offseason. As for tonight…is this the wedding I imagined as a little girl in a big church with a stunning white ball gown? Not even close. But it's more perfect than anything I could have ever imagined.

My eyes trace every inch of the space. This bar and the people here to celebrate us, has my heart stuck in my throat. Walt and Johnny. Kristi and the Riders. Maggie. And, most of all, Hayes. The man who found me at one of my lowest points and turned it into one of the best moments of my life. The man who encourages me to live without fear, believes in me, and wants a future with me. The man who saw the broken pieces within me and painstakingly glued them back together.

"Hayes Larson, I thought you'd never ask."

44

hayes

"We are gathered here today, before family, friends, coaches, teammates, and pinball machines to celebrate the joining of Hayes Larson and Olivia Brooks," Zack says, standing in front of the guests gathered here at Button Bashers. He apparently became an online-ordained minister during the pandemic since a lot of his friends' weddings were being cancelled. He also got his realty license, which also may come in handy.

"Being a captain is a lot like being the captain of a ship. You guide the team in a good direction, give them advice. You also have the authority to marry anyone aboard the ship according to maritime law. I know to some of you, this wedding may seem fast. But I would have married Kara the first night we met, and I see that same spark in Hayes and Olivia. Kara and I made it a few months before tying the knot, you two just *had* to do it in less time and show us up," he says, getting a laugh from everyone.

"Being married for ten years, I can tell you there isn't a day that goes by where I regret marrying Kara. And my instincts tell me you two will feel the same way in ten years."

I squeeze her hands in mine, rubbing my thumb along her knuckles. *I still can't believe this is real.*

"I've always known who Olivia was, but only as a singer. The Weapon. As our unofficial second mascot; when Olivia wasn't at our home games anymore, we struggled as a team. I'm not as superstitious as some of the Riders, but something felt off. The ice felt empty. Others tried to fill the void, but it was never quite right. Just like there was an empty place in your hearts until you found one another. Only then did they truly begin to beat."

My eyes are fuzzy, tears threatening to fall down my cheeks. *Fuck Zack for making me cry.* But dammit he's spot on. *Fuck it.* I let my tears fall, choking back sobs. My heart never truly beat until I saw the redheaded siren standing before me. I tilt my head to wipe the tears off on my shoulder, not dropping Olivia's hand for even a second. Her tear-filled gaze beaming right back into mine.

"And now, if I could please have the rings," he says as Maggie steps forward. I see Olivia start to panic, and I squeeze her hand reassuringly a small smile on my face. But Maggie extends her hand revealing two black plastic spider rings.

Olivia lights up grinning from ear to ear.

"We can pick out rings soon, but I wanted to have something for the actual ceremony," I whisper, my own cheeks lifting as I remember our first date.

"This is actually the most perfect ring. I am keeping this one forever," she says, still sporting the biggest smile.

We repeat the vows Zack reads out loud, promising to be there for each other no matter what. He, of course, threw in some mentions of caring for each other for a variety of ailments including common hockey injuries and carpal tunnel syndrome from playing piano. He also made a joke about Kara swearing Olivia in as an official WAG.

"Now, as we stand before this holy skeeball machine, surrounded by those who are here to witness this declaration of love, I now pronounce you husband and wife. Larsy, you may kiss The Weapon."

I give Olivia a church appropriate kiss, but it's not a peck by any means. I draw it out a little for the crowd…and myself, knowing I would much rather be kissing her like the first time we were here in the back hallway.

"Ladies and gentlemen, I present to you Hayes and Olivia Larson!"

We walk down the makeshift aisle set up in the bar to a chorus of "Way to go, Larsy!" being shouted by several of my teammates, none louder than Bougie. Vladi catches my eye with his nod of approval.

My heart swells as I spin *my wife* around, pulling her into my arms. "Well, Mrs. Larson, what would you like to do for our first act as husband and wife?"

"I assume I should kick your ass at skeeball again. Show everyone how your wife is the superior athlete," she says with that smartass tone of hers I love so much.

Pulling her closer, I trace my nose along her jaw, nipping at her ear. "Do you remember what happened after the last time you beat me at skeeball?"

"I'm sorry, Mr. Larson, but I don't seem to recall the details of that particular event." Her eyes spark in the low light of the bar.

Narrowing my brows at her, I place my hand on her cheek, my thumb rubbing along her bottom lip. *I'll never tell her, but I fucking love it when she acts like a brat.* "Did you just say you're sorry, siren? I cannot have my wife apologizing for things she should not be apologizing for. I'll have to remind you later of that later tonight."

"Promise?" she teases, leaning in to press her lips into mine.

She's officially my wife.

"Now let's go show up all our friends and family with a high score on skeeball."

45

hayes

My fingers tap furiously on the empty beer glass in front of me, my knee rapidly bouncing up and down. A cold rush of air from outside hits my cheek, sending a chill up my spine as my heart races. Glancing over my shoulder, I zero in on the door. *Damn.* My knee bounces harder. *Not her.*

"Watching the door won't make her show up faster," Vladi snarks as Johnny walks over with another round.

"I am not watching the door, Vladi." *I'm absolutely stalking the door.*

"The fuck you're not. You look like you're watching a ping pong match the way your head keeps turning back and forth."

"The Wolf's right, Larsy," Johnny pipes in. "You haven't stopped lookin' at that door since you sat down. Don't worry; she's never once been late. She'll be here shortly."

"Someone's blue balls are crabby today. You don't want to spend some alone time with me, Larsy? I've barely seen you since you've been a married man…I'm so lonely without you," Bougie whines, his voice thick with sarcasm.

"How about you all just mind your own goddamn business?" I grumble, nodding my thanks to Johnny for the full beer. "You can all go fuck yourselves. We just got back from an away game; I've had to be around your annoying asses for the last two days. Excuse me for being excited to see *my wife*."

The day after the wedding, we had a day off, leaving me a full twenty-four hours to consummate our marriage in every way imaginable in our apartment. *God I can't wait for the offseason.* Then we had a travel day for a game in San Jose. We won, and I got my tenth career hat trick, the hockey universe's wedding gift to us. After the game, we took a late-night flight back to Milwaukee, but didn't arrive until Olivia was already at work. *Stupid time zones. I have been waiting for two fucking days to get my hands on my wife.* I tighten my jaw trying to hide the smile my teammates will no doubt give me shit for. But I can't keep it contained. *I have a wife.*

The door flies open again, but I don't turn around, trying to prove my point. I sit patiently at the bar and take a big sip of my freshly poured beer. Johnny looks at the door, then back at me with a cheeky grin. I sit up straight in my seat, my heart pounding against my chest. Warm arms wrap around my waist as a familiar scent surrounds me. I place my hands over the tiny ones gripping my abs, my cock jumping in my slacks. Slightly turning my head, I see flowing auburn hair behind me and nothing else in the bar matters. I swivel my stool around to face the feisty siren standing before me, being gentle enough to not break her hold despite my excitement. *Damn, I've missed this view.* I place a hand on her cheek as I press my lips to hers. *Fuck my teammates. I'll slam any one of them into the boards if they give me shit about this.*

She smiles against my lips. "Miss me Hayesy-poo?"

"Every minute of every day, siren." I drop my forehead to hers, refusing to break contact with *my wife. I'm never going to get over that.*

"He's got major blue balls, Liv! They're making him really cranky; if you can do the team a solid and help him out, we'd appreciate it!" Bougie shouts across the bar. I keep my gaze fixed on Olivia, as I flip Bougie off, seeing Vladi quickly smack him on the back of the head from the corner of my eye.

Fucking rookie.

"What?! I'm just being honest; he's been a damn grump the past two days. He needs some action. Hell, I need some action."

Olivia's cheeks are flushed, but I notice the slightest glimpse of mischief in her eyes. She looks at me, as if asking for permission to reply, and I nod, taking another sip of my beer.

"Thanks for the heads up, Bougie, but since you guys only play with pucks, you can leave the ball-handling to me. It happens to be my specialty."

I choke mid-sip, coughing up my lager at the audacity of what just escaped her mouth. She just gave the perfect response to shut Bougie up. *Damn...I need to take some notes.* His eyes go wide at her boldness, his mouth dropping open without any signs of it coming back up anytime soon. Vladi laughs harder than I've seen him laugh in a long time, and Johnny walks away shaking his head, probably off to find Walt and fill him in. Once I catch my breath, I pull her in close and whisper in her ear, "Olivia Larson, what the hell has come over you?"

She lets out a slight chuckle, burrowing deeper into my chest. "Someone helped me come out of my shell. Plus, you know it's true."

"Fuck yeah it is," I say, desperate to feel her lips on mine once more.

"Here's your Strongbow, Liv." Johnny slides a glass across the bar to Olivia. "I know you're not singing tonight, but figured you'd like one."

It warms my heart to see the family she has with Johnny and

Walt. It's comforting to know there are people looking out for her while I'm on the road. And now they are all part of my family too.

"You're the best, Johnny." She takes a sip, her eyes rolling into the back of her head and making me incredibly jealous of her damn drink. "By the way, sorry I kept you all waiting. Bill called a meeting at 4:30 and it ran long. He wanted to talk about the new cloud storage we're moving to. He doesn't understand it. I almost told him to go outside and pick his favorite cloud and that's where his documents would be stored," she says rolling her eyes. "Maggie was coming too, but she has a big deadline tomorrow, and she doesn't have time to stop by."

"Aww, no Mags tonight? At least Bougie's here to keep us on our toes, eh, Vladi?" Johnny looks to my stoic friend, who turns to me with a puzzled, pleading look on his face.

That's fucking weird. I guess he really doesn't want to hang out with Bougie.

"Mr. Larson, would you follow me outside for a moment?" Olivia asks, pulling me from my thoughts.

"Outside? In the dark? With you? How do I know you're not trying to murder me like on Dateline?"

"You don't," she says, sauntering toward the door with a playful smirk. I nearly fall off the bar stool in a rush, weaving through tables and dodging customers as I race toward the exit after her.

Bolting into the alley where I helped her to her car what seems like yesterday, I catch up, wrapping my arms around her and holding her tight. "What are we doing here, Mrs. Larson?"

"I was just thinking…" she glances around, her cheeks red from the chill. "We never got to finish what we started here. I wanted to kiss you that night. I figured we could try again."

A guttural moan escapes me. "Oh siren, I wanted you so bad that night. But I couldn't have you," I say, caging her against her car. "I would have cut off my right arm to have kissed you that night, but that wasn't how our story was meant to be written." I press my leg between hers, placing my lips on her sensitive neck.

"It wasn't?" she whispers, her breaths short as I kiss along her jaw.

"No. That night was just the beginning. The ending is ours. We're living it."

Olivia crushes her lips to mine in one quick move, both of us eager to complete this unfinished moment in the place we met. Our tongues collide as she fully wraps her arms around me, grinding her sweet cunt into my leg. *I bet she's dripping wet.* I press against her, pissed at the layers of clothes separating our skin. *Fuck, I need to get her home and in-*

BOOM!

We jump apart, our kiss interrupted by the slam of a dumpster lid eerily similar to the first night we met. Glancing towards the sound, I see Johnny taking out the trash once more. *This guy has terrible fucking timing.*

"Sorry!" he yells over to us with an embarrassed wave. "It was completely unintentional…this time!" He winks as he walks away, his shoulders shaking with barely controlled glee.

Looking at Olivia, we both double over with laughter. "Okay, siren, let's say goodbye to our friends and head home. I believe you made a promise to my teammates to get rid of my crabbiness, and I'd like to make good on that."

46
olivia

"And now, let's get loud for your Milwaukee Steel Riiiderrrsss!!" the announcer shouts as the players skate out onto the ice for the starting lineups to be announced. Breathing in deeply through my nose, I didn't realize how much I missed it. I love the cool air whirling up as the players skate in a circle coming onto the ice, warming up their muscles one last time before the game. I love the shiny rink that hasn't been sliced into. I love standing on the little Milwaukee Steel Riders carpet, placed just for me, knowing I am the last person out there who isn't playing in the game.

But now, I have a new love on the ice, and he happens to be my husband. In the past, I've always seen the players standing here on the ice, but never really paid them much attention, until 22 stood across the ice and caught my eye. This is normally my chance to take a deep breath, make sure I have the pitch for my starting note, and remind myself of the lyrics one last time. *The second verse is 'whose broad stripes' right?* I have never messed up the words, but I always go over them one last time just in case. Tonight, I throw my routine out the window, listening to the starting lineup. Swaying back and forth, I wait for them to announce the players. As they say his name, I clap against the mic and do a quick little 'whooooo' for Hayes as he skates out and gives me a quick wink. Once the players are announced, I'm up. I nervously rub my fingers along the seam of the jersey I'm wearing. The only one a guy's ever asked me to wear. I couldn't be prouder to have the last name Larson on my back. *Now it's my name too. I'm married to a Rider.* The slight butterflies I usually get before singing seem more like a swarm of bees in my stomach. The stakes seem higher now. But as I breathe in the chilly air, I calm myself knowing everyone on this ice is cheering me on.

"Please rise and remove your hats as we honor America with the singing of our national anthem. Tonight, we are pleased to announce the return of our beloved singer with a shiny new last name! Please welcome the wife of our assistant captain, Hayes Larson - Mrs. Olivia Larson!"

Okay, I was not expecting that. It makes me smile knowing David and Hayes arranged this to make my first day back more special. The crowd goes crazy cheering, the roar nearly deafening in the arena. Normally, this would make me tear up, my eyes burning, but just like an athlete, I have my game face on. It's virtually impossible to cry and sing at the same time. All emotions need to get shut off with a little switch in my brain until the song is over. *I can cry in the WAG suite with Kara and Maggie later; first, I need to remember the words and sing my heart out for my husband…and I guess also America.*

The crowd finally quiets enough for me to start the song, the first few notes ringing throughout the arena. As I hit the high note the crowd goes wild once again, goosebumps rippling across my flesh at the sound. *I've never had a response like this.* I finish the song, do my wave to the crowd, and prepare to walk back into the tunnel. But, before I can even turn, I see Hayes skating towards me, a mischievous look on his face. Spraying the carpet with ice, he dips me back and gives me a huge kiss in front of the entire crowd. I thought the cheer after I finished singing was loud, but it doesn't compare to the roar echoing around the rink. *I don't think he is supposed to be doing this.* I smile against his lips, wrapping my arms around his neck and losing myself in his kiss. *Then again, we've broken quite a few rules in our time together.* He may get a fine for delaying the start of the game, but I know he's willing to pay good money to show everyone I belong to him.

I still can't quite figure out how a super-hot hockey player fell for a singer like me. But as he skates on the ice, I know this very rink brought us together. I don't know what the future holds for us, but I am excited to spend the rest of my days figuring it out with the center forward who is now the center of my whole world.

epilogue

Maggie

"Liv, I cannot believe you live in this giant hockey money mansion," I grumble as we stand in the massive kitchen directing the movers where to put the multiple boxes of their belongings.

"Mags, it's not a mansion. It's just a house," Olivia replies.

"Yeah. Just a *five-bedroom* home with an indoor basketball court that is getting turned into a hockey rink/gym, a pool, an outdoor kitchen, and a basement theater room complete with a fountain soda machine. Oh, and it's *on* Lake fucking Michigan. I think we can call it a mansion."

Liv smiles, rolling her eyes at me, as we unwrap dishes from packing paper. *How many damn coffee mugs does she own?*

"Okay, maybe you're right. I have to admit, somedays it's like I'm in a dream. It's not even been a year, and I went from being in the world's shittiest relationship to meeting the man of my dreams, getting married, and moving into this amazing space. I still have no clue how I got here."

I snuggle into Olivia, resting my head on her shoulder and closing my eyes. "You're one of the best, most kind-hearted people I know, so I'm not one bit surprised. You deserve this, Liv. I'm so happy for you."

I really am happy for Olivia. Cayden was such a douchebag for so long, but Hayes is the perfect man for her. He's so attentive, so sweet and loving. Plus, he's cool as fuck to hang out with. I pull away, giving her a genuine smile as I bask in her joy. Getting to know Hayes over the past few months has solidified the fact that the two of them are soulmates. *She deserves nothing less.*

"Hey sweet girl." Hayes joins us in the kitchen, talking to Liv as he gives her a kiss like he hasn't seen her in a week. *Okay I'm happy for her, but I don't need it flaunted in my damn face.* I'm still single as a Pringle over here and maybe just a *little* jealous. I swear if one more person tells me there's a great guy out there for me somewhere, I'm gonna fucking lose it.

"You guys bought a giant house, so I feel like it's appropriate for me to beg you two to get a room."

"Well, if it isn't Maggie James gracing us with her presence," Hayes teases as he walks over to give me a hug, easily welcoming me into their new home. "Always throwing out the compliments aren't you? Seriously, though, thanks for helping us out today. Some of the team is coming over later to move some of the bigger pieces into place. Hopefully when the movers are done, we can all grab a bite to eat."

"Who's all coming over?" I ask, my gaze focusing only on the dishes I'm unwrapping, hiding the fucking agony of a certain player being in my general vicinity.

"Zack and Kara. Zack's parents are in town watching the kids, and Kara is dying to get out of the house to help us put towels in a linen closet just to get a break from the kiddos for a bit," Hayes says. "And I think Bougie, Vladi, EJ, and Tay should all be here shortly."

Shit. Shit. Fucking shit.

I force a tight smile, praying Olivia is too distracted to pick up on it. *Of course* he's *going to be here*. He's one of Hayes' teammates and good friends. Why wouldn't he be here helping them move into their new home? I've only been doing everything in my damn power to avoid him for months, and now I don't know how I can get myself out of this situation.

Fuck, fuck, fuck.

One of the movers asks them where a box of photos should go, distracting them both as I fight to catch my breath. *I should just tell Liv.* I should just tell her that I slept with one of Hayes' teammates. We are all consenting adults here. Liv and I don't keep secrets from one another. But *he* asked me to keep this between us. Why am I keeping this man's secret? Why can't we just tell everyone what happened and move on with our life?

More importantly, why am I keeping his secret when I fucking hate him?

There was *a lot* of bourbon served at the gala. I had enough to drink where everything is a little fuzzy, but I remember every moment of that night. One fantastic night of the most mind-blowing, toe curling, orgasmic sex of my life. Only when I woke up, more than ready for round four - he was gone. Fucking *gone.* No note, no text, no calls. Just gone.

The Riders season is over, so I thought this was the perfect opportunity to get more time with Liv without having to worry about running into the man who broke my heart. But the asshole decided to stay in Milwaukee for the summer, and now he's going to be here helping my best friend and her husband move into their new fucking house.

Motherfucker only gives a damn about Hayes *apparently.*

Sucking in a tense breath through my teeth, I open a box and start putting dishes away in the cupboard above the dishwasher. *You can do this.* You are Maggie fucking James. You are a badass bitch, and you don't need to act like a wounded fawn in front of him.

"You okay, Mags?" Olivia asks, her eyes narrow with worry. She knows something is up and has been trying to tear down my reinforced brick wall since the wedding. I've held strong, but I'm not sure how much longer I can.

I don't know if I can keep doing this without my best friend.

I let out a sigh, flinging myself across the kitchen island. "Yeah. I'm just hangry," I mumble with my face flat down on the granite. "Do you have snacks in this place yet? Do I need a museum docent to direct me to them?" I ask using my humor to, hopefully, deflect the terror in my stomach.

"Larsy, you in here?" a familiar voice booms from the hallway, my stomach dropping as my traitorous pussy clenches with need.

I know that voice. That voice haunts me in my dreams. The voice I still hear whispering in my ear. I jump up from the countertop. My fists shake at my sides, my teeth grinding as I fight to look unaffected. The voice that disappeared when I woke up alone in my bed.

"Yeah, man, in here!" Hayes yells back, a wide grin on his face.

His tall figure appears in the doorway to the kitchen. *Well fuck me sideways with a pineapple.* His dark black hair has just the slightest wave, begging for my fingers to tug at the soft strands, his tight-as-hell white t-shirt and full sleeves of ink on his arms fully displayed, doing little to hide the Adonis build underneath.

Why does he have to be so fucking good looking? This would be so much easier if he was disfigured from too many pucks to the face.

"Nice place, Larsy. I approve," he says as he walks over to shake

Hayes' hand and give Olivia a hug. He steps back and leans against the countertop, staring at me with those green eyes I've never been able to forget. "Hey Maggie. Nice to see you again."

It's nice to see me? Fuck him. I want to cry. I want to throw up. I want to punch him in the throat. And I want to run. I want to run right into this man's arms and kiss those soft lips. But I can't. Because I fucking hate him.

I shove it all down and suck it up like the bad ass bitch I am.

"Hey Vladi. Long time, no see."

in the way - lyrics

Verse 1
You think you're the life of the party
Well honey hardly
You're just a selfish prick
You think you can do better than me
someday they'll all see
You can be a real dick
And I sure don't wanna keep you
From hanging out with all your boys
I hope they makeout with you
And bring you happy ending joy

Chorus
I'm done standing in your way
I'm done hoping some day
You'll come crawling back to me
'Cause honey
It's already way too late

You're not worth the wait
'Cause in your eyes I'd always just be in the way.

Verse 2
Talkin' to me always seemed like a burden
Maybe 'cause I'm a real person
And not a damn video game
But lying to me, oh you seemed like a natural
Acting all coy and bashful
But honey I got brains
So it didn't take me long to find out the truth
That you're more than just a nice guy
You're a super fucking douche

Bridge
And now you're free, free to do as you please
Free to get drunk 'cause you think you're cool
Free to feel like shit 'cause you're a tool
And now I'm free, free to finally live for me
You know I didn't see it all along
But now it's oh so clear as I write this song

Chorus 2
You've been standing in my way
I'm done hoping some day
You'll come crawling back to me
'Cause honey
It's already way too late
You're not worth the wait
'Cause in your eyes I'd always just be in the way.

also by ellie k. drake

Want to read more about the Milwaukee Steel Riders? Maggie and Vladi's
story is up next!

Book Two is scheduled for release in Fall 2025 and
you can pre-order it now on Amazon!

Follow me on Instagram @elliekdrake for updates.

Subscribe to my newsletter at www.elliekdrake.com
for bonus content, sneak peaks, and all the latest news
in the Ellie-verse!

acknowledgments

Holy crap I wrote a novel! I've always been a creative person, but never in a million years did I think I would get to this point. This is a story I've wanted to tell for a long time, but never really knew how. I would read books and think, "I wish there was one about a national anthem singer in a hockey world." The idea bored a hole in my brain and never left. I sat down one day and thought "I think I'll write a book" and now I've written 80,000 words and have two more books in the works.

I'm sincerely thankful for everyone who has taken the time to read this book! I hope you find the confidence in yourself to accomplish something you never thought you could.

To my my husband, who is my Hayes. Even though you aren't a hockey player, you stole my heart. You are my best friend and helped me find the confidence in myself that Olivia found with Hayes. Smooch.

To my mom, (who I hope does not read this) who has always supported me. You have always been a guiding force in all your kids lives, especially mine.

Thank you to my incredible sisters and my extended family (also hoping they don't read this) who have encouraged me to be creative and funny. Humor is our love language and I think that really shines in this book.

To my editor Casey at Inked Edits Developmental. I don't even know where to begin. You helped me take my story to a place I never thought it could go. You helped me find voices for my characters. I am so thankful I joined a random group on social media and found you. I am such a better writer having worked with you. You are an amazing human and I'm so grateful for all you did on this book. And we solved the mystery of the vanishing plate of brownies. Thank you for helping me build my sandcastles!

To Sandra at Maldo Designs for the stellar cover art and rolling with the hot pink.

To Ashley at Geeky Girl Author Services for the proofread and the encouragement!

To Mudge at Kindles & Coffee for helping me navigate the world of Bookstagram, being a cheerleader for my book, and just being an overall awesome and hilarious human being.

To Amy, Leigh, and Christian, the first people I ever trusted to read my book baby. I will be forever grateful for your feedback and your encouragement!

To Misty, Ashley, and Megan for unintentionally giving me fantastic ideas for a few of the hilarious lines that made their way into this book. And for listening to me talk about my book non-stop for months (sorry, not sorry, more books are on the way).

And finally, to the inspiration for the 'villain' in this work of fiction. I'm not here to thank you, but to remind you that you once said 'don't date a songwriter if you don't want to end up in a song'. I bet you never thought I'd write a book! Enjoy!